DELETE

water,
stone,
heart

**Center Point
Large Print**

**This Large Print Book carries the
Seal of Approval of N.A.V.H.**

water, stone, heart

WILL NORTH

CENTER POINT PUBLISHING
THORNDIKE, MAINE

This Center Point Large Print edition is published in the year 2009 by arrangement with Shaye Areheart Books, an imprint of the Crown Publishing Group, a division of Random House, Inc.

This is a work of fiction. Names, characters, places, and incidents either are the product of the author's imagination or are used fictitiously. Grateful acknowledgment is made to Fogarty's Cove Music for permission to reprint an excerpt from "The Mary Ellen Carter" by Stan Rogers, copyright © 1978 by Fogarty's Cove Music.

The text of this Large Print edition is unabridged. In other aspects, this book may vary from the original edition. Printed in the United States of America. Set in 16-point Times New Roman type.

ISBN: 978-1-60285-533-5

Library of Congress Cataloging-in-Publication Data

North, Will.
  Water, stone, heart / Will North.
     p. cm.
  ISBN 978-1-60285-533-5 (library binding : alk. paper)
  1. Sexual abuse victims--Fiction. 2. Americans--England--Fiction.
   3. Natural disasters--England--Fiction. 4. Cornwall (England : County)--Fiction.
   5. Large type books. I. Title.

PS3614.O778W38 2009
813'.6--dc22

2009011480

To Hazel,
"me dear old mum,"
for a lifetime of love and encouragement

August 16, 2004
5:10 p.m.

Pass to all emergency services. This is a major incident. Repeat, major incident. We require all the standby aircraft and all available land-based emergency crews as we are in danger of losing Boscastle and all the people in it.

Captain Pete McLelland, RNAS Culdrose rescue helicopter 193, to RAF Kinloss Aeronautical Rescue Coordination Centre

August is statistically the second hottest month of the year, just behind July . . . but August 2004 also turned out to be the wettest since 1956. A combination of humid sub-tropical air masses, slow-moving frontal systems and several hurricane remnants were reported as possible reasons for the exceptional precipitation conditions. . . .

Boscastle Flood Special Issue,
Journal of Meteorology 29, no. 293

one

"You all right down there?"

Andrew Stratton looked up toward the cliff top, ten feet above his head, but the afternoon sun was in his eyes and all he could make out was the silhouette of a woman's head and shoulders, etched against a Wedgwood-blue sky. Stratton was standing on a narrow grassy ledge above the sea, which he shared with a loudly bleating, black-faced sheep. The shape of a dog appeared beside the woman. The shape barked.

"Um, yes," he called back. "I was just walking along and saw this sheep stranded down here."

"And you decided to join it?"

"Yes . . . well, no . . . I mean, I thought I'd try to help it back up to the top. But whenever I get near it, it looks as if it's going to jump."

"Do you always have that effect?"

"What?"

"Oh, nothing."

From the slender shelf he and the sheep occupied, it was, he guessed, at least two hundred feet straight down to the Atlantic breakers crashing far below—so far, in fact, that he could barely hear the thudding combers above the whistle of the wind. He'd been walking along the cliff path just north of the Cornish village of Boscastle and had paused to watch the waves roll in and dash themselves to

9

foam and mist on the jagged rocks at the base of the cliff when he'd heard the sheep. There was a scar of loose rock and torn vegetation where the sheep had descended to the ledge, on the theory, Andrew imagined, that the grass there was greener.

"That's Darwin's sheep, that is," said the voice above.

"You know the farmer?" Andrew was suddenly more hopeful.

He heard the woman laugh. "No, I mean that what you have there is the dimmest sheep in the flock, the one that has to die to protect the gene pool and assure the survival of the species."

"Oh."

There was something in her tone that implied she thought he and the sheep had more in common than just the thin sill of grass they shared.

"Any suggestions?" he called.

"Not a one. The general idea is to let nature take its course."

He let this sink in.

"Right, then," she said. "As long as you're okay, I'll leave you to it." And with that the head pulled back from the cliff edge and disappeared. He could hear her whistling as she crunched off along the path.

Andrew Stratton—professor, from Philadelphia— did not know a great deal about sheep. He hadn't a clue, now that he was down here, how he would get the sheep back up. Come to think of it, he wasn't at all sure how he'd get *himself* back up, either. He approached the skittish animal once more and it backed away again, its rheumy red eyes wild with fear, until it was perched at the very lip of the precipice.

He gave up. He turned toward the cliff face and started climbing, only to slip back almost immediately when a chunk of rock came off in his hand. He could almost hear his wife Katerina's voice— ex-wife, to be accurate: "Never climb shale or slate if you can help it. It flakes off and you fall." She had taken up rock climbing more than a year earlier—taken up with a rock climber, too, and left Andrew for him shortly thereafter. Now he remembered some of her safety rules: Plan your ascent several moves in advance; maintain three reliable points of contact with the rock before you reach for the next hold; test each hold before you use it to bear weight. He'd often wished, in the weeks following her departure, that there had been similar rules for protecting oneself in the case of domestic landslides.

In a few moments of more-careful climbing, he regained the rim and hoisted himself up to the footpath. In the far distance, he could see a figure, a woman, striding along the cliffs, a large brown and white dog running circles around her. For reasons he could not fathom, she was waving her arms, as if in urgent communication with the dog.

He looked down. The sheep had returned to

munching, utterly oblivious to the fact that it would soon be out of grass and luck. The woman had been right: This was a very dim sheep—although in his experience, limited though it was to the few days since his arrival in Cornwall, in the stupidity sweepstakes all sheep seemed equally qualified. He resolved to tell the manager at the Visitor Centre in the village about the stranded sheep and let someone who knew what he was doing rescue it.

THE DAY HAD begun pleasantly enough: He'd taken a guided tour of the Valency river valley. His tour guide was an expert who knew every twist and turn of the tumbling stream, every nook and cranny in the valley: the places deer came to drink early in the morning; the springs and bogs that were the best spots to find frogs; the pool of deep water where, if you kept very still, you could sometimes see fish hanging motionless below the mirrored surface. Her name was Lilly Trelissick, and the Valency valley was her favorite place in the whole world. Lilly was nine. She hated her name and preferred to be called Lee. Naturally, she called Andrew Drew.

Lilly—or, rather, Lee—was the only child of Roger and Anne Trelissick, who lived at Bottreaux Farm on a hill above Boscastle, a small village in a steep-sided, V-shaped valley on Cornwall's stormy Atlantic coast. On the lush pastures above the valley, Roger raised Devon Ruby Red cattle, a breed much prized for its flavorful meat, and Anne worked part-time as a freelance illustrator of children's books. Andrew was renting a seventeenth-century stone cottage off in one corner of the farm, which the couple had renovated. Roger and Anne's house was newer—Georgian, Andrew thought, given its tall windows and pleasing proportions. He suspected his cottage, which seemed to have grown out of the ground rather than having been built upon it, was the original farmhouse.

Lee Trelissick charged a small fee for her tours, payable in the form of an ice cream bar—specifically a Chunky Choc Ice—readily purchased from the newsagent's shop just up the main road from the harbor and conveniently situated near the beginning of the footpath up the Valency valley. A few steps downhill from the shop, just above the narrow stone bridge that carried the only road through the village, the Valency met the Jordan, a smaller river that tumbled down the lesser arm of the valley toward the sea. In truth, both were little more than streams. Normally, at this time of year—for it was high summer—water levels in both streams would be low. But August had begun with unusually muggy, sunny days punctuated by sudden, short rain squalls, so the ground was saturated and both streams were flowing picturesquely fast and full.

Below the bridge, the conjoined streams followed an arrow-straight channel neatly bounded by ancient, hand-laid stone embankments. The little river clattered over rock shelves, ducked under another, even smaller stone bridge, and then lost itself in the harbor. Eons of water relentlessly seeking sea level had exploited fault lines in the towering slate cliffs of Penally Point and carved a narrow dogleg gap that formed the harbor mouth. Tiny and tidal, protected by two massive stone jetties, Boscastle harbor was the only protected cove along twenty miles of wild, shipwrecking Atlantic coast. The harbor had once been a bustling little cargo-shipping port, supported a modest coastal fishing fleet, and, in the old days, trafficked in no small amount of smuggled tea, tobacco, and brandy.

Standing on the cliff above the harbor entrance on the day he arrived, Andrew had thought about exhausted fishermen returning home, pitching through the tide rips and coastal swells after a long day out on the heaving ocean, only to face the daunting prospect of negotiating the diabolical harbor mouth. The first hazard to avoid was Meachard Rock, a massive outcrop of ragged, knife-sharp slate several stories high and situated squarely in front of the narrow entrance. Then the passage turned ninety degrees to port and ran a good hundred yards north between beetling crags before turning another ninety degrees to starboard and around the tip of one of the jetties, finally reaching a tiny area of protected water. It would be difficult and perilous enough to navigate this approach with today's sturdy, snub-nosed, diesel-powered fishing boats; he couldn't imagine how they'd done it during the age of sail.

What was hell for mariners, though, was heaven for tourists. The tortured sedimentary cliffs, the crashing sea spray, and the scenic harbor netted the quaint old fishing village great shoals of visitors every summer. These days, Boscastle's economic survival depended on the tourist trade. August, with schools closed and many Europeans on holiday, was high season, the make-or-break month for the gift shops and cafés that lined the narrow street, the month that would measure how some of the residents would fare the rest of the year.

Lee, however, was having none of it.

"I can't *wait* till all these people *leave!*" she hissed between licks along the exposed vanilla core of her chocolate-coated ice cream bar. She and Andrew were standing outside the newsagent's, just uphill from the big car park that had been built along the north bank of the Valency to accommodate the tourists.

"And anyway, just *look* at them," she sputtered as another tour bus stopped to disgorge a stream of travelers who then waddled off downhill like so many overnourished ducks, "Bet you none of them makes it to the top of Penally; they're all too *fat!* "

"I dunno, Lee; keep eating those ice creams and

you could end up the same way," Andrew said calmly.

The girl lifted an eyebrow. "You want the tour or not, Drew?"

Andrew laughed. "Okay, okay; you're the boss. Lead on."

Stratton had only been in Boscastle for a few days, but he'd already developed a fondness for the wiry little girl. There was nothing fussy about this kid. She seemed to live every day in the same worn khaki shorts, a T-shirt from someplace called the Eden Project, and olive-green rubber wellies—the better to wander through the woods below the farm and along the river's soggy upper reaches. Her arms and legs were bony and browned by the sun, and her sandy hair was cropped close to the skull, with a ragged fringe at the forehead. When she looked up at him, and especially when she smiled, her eyes narrowed to slits so thin he marveled she could see out of them at all. He never saw her with any other children; she seemed perfectly happy in her own company. And whenever he saw her crossing the fields beyond his cottage, her strides were strong and determined. No loitering among the meadow flowers or daisy-chain making for this one; Lee always seemed to be on a mission.

It worried him a bit that she wandered the countryside all alone. It was a city-dweller's worry, he knew, and, anyway, Anne had told him she'd long since stopped trying to keep track of her daughter. "She's a bit of an old soul, is our Lilly; she goes her own way," Anne had said, with what Andrew thought was a hint of awe, as if her daughter was something of a mystery to her. "Mind you, she's a good girl, smart and strong and trustworthy, but stubborn as a goat. And she either likes you or she doesn't."

Apparently, she liked Andrew. At least, he guessed she did, since most mornings he found her sitting on the stone wall by the gate to his cottage, facing the front door as if impatient for him to get a move on. She'd been there the first day after he arrived from the States. Jet lag had kept him asleep until nearly midmorning. Yawning, a cup of tea in his hand, he'd opened the top half of the split door at the front of his cottage and been greeted with "Who are you?"

He'd had no idea who she was.

"I'm Andrew; who are *you?*" he'd replied.

"Lee. I live here."

"No you don't; I do."

"On this farm, I do."

"I see. So Anne's your mother?"

"Uh-huh."

"But Anne told me her daughter's name was Lilly."

The girl screwed up her face in disgust. "I *hate* that name."

"I see."

"What are you doing here?"

"I'm renting this cottage."

"Are you on holiday?"

"Not really; I'm taking a course, starting Monday. It's like being at school."

"School? In the summer? That's daft."

"Oh, I don't know; I think I'll enjoy it."

"What are you going to school for?"

"Stone-wall building. I'm learning how to make walls . . . like the one you're sitting on."

"Why? We've already got plenty of them."

Andrew could see the door opening to a very long discussion, one he wasn't really prepared to enter, especially with an inquisitive little girl. The plain fact was, at least part of his brain worried that he was simply running away from his grief. That, and what he was sure were the unvoiced theories of friends and colleagues about why Kat had left him—was he a wife beater, a lush, a failure in bed? *Why,* he realized, was a very complex question. So he dodged it.

"Would you like a cup of tea?"

"Had some already."

"Like some more?"

"Nope. Gotta get going. Busy day." And with that, her curiosity apparently satisfied at least for the moment, the girl hopped down and dashed off across the meadow beyond the wall.

And ever since Wednesday, that's how their days had begun. He'd throw open the top half of the door and shout, "Good morning, madam!" (She liked that.)

"Guess what, Drew?!" she'd begin, hopping off the wall and skipping to the door. Lee seemed to think every new thought needed to be introduced this way: "Guess what?! The cat's had kittens." "Guess what?! Gonna rain later." "Guess what?! Dad's movin' the calves today."

Andrew had taken to answering. "I don't know, *what?*" just to tease her, but she just ignored him and launched right into the latest bit of local news. It was better than any morning newspaper. The news was always varied, interesting, and unexpected. It was a delightful way to start the day: a cup of hot, sweet, milky tea, and Miss "Guess What?!"

That's how today, Saturday, had started.

"Guess what, Drew?!"

"I don't know, *what?*"

"It's a good day for you to have my famous and ex-*clu*-sive guided walking tour of the river valley. Complete with sacred wells and witches!"

"Famous is it?"

"It is. Far and wide."

"How often have you conducted this tour?"

"Loads of times."

"Hmmm. Doesn't sound very exclusive."

She hesitated.

"A few times, then?" he ventured.

"Nearly once!" she said, giggling behind her hand.

19

"Ah, now that's what I call exclusive. When do we leave?"

"Soon's you finish that tea, because—Guess what?!—Mum's taking me to Wadebridge this afternoon to get new wellies; my feet've got too big for these ones." She hopped around on one foot and shook the other by way of emphasis.

"Well, then, I guess I'd better get a move on. I'll just get my boots."

When he emerged again, a day pack slung over one shoulder, she was waiting by the gate.

"Where shall we begin?" he asked.

"At the bottom, of course. In the village."

Given that he knew there was a back route from the farm directly into the valley, this seemed odd to Andrew, but he didn't argue; he liked the girl's company too much. "Right, then. Down to the village it is!"

It was a luminous morning; a bit of ground fog drifted up in wisps from the cooler fingers of the valley, evaporating quickly in the warming air. They followed a narrow lane that dipped into the side valley cut by the little River Jordan, passed a whitewashed old mill perched above the stream, briefly joined the main road from Camelford, then turned into steep, one-way Fore Street and followed it as it twisted downhill. Over the centuries, Boscastle had evolved two centers: "Top Town," high above the valley, where they were now, and "Quay Town," down around the harbor, though hardly anyone called them that anymore. Fore Street—which, somewhat confusingly changed its name to Dunn Street halfway down the hill—linked the two. Andrew loved the almost medieval character of the narrow street, lined as it was on both sides with squat stone cottages leaning one against the other, as if exhausted by time. They passed the village hall, the old Methodist chapel, the primary school Lee attended, and the post office. Lee rapped on the window with her knuckles and waved to Sam Bonney, who was behind the service window at the back. Beyond the post office, the street turned sharply right and plunged downhill even more steeply, paralleling the course of the Jordan, which clattered through the valley far below. Although it was barely ten o'clock when they reached the bottom, tourists already packed Quay Town as tightly as salted sardines in a barrel.

It was here that Andrew was informed matter-of-factly by his guide that there was a small fee for the tour. Ice cream seemed to Andrew a fine breakfast, so he bought Chunky Choc Ices for them both. Soon they'd left behind the crowded car park and were heading upstream through the trees bordering the Valency. The tourists all seemed to have been drawn like iron filings by the magnetism of the cliff-ringed harbor, and Andrew and Lee had the leafy riverside footpath to themselves.

Trees arched overhead, their branches cloaked in gray-green lichen, their trunks often wrapped in glossy green ivy. Here, just above the port area, the valley's wooded slopes climbed steeply up from the banks of the stream, leaving just enough room for the riverbed and the narrow footpath. But a little farther on, the floor of the valley opened, and the path meandered through a grassy meadow. Here and there, massive boulders of creamy, apricot-veined quartz lay about in the riverbed like some giant's abandoned marble collection, washed down from who knew where by some terrible force.

"You've missed most of the flowers," Lee said, as if Andrew hadn't been paying attention.

"What do you mean?"

"There are masses and masses of primroses, and daffodils, and bluebells, and things here in the spring. You should see Minster churchyard then; there's so many daffodils then you can barely see the gravestones. But they're all gone now. You came too late."

Andrew felt as if he should apologize. "Still lots of flowers here, though," he countered, somewhat defensively. "Like this, for instance." He pointed to a bush flecked with pale pink blossoms maturing to ivory.

Lee snorted. "That's just dog rose. It's a weed, like these nasty, prickly blackberry brambles. They get everywhere. I hate them."

"Your mother told me she makes blackberry wine."

"Lotta good that does me."

Andrew couldn't argue with this line of reasoning.

They passed through a wooden gate in a stone wall.

"Mind the stinging nettles," Lee warned.

"Which are they?" He pushed aside the branches of a fringe-leafed plant that clustered around the gateposts and his hand suddenly felt on fire. "*Damn!* I think I just found out."

Lee stopped and shook her golden head with disgust. "I *told* you! Now I'm going to have to find you some dock." She stomped off up the path, then bent and snapped off a broad, bladelike, greenish-yellow leaf. Andrew followed.

"Here. Crush this and rub it where it stings."

He did so, and in moments the pain vanished.

"How'd you know that would work?" he asked, amazed.

The girl looked at him as if he was brain-damaged. "Everybody knows dock cures nettle stings. Why do you think they grow near each other?"

Having no idea what either nettles or dock were, Andrew had never given this question much thought.

"Come on," Lee said. "I don't have a lot of time to waste."

"Yes, ma'am!"

A gentle bend revealed a pool created by a low stone dam that slowed the stream's flow. They stopped and sat on a rock, where Lee said you could see fish in the still water. Andrew stared at the surface intently.

"I don't see any," he said finally.

"They're shy sometimes."

"Are they big?"

"I should say so; really big."

"How big?"

"That's a weir, that is," Lee volunteered, changing the subject and pointing toward an outlet just upstream of the dam. "It used to shunt water to the leat."

"Leat?"

"You know, *leat* . . . what carries the water to the mill. I thought you Americans spoke English."

"I used to think so," Andrew said, "but now I'm not so sure."

"Okay, you know that big red wooden water-wheel by the leather shop, down near the car park? Used to be a mill there. Water that ran it came from here."

"What kind of mill?"

"A mill that grinds stuff, silly."

"What kind of stuff?"

"You sure have a lot of questions for a grown-up."

"You sure know a lot for a kid."

"Is that a compliment?"

"I never compliment before lunch."

Lee smiled. "You remind me of my friend Nicki.

24

She says things like that. You'd like her. She's funny."

"Am I funny?"

"Not before lunch."

Lee hopped off the rock and spun off up the path again, sometimes walking, sometimes skipping. From time to time, she'd stop and peer at something in the bushes—a bird or a butterfly—and name it.

Andrew was amazed at how much Lee already knew about the natural world. "Where did you learn all this?" he asked when he caught up with her.

"Mostly from Elizabeth. Mum says I'm to call her 'Mrs. Davis,' but she says I can call her Elizabeth. She runs the Visitor Centre and knows loads of stuff."

"But wait, you're not a visitor."

Lee looked at him a moment, as if trying to decide whether he was teasing or just stupid.

"That's silly," she said, and off she skipped again.

Andrew followed happily, his eyes sweeping the hillsides. The trees climbing the slopes included ash, beech, and hazel, but mostly they were gnarled sessile oaks, which looked to him like something from a fairy tale, their mossy branches thick, twisted, and dense. It was the kind of woodland that should have fairies and elves, and he said so.

"I never saw none, but Nicki says there are piskies down here."

"Piskies?"

"You know; little folk."

"Has she seen them?"

"Never asked. Mostly, if Nicki says something, that's good enough for me."

Andrew was admiring the elaborate structure of one particular oak, a very old one that overhung the river, when Lee piped up.

"Guess what, Drew?!"

"I don't know, *what,* Lee?"

"That's my secret tree."

"Is it indeed?"

"Uh-huh. I climb way high up in it sometimes with a book and read there."

"I bet it's peaceful up among the leaves."

Lee's secret tree was made for climbing; its branches began low and continued, ladderlike, far up its thick, knobby trunk. Andrew swung up onto the lowest branch and said, "Come on; show me where you sit!"

Lee scrambled up past him with the sureness of a monkey, until the two of them were deep in a cylinder of green leaves, virtually invisible from the ground.

Lee settled into the crotch of one of the branches and leaned against the trunk. Andrew balanced on a branch beside her.

"Maybe I'll come up here and read sometimes, too," he said.

"Better ask me first," she said with a proprietary frown. "It's my tree, after all."

"Of course."

She leaned toward him and confided, "Sometimes I sit here and spy on people walking along the footpath."

"No kidding! See anyone interesting?"

"Uh-huh. Saw the vicar once."

"What was he doing?"

"Not 'he,' silly, 'she.' He's a *she!*"

"You're joking."

"Don't you go to St. Symphorian's?"

"I've only been here a few days, Lee; gimme a break."

Her eyes narrowed to slits. "You're not one of those Methodists are you?" She asked this as if Methodists had horns.

"No, I'm not. Wait a minute; how can St.—what was it?"

"Symphorian's."

"Right, Symphorian's. How can they have a priest who's a woman? I didn't think Catholics allowed that."

"It's not Catholic; it's C. of E., innit!"

"Huh?"

"Church of England. You don't know a whole lot, do you?"

"Geez, I guess not."

"Me and Mum, we're C. of E. Dad is, too, I think, but he's too busy with the farm most Sundays to go to church. Goes Christmas and Easter, though."

"And the C. of E. has lady priests?"

"Uh-huh."

"Wow."

The girl shot him a look. "You got a problem with that?"

"No!"

"'Cause some people do, I guess. My friend Nicki, she calls them 'nanderthals.'"

"*Ne*-anderthals. Boy, your friend sure uses big words." He wondered whether all the kids in Boscastle were as precocious as these two.

"Yeah, *Neanderthals;* that's it. It means backward, sort of. You're not one of them, are you?"

Andrew placed his right hand over his heart. "Neither a Methodist nor a Neanderthal, to the best of my knowledge. Promise."

This seemed to satisfy Lee. Back on the ground, the two of them continued along the riverbank until they reached a narrow wooden footbridge that crossed the stream to a path that led up the thickly wooded hillside opposite.

"End of tour," Lee announced.

"That's it? What about the wells and witches?"

"Have to wait till next time. Got to meet my mum so's we can go to Wadebridge. For the boots."

She dashed across the footbridge.

"Thanks for the ice cream," she called over her shoulder.

"I'm going to complain about this to the Visitor

Centre," Andrew called after her. There was no reply, but he thought he heard a distant giggle.

He slipped off his day pack, unzipped it, and pulled out an Ordnance Survey Explorer Map. He checked it for a moment, shouldered his pack, and continued upstream. At a tiny cluster of cottages the map identified as Newmills, he climbed out of the valley and turned seaward. He was heading for the coast path and, unbeknownst to him, an encounter with a stranded sheep.

Flash floods are sudden and often unpredictable events resulting from massive and sudden rainstorms, a rapid snowmelt in mountain regions, or a failure of natural or man-made water defenses. Although these events are relatively rare in the UK, flash floods do occur, often with devastating consequences.

Boscastle Special Flood Issue,
Journal of Meteorology 29, no. 293

Nicola Rhys-Jones was berating herself. And not quietly. She was shouting into the wind.

"Idiot! Bloody idiot! Meet a nice-looking guy with a conscience, toss off a few wisecracks, walk away. Brilliant!"

Randi, her seven-year-old Siberian husky, rocketed around her, barking, as she tramped along the coast path. Randi liked this game: His mistress yelled and waved her arms, and he ran in circles. Any minute now, he knew, she'd stop, look at him, and say, "What the hell do you think you're doing, you crazy dog!" Then she'd kneel down and give him a big hug, because she felt even more foolish than he looked. He knew this. He loved it. Especially the hugs.

Nicola did exactly that, then stood up and looked back along the cliffs to the north. High above Pentargon, near the stream of the same name that flung itself over the cliff edge, becoming no more than mist by the time it reached the beach far below, she saw the tiny figure of a man. The handsome man who'd tried to help the idiot sheep. The handsome man with the thick, curly, salt-and-pepper hair and the gentle, caring face. She would not wait for him to catch up. She wanted to, sort of, but mostly she didn't. Too obvious. She passed the tall pole with the fish-shaped weather vane at the top of Penally Point, then trudged down the steep path toward Boscastle harbor and her tiny stone cottage–cum-studio near the jetty.

Nicola Rhys-Jones, single—divorced, if you wanted to be technical about it—was rapidly approaching "woman of a certain age" status and pretending it didn't matter to her in the least, though it did. Anyone—any man, at least—passing her on the coast path would have observed a woman beautiful by any definition but her own: long, softly wavy dark-brown hair; big brown eyes beneath thick, expressive brows; a handsome nose admittedly a bit too big for her face; high, angular cheekbones; skin slightly olive and remarkably unlined; full lips that curved up at the corners with the perpetual hint of a smile, as if she was keeping a secret; the beginnings of softness beneath the chin—the only part of her, so far, that was giving way to gravity. She was nearly forty, but didn't look it. Yet. She stood three inches shy of six feet (a little too tall, she thought) and had broad shoulders (a little too broad, she worried), generously proportioned breasts (too generous—her Italian heritage), and slender legs attached to shapely hips she worked hard to keep from spreading (thus the dog walking, not that she didn't enjoy it). Her ex-husband, Jeremy, used to say something coarse she had secretly enjoyed, before she began hating it: "I like seeing daylight between your thighs."

Nicola unlocked the low wooden door to her tiny

stone cottage, went into the kitchen, filled a bowl with water for Randi, then mixed herself a gin and tonic and climbed the steep stone steps to her studio. She loved the house, especially the light-filled studio with its view of the harbor. She lay back on the chaise opposite her easel and put her glass on the floor. The upper story of the cottage had once been a loft for drying fishing nets. The ground floor had been an office and a storage room for crab pots. The place suited her at this stage of her life, though it was a far cry from the gracious home she had shared with Jeremy.

Jeremy. What a disaster. Ten years of marriage to a rich, well-educated, hopelessly narcissistic Englishman who also happened to have an abusive streak. As if she hadn't had enough of that as a girl.

Nicola DeLucca, graduate student at the Art Institute of Boston, had met Jeremy Rhys-Jones, son of an English peer, while she was on a fellow-ship in Florence, Italy. His family had a modest estate on Cornwall's rocky, wind-wracked Penwith peninsula, near the artists' colony of St. Ives. She was the sole daughter of a working-class immigrant family from the claustrophobic Italian enclave that was Boston's North End. She had had two brothers: one younger, James, the older one, John—named after apostles, saints, though only James would later warrant that honor. Her father, Anthony, had abandoned his family when she was only six, and her mother, Angela, had been forced to go to work cleaning offices in the State House at night—an unspoken source of shame in the neighborhood.

After high school, Nicola had won an art scholarship to Boston College. Four years later, she graduated and landed a part-time job as a book jacket designer for a publisher. In her free time, she took advanced painting courses at the Art Institute. Winning the fellowship freed her from the need to work and forced her to take seriously her talent as a painter.

In Florence, she floated in a nearly perpetual state of sensory overload. Her breakfast was cappuccino and biscotti amid the continuous hiss of the espresso machine behind the long marble counter of the steamy corner café near her student rooms. Then she wandered out into the city. She quickly realized that the elaborate palaces left her cold. Even the glorious Duomo felt strangely oppressive. The places that stirred her were far more pedestrian: tiny shops lining the narrow stone-paved alleys and arched arcades; the agricultural abundance of the public markets at the Piazza Lorenzo Ghiberti; the black and red capes the Florentine police wore as they sat astride horses so white and muscular they seemed carved from the same dazzling Carrara marble as Michelangelo's *David;* the street artists chalking pastel reproductions of Renaissance masterpieces on the pavement of the Via Santa Maria; and the equally brilliant artistry that went into the product displays in every cheese and smoked-meat shop in the city, as if their owners considered artful merchandising as important as the mouthwatering quality of their foods. She spent hours sketching the alleys, rooflines, the window displays, and the milling crowds in the piazzas of the city for oil studies she would later complete in class.

Jeremy was not in Florence studying art; Jeremy was in Florence studying Italian women. It was just her luck that he preferred his Italian women to be English-speaking. Though a year younger than she, he was mature, and cultured, and charming. And tall. And dishy. And unlike anyone she'd ever met in the North End. His accent, which exuded solicitude and breeding, reached her in a way the salaciously insinuating voices of her Italian class-mates never could.

Nicola fell hard. Many afternoons, she and Jeremy climbed the hill opposite the city to the ter-race of the Piazzale Michelangelo to watch the set-ting sun gild the stone and stucco walls and red-tiled roofs stretching toward the distant, mauve hills. One evening, Jeremy took her to the Ponte Vecchio to see the statue of Cellini, the famous goldsmith. Every post and railing of the cast-iron fence surrounding the statue was trimmed with padlocks. Lovers, he said, sealed their love by attaching locks inscribed with their names to the fence and then throwing the key into the Arno

River, far below. And when he presented her with a similar lock etched with their names, she was surprised. She was even more surprised when she clasped the lock to the fence, turned the key, and flung it into the river.

Jeremy returned to England while she continued studying and painting in Florence, but he wrote ardent letters to her almost daily. No one had ever done that for her before. He flew down every few weekends. Then, as winter approached, he invited her to spend Christmas with his family in Cornwall. Charmed by the cookie-tin image of Christmas in England—the thatched cottages, the mistletoe, the horse-drawn sled tracks in snowy lanes—and unable to afford the airfare back to Boston anyway, she accepted. She flew to London, then took the long train ride down nearly to the tip of Britain's southwest peninsula. Jeremy met her at the station in St. Ives in a drafty, beat-up Land Rover. He was wearing an oily-smelling, waxed-canvas waterproof jacket, a flat tweed cap, and green rubber boots she learned were called Wellingtons, though she didn't know why.

Jeremy had described his family's home as a "country house," and Nicola had in mind something small, sweet, and ivy-clad. So when they passed through pillared gates, she was completely unprepared for either the scale or the grandeur of the granite mansion to which the long, tree-lined drive led. Compared to the cramped row houses of the North End—or, for that matter, to the houses in Florence—the house seemed to her palatial.

Trevega House, as it was called, lay in a sheltered valley cut by a stream that raced west from the high moor tops before emptying into the sea. The estate ranged for several hundred acres and included a clustered hamlet of former tenants' cottages, a farm complex, even a disused water mill. Over the generations, the Rhys-Joneses had created lush landscape gardens and broad lawns around the manor house, as well as a massive walled vegetable garden. Even at Christmas there were fresh herbs, salad greens from glass-topped cold frames, beets, kale, turnips, rutabagas ("Swedes," the cook called them), and arm-thick leeks.

Inside the house, the rooms were high-ceilinged and spacious. From her time in Italy, Nicola recognized the gracious, almost mathematical symmetry of the building's facade as influenced by Andrea Palladio, the great Italian Renaissance architect. The interior of the house, though, was saved from being austere and intimidating by its furnishings, which were informal, comfortable, and decidedly English—a hodgepodge of patterns, colors, and textures that somehow worked as a whole. There were big, over-stuffed sofas and plush chairs, thick drapes, sturdy and well-used antique oak and pine tables and cabinets, worn but beautiful Persian rugs, shelves and shelves of books, and cozy fires in the wide, stone-linteled fireplaces that anchored each room.

For the holiday, evergreen boughs, red-berried holly branches, and ropes of ivy were arranged on windowsills and tabletops. The evergreen clusters were studded with tiny bunches of dried baby's breath, which made them look dusted with snow. In the stone-flagged reception hall, the floor was strewn with lavender sprigs and bay leaves, so that every time you entered or left the house, fragrance rose in your wake. There were candles everywhere.

The coastal landscape beyond the valley, however, was a far cry from the "green and pleasant land" Nicola envisioned when she thought about England. The hills around the Rhys-Jones estate were rugged and wind-whipped. Miles of ancient stone walls crawled across bare, rocky slopes, which rose to massive granite outcrops that looked like the bleached bones of some prehistoric beast sticking up through the skin of the earth. Where the terrain was too rough to be grazed, it was scabbed over with dense, dun-colored blankets of heather and prickly gorse. What trees there were, and they were few, were twisted and salt-stunted, their trunks and limbs bent away from the wind screaming in from the Atlantic. Their bare winter branches put Nicola in mind of the frozen tresses of a maiden standing on a cliff top, face-on in a winter gale.

And wherever Nicola walked there were remnants of Bronze and Iron Age settlements: stone hut circles, rings of standing stones, hilltop burial quoits, and enigmatic granite monoliths, all of them, Jeremy explained, thousands of years old. Some of the buildings in Boston's North End dated to before the Revolutionary War, but this was antiquity beyond anything in her experience, beyond even Florence—a landscape steeped in mystery and magic.

Then there were the place-names—Pendeen, Zennor, Morvah, Porthmeor, Treen—as rough-edged and raw-sounding as the landscape itself and as alien to her as if they were in some foreign language. And indeed they were. They were Cornish, an ancient Celtic tongue closely related to the original languages of Wales and Brittany. Other villages were named after obscure Celtic saints: St. Just, St. Buryan, St. Sinar, among others.

Someone else might have found this midwinter world impossibly bleak, but Nicola felt strangely at home. It took her a few days of wandering to understand why: The rocky crags and the windswept cliffs, she realized, were simply colder, windier, wetter versions of pictures she'd seen as a child of the sparsely clad hills her father and mother had come from in Sicily.

For all the estate's ruggedness, though, the grazing meadows nestled within its snaking stone walls were, even at Christmastime, impossibly green. The climate here was gentle, even if the wind wasn't, and the rainfall plentiful. So, though the soil was shallow (the granite bedrock was only a few inches below the turf), the coastal plateau was prime grazing land, and Jeremy's father's farm manager, Nigel Lawrence, ran a large herd of Black Angus cattle on this land.

Jeremy's small family—his father, Sir Michael, and his younger sister, Nina—received her warmly. Nicola knew that his mother, Jemma, had died years earlier not far from their London town house when she flipped her antique MG convertible while driving too fast—"As usual," Jeremy had said with disgust—along the Thames Embankment. Nicola liked Nina immediately. Jeremy's sister was a talented landscape designer who had helped in the restoration of the long-abandoned Victorian-era gardens at Heligan, outside nearby St. Austell.

And, after a few days (and a few large whiskies), his father, Sir Michael, a large man in his midseventies with an unruly mane of white hair and a sparkle in his clear, blue eyes, told Nicola that she reminded him of his wife. "Strong-minded and high-spirited, she was," Sir Michael had rumbled, his gentle, jowly face creasing in fond remembrance. "Just like you, my dear, just like you; fine thoroughbred stock, both of you." Nicola thought about the near poverty in which she'd been raised and simply smiled, not even knowing how to respond.

Jeremy had described his mother as wild and his father as intimidating, but Nicola and Sir Michael got along famously right from the start. He was courtly and kind and made her feel at home. She simply adored him—as the father, perhaps, she'd always dreamed of but had been denied. Nicola and Sir Michael shared a language of aesthetics that Jeremy did not comprehend. Sir Michael's artistic passions were on display on walls throughout the great house. He was a lifelong collector of the works of the English artists who had painted in the Cornish coastal art colonies of St. Ives, Lamorna, and Newlyn at the beginning of the twentieth century: Stanhope Forbes, Frank Bramley, Laura Knight, Borlase Smart, and Alfred Wallis, among others. But it was Laura Knight's talent for capturing the clarity, intensity, and purity of the light unique to the far southwest of Cornwall that affected Nicola most—and later influenced her own painting.

On Christmas Day, Jeremy gave her a complete set of Winsor & Newton oil paints and a portable easel. Sir Michael gave her a charcoal sketch of a woman with a small boy in her lap. It was some days later that she learned, from Jeremy, that it was a portrait of his grandmother and his father as a boy, by Stanhope Forbes.

Then, on New Year's Eve, Jeremy surprised her

by asking her to marry him, and Nicola surprised herself by accepting.

Her mother disapproved: Why couldn't she marry someone from the neighborhood, someone whose family they knew? And these people weren't even Catholic! But Sir Michael wrote Nicola's mother a long letter full of admiration and affection for her daughter, and it charmed Angela DeLucca completely.

NICOLA LOOKED DOWN at her gin and tonic and was surprised to find the glass empty. Should she make another? The day had been strangely hot and close. Maybe it was global warming. It wasn't supposed to be humid in Cornwall, even in August.

She worried she drank too much. It hadn't always been that way. Only since St. Ives. She went to the tall window overlooking the harbor and saw below her the man from the cliffs. He was walking along the path on the opposite side of the river, past the youth hostel and the Harbour Light, toward the center of the village. His stride was easy, loose-limbed. She wondered who he was.

AT THE BEGINNING, everything seemed perfect. The wedding was in late May, just after Nicola's fellowship ended. The ceremony was performed at the eleventh-century church in Zennor, the hamlet closest to the Rhys-Jones estate. The Anglican rector graciously allowed Nicola's brother James, who'd recently been ordained a Catholic priest, to participate in the ceremony. Sir Michael had flown both her brother and her mother "over the pond" for the event. The stark stone sanctuary had been bedecked with white roses and chrysanthemums. Her mother had cried.

After a damp honeymoon of island-hopping in Scotland's Outer Hebrides, she and Jeremy moved into Trevega House. It wasn't her husband's first choice. Jeremy had taken an economics degree at Cambridge and planned to work at the London headquarters of his father's financial-management firm, tending to the arcane investment problems of his father's many wealthy clients by day and enjoying the city's social scene by night. But Sir Michael had other ideas. He sent Jeremy off to apprentice at the firm's Penzance office and gave them the country house in which to live. Sir Michael tended to stay in London, close to the House of Lords and his club.

Jeremy was furious with this arrangement, but Nicola was thrilled. She loved the rambling old house, the gardens, the peaceful evenings by the fire, the long walks along the coast, and the horse-back rides deep into the prehistoric granite hills. And then there was Sir Michael's wedding present to her: a little painting studio of her own over-looking the harbor in nearby St. Ives, where the light was diamond bright and the aquamarine water in the little port looked positively

Mediterranean. The truth, of course—the white sand beach notwithstanding—was that the water sweeping in from the Atlantic with each tide was so cold, even in midsummer, that only children (whose nerve endings seemed yet to have developed) could tolerate it for more than a few minutes.

Children. They'd had none, though not for want of trying. Nicola's secret was that her own sexuality was complicated and fraught—she could be frisky and flirtatious one moment, remote and disengaged the next. It troubled her, but she kept it to herself, and the fact was that her husband was too involved in his own needs to even notice the shifts. Then, a few years into the marriage, years in which her husband increasingly lurched from solicitous to abusive, Jeremy decided it was time they started a family. After that, sex became his obsession. And when months passed with no pregnancy, he turned brutally primal, hammering away at her like a machine, as if his sheer determination were all it would take to plant new life. The harder he pounded her, though, the colder and more distant Nicola became. She could feel her consciousness detach itself from her body and rise above the bed. That wasn't her down there; it was someone else, a ghost—a ghost she recognized, one who had done this before, who had had this done to her before. She floated high above and away from it all, to safety.

And as she had once before, she stopped eating, as if to purify herself, as if the pain of hunger could expunge whatever it was that she had done, whatever sin she had committed, to bring this abuse upon herself. When Jeremy began to take ever-longer business trips to London, she found herself relieved. She suspected that he had a lover in the city, and she realized she didn't care. It should have felt like loss, but instead it felt like relief.

NICOLA'S ONLY CONFIDANTE in those days was Annabelle Lawrence, the farm manager's wife. A leggy, tomboyish blonde, Annabelle was several years younger than Nicola, but she and Nigel already had a child, Jesse, who, at two, seemed to be permanently and happily grafted to Annabelle's left hip. Annabelle was one of those relentlessly upbeat, energetic women who take everything easily in stride. Faced with some difficulty, whether with the cattle or with her life, her perennial comment was "Oh well, it's a temporary problem," as if the only thing worth giving much serious thought to was death itself.

Annabelle liked Nicola and was worried about her. In recent months, Nicola had lost weight and seemed to have gone pale, as if the inner warmth of her Mediterranean skin, a radiance Annabelle so envied, had turned wintry. One dreary autumn morning at about eleven, when she noticed Nicola hadn't driven to her studio in St. Ives, Annabelle paid a visit with a plate of freshly baked currant scones. She let herself in through the back door, called out, and found Nicola sitting alone at the scrubbed-pine trestle table in Trevega House's cavernous kitchen, staring out a window toward the ocean as a cold mist crept in from the Atlantic.

"Foul day is what it is out there," Annabelle announced gaily as she stripped off her wet jacket and set Jesse down in his carrier chair. "What say we girls have tea and get fat on these scones?"

Nicola looked up and gave her a wan smile.

"You all right, then, luv? You're looking right peaked lately."

"I'm fine, Annabelle, really; just tired."

"You're spending too much time in that studio of yours, that's what it is. Wearin' yourself right out getting ready for that exhibition."

Nicola had been working hard preparing canvases for an opening at the Great Atlantic Gallery in nearby St. Just, but that wasn't it.

"I'll just put the kettle on," Nicola said, rising and heading for the counter where it sat.

She never made it. She had only gone a few steps before the room began to swim around her. She shot an arm out for support, found nothing, and collapsed. She never felt the floor when it rose to meet her; she had blacked out.

"Mother of God!" Annabelle cried. Having had some training as a nurse before she'd married Nigel, Annabelle checked Nicola's breathing and pulse, then raced to the sitting room, grabbed pillows from the couch in front of the big granite fireplace, and returned, using one to support Nicola's head and the rest to prop her legs above her heart. It was when she unzipped Nicola's hooded sweatshirt to help her breathe that Annabelle saw the bruises on her neck and collarbone. Someone had throttled her. There was only one likely candidate. Instinctively, Annabelle pulled the zipper up, then changed her mind and exposed the welts again. A fury built inside her. She was holding a cool, damp cloth over her friend's forehead when Nicola came to.

"Well, that was stupid, wasn't it?" Nicola said, blinking and struggling to sit up.

"No, sweetie," Annabelle whispered, pulling Nicola close. "Stupid is letting him do this to you and not telling anyone."

It had taken months, Annabelle's persistence, and several visits to a social services adviser in Penzance for Nicola to leave her husband. When she did, in the middle of a freakishly cold March, she did it quietly one day when he was away. She took only her car, her clothes, and her art supplies.

She drove north along the coast, following narrow, rural lanes. From time to time, like someone testing the water temperature with a toe, she'd dip down into a tiny fishing village tucked in a cleft in the cliffs to see how she liked it. She was intuitively unwilling to stray far from the sea that gave her so much pleasure and that informed so much of her art. On the third day of her meandering journey, she turned down a steep hill and found herself at the harbor in Boscastle at low tide. Something about it was right: the way the colorful local boats leaned this way and that on the mudflats, waiting for the tide to turn; the pretty river twisting through the village; the protective folds of the valley. The trees had just begun to break leaf and the slopes were furred in pastel green. Daffodils and lemon-yellow primroses bloomed along the river, as if their color alone could bring warmth. Tucked beneath the cliff on the south side of the little harbor was a small, honest, stone building with a WELL-APPOINTED COTTAGE TO LET sign in the window. She punched the number into her cell phone and discovered there was no signal there at the bottom of the valley, so she phoned from a public phone in the Wellington Hotel. She agreed to rent the place for a week. A few days later, she extended her stay another week. Eventually, she came to an understanding with the owner, a born-again Christian who owned a gift shop in the lower village, for a year-to-year lease. What the owner lost in high-season rates was offset by the cottage's no longer being empty during the winter and the fact that she no longer had to clean the place every week.

About a month later, Nicola was working in her upstairs studio when she heard a knock at the door.

She had no friends at that point and couldn't imagine who it might be. When she got downstairs and opened the door, she found Sir Michael there, leaning on his cane in the rain, with a large parcel under his arm.

"Good afternoon, my dear," he said, his great head tilting downward, almost shyly. "Do you suppose I might come in out of the elements?"

Nicola felt a surge of fear. "Jeremy?"

"I come alone, Nicola. I should like a word with you, if you'll permit me."

Nicola stepped back from the door and the big man entered. He set down the parcel, leaning it against the wall with great care, straightened, and shrugged off his wet coat. Finally, he turned to her and smiled, his sagging, bloodhound face transformed with warmth.

"Hello, dear Nicola," he said softly. "I have missed you."

Tears slipped down Nicola's cheeks and Sir Michael took her into his arms.

"Oh, Dad," she said into his shoulder. "I'm so sorry. It's just that I couldn't . . ."

"I know, dear one. You couldn't tell me. But I found out. Nigel told me, in the end. He didn't want to, of course; managing the farm is his life, and he didn't want to jeopardize that. Annabelle made him. He went after her, you know."

"Nigel did?" Nicola was confused.

"No, dear girl. Jeremy. Made a play for her, you

49

see. Well, attacked her, actually. First you, then the staff. Disgusting. My own son."

Sir Michael looked around the tiny sitting room and dropped into a chair by the coal fire.

"I don't suppose you have a whisky?"

Nicola shook herself out of her shock. "Um, no. Brandy? I have a nice cognac . . ."

"Splendid." He inched the chair closer to the fire.

When she returned, Nicola sat on the floor and wrapped her arms around her father-in-law's knees.

"How did you find me?"

The old man shrugged. "Not so difficult, really, for a man in my position. Put in a word at the Yard. They traced your auto, you see."

"But why?"

Sir Michael looked at her, placed a wrinkled, age-spotted hand upon her shoulder, and chuckled. It was more a rumble. It came from somewhere deep within him, somewhere rich and sonorous. It was a sound that wrapped around her like a goose-down duvet.

"Thoroughbred stock, my dear; thoroughbred stock. Knew it from the moment you walked through the door. Told him that Christmas someone like you came along once in a lifetime and it was time he settled down. But I had no way of knowing my only son was a brute, I promise you. How could I? What do we ever really know about our children, except what they allow us to know? Feel like a fool, and worse. Lost someone very dear to me when you left. Love my daughter, of course, but you . . . well, you were—*are*—something else entirely."

Nicola saw the watery shimmer in Sir Michael's eyes and hugged his knees closer.

"I can't come back, Dad. I won't."

"I know that, my dear, and have no intention of asking you to."

"Then why are you here? Why did you track me down?"

"My son, I am sorry to say, is not a gentleman. But I am. It is my responsibility—and my great joy—to ensure you are provided for."

"I don't want anything from—"

"Hush, Nicola. I know you don't. Don't you see that's partly why I am here? You conducted yourself throughout this horror like a perfect lady. In some respects, I rather wish you hadn't; I would have understood what was happening sooner. I've come to tell you that I have arranged for the divorce and made Jeremy sign the papers. That is what you desire, is it not?"

Nicola nodded.

"Good. That's sorted, then. In addition, I aim to make sure you experience no further hardship. You've had quite enough."

"But—"

He put up a hand. "There will be a small stipend—nothing embarrassing, I assure you—but you will not be uncomfortable. It will be deposited to an account in your name every month. I have also kept your studio in St. Ives, and am leasing it out. Of course, should you ever wish to have it again . . ."

"Dad, you know how I love St. Ives and that studio—oh, the light! But so long as Jeremy is at Trevega House, I couldn't possibly . . ."

"I know. I haven't yet decided what to do about him. But in the meantime, I'm doing quite well on the studio rental, if I do say so myself!" His old eyes sparkled like those of a thief with a diamond. He took another sip of the brandy. "Oh, and there is one more thing."

He hoisted himself from his chair, groaning from the effort, and moved slowly toward the door, where the parcel leaned against the wall.

"Nicola, I want you to have this. I know you love it, and it would please me to no end to know it was with you. Besides, should you ever find yourself in difficulties, Christie's will, I'm sure, be happy to auction it at some princely sum."

He lifted the parcel, which was wrapped carefully in heavy brown paper, and set it before her. Nicola unwrapped it slowly, but thought she knew what it was. It was the painting she admired most in Sir Michael's collection: Laura Knight's exquisite *Ella, Nude in Chair.* When she lifted it from its wrapping she stared at her father-in-law, shaking her head.

"No. I couldn't—"

"I'm afraid you must, my dear; it's already written into my will. It was, actually, long before any of this trouble began. Do you know the story behind it?"

Laura Knight and her husband, Harold, Nicola knew, had been members of what became known as the Lamorna school, a group of painters who settled in the leafy Lamorna Valley, on the coast a few miles west of Penzance, in the years before World War I. Their painter friends included S. J. "Lamorna" Birch and his family, and Charles and Ella Naper. Most of these artists, drawn by the natural setting and the scintillating light, painted coastal landscapes and scenes of fishermen at sea or bathers along the shore. But Laura Knight also produced a number of studio paintings, including this nude of her best friend, Ella Naper, whom she'd posed in a gilded armchair draped with a black and red silk robe. The painting had a slightly unfinished look; though the figure in the chair was perfect, and Ella's skin was luminous, much of the background was filled in roughly, with broad brushstrokes. Nicola loved its freedom.

"Turns out," Sir Michael began, "Laura's husband, Harold, never loved her. Oh no. He was head over heels for Ella, his friend Charlie Naper's wife. Times being what they were, of course, friendship was as far as it got. Always felt sorry for Laura, though. Knew them all, you see; Mother was part of their circle. Told me she thought the complexity of the relationship spurred Laura's art. The nude's splendid; she painted it in one sitting, is what Mother told me. Can you imagine? Pleasure to give it to someone with your talent." He glanced again at the painting. "Maybe she'll be your muse—eh, my girl?"

NICOLA ROSE FROM the chaise and descended to her kitchen. Outside, the sun had set, and the harbor was in shadow. She fed Randi, refilled his water bowl, and made herself another gin and tonic. Then she went into her sitting room, lay down on the sofa, sipped her drink, and stared at the painting of Ella Naper that now hung above the rough granite mantel. She thought of Ella as her spiritual companion, though one nearly a century removed—a free spirit, naked and confident in her world. It was who she wanted to be. It was, in fact, who she'd become in the nearly four years she'd lived in Boscastle.

Moments later, she was asleep. After a while, Randi came in from the kitchen, nuzzled his mistress's hand, got no response, and curled up in his usual place, on the rug in front of the hearth.

. . . flash floods arise when the ground becomes saturated with water so quickly that it cannot be absorbed. This leads to "run-off." Run-off is part of the hydrologic cycle connecting precipitation and channel flow. It occurs when the infiltration capacity of the soil surface is exceeded, and the subsurface can no longer absorb moisture at the rate at which it is supplied.

Boscastle Flood Special Issue,
Journal of Meteorology 29, no. 293

three

"Guess what, Drew?!"

Andrew had just opened the door of his cottage to a soft August Sunday morning. Lee was in her usual place. She had on her new wellies.

"You're going to finish the tour today and take me to see the sacred wells and the witches?"

"No, silly; it's nearly time to go to church! You'd better hurry up."

"Well, thank you for that reminder, but I'm afraid I have other plans. I'm going walking this morning, since somebody I know cut short yesterday's outing. . . ."

Lee squinted at him from the wall. "You *sure* you're not one of those Methodists?"

"Positive."

"Well, suit yourself, then. I'm off."

And she was. She pivoted on the stone at the top of the wall, legs outstretched, hopped off the other side, and dashed across the meadow toward home.

Lee Trelissick made Andrew's heart ache, the way it does when you long for something you know you will never have. Lee was exactly the kind of child he'd dreamed of having with Katerina—and was glad they hadn't. Andrew was a professor of architecture at the University of Pennsylvania when he and Katerina Vogel met, at an awards dinner for the school's most promising graduate students. She'd worked in real estate but had discovered that her strength was in finance, not selling property. When she completed her MBA at the top of her class, Mellon Bank snapped her up and put her on their executive fast track.

Katerina—"Kat" to her friends; "the Ice Queen" to those jealous of her poise and style—was older than her fellow students and far more sophisticated. When Andrew first saw her, it seemed to him as if she'd been created by a Cubist. She was all sharp angles and hard edges. Even her shiny, jet-black hair was asymmetrically cut. Almost painfully thin and taller than average, Kat stood apart from her classmates and, Andrew noticed, spent most of her time talking with the professors. That evening, she was wearing a simple sleeveless sheath dress in smoke-gray silk charmeuse. It fell to her calves and was kept from simply pooling on the floor by two thin spaghetti straps that emphasized her broad shoulders. When she turned away, he realized that the back plunged in soft, draped folds almost to her waist. The only color she wore was a small red clutch purse that matched perfectly the scarlet of her lipstick. She was the kind of woman who, had she smoked, would look perfectly normal holding her cigarette in a long ebony holder. She stood as if she was waiting for someone with a lighter. It put him in mind of old black-and-white movies. When she noticed him in the crowd, she simply lifted an eyebrow. He was mesmerized.

When they married a year later, she was far too busy with her career to consider children. That made perfect sense to him at the time; though he was a full ten years older than she, Katerina, at thirty, had plenty of time left on her biological clock. But he also sensed that she was ambivalent about children, as if she feared she wasn't mother material. This surprised him because whenever they socialized with his colleagues, she was imaginative and playful with their children. It made him happy and proud. But later she'd say, "I love to be with them, and then I love to leave them with their parents." When she passed her thirty-fifth birthday, Andrew began to resign himself to childlessness.

Then she left him. Now, he'd learned, she was pregnant.

It was hard to know which had been more of a surprise. Or more painful.

HE FINISHED HIS tea, laced on his boots, grabbed his day pack, and headed north along a single-track lane above the farm. After a half mile or so, he turned left onto the path that led down through Minster Wood to the footbridge over the Valency where Lee had left him at the day before. He was headed for St. Juliot's, an isolated parish church the young architect Thomas Hardy had restored before he became a novelist and poet.

• • •

ANDREW HADN'T SEEN the end coming. Yes, Kat had been distant for some weeks, but he put that down to mourning: Her mother, a lifelong smoker, had died of lung cancer three months earlier. Katerina had grown quiet, distracted, and cold— not that she'd ever been especially passionate, come to that. When she announced she was leaving, one Saturday just before the end of the spring term, he had been so stunned, so utterly blindsided, he'd simply stared at her. He felt poleaxed.

"When?" he'd finally said.

"Today. Now. I've already packed my car. My lawyer will contact you. Don't worry; I don't want anything that's yours."

But Andrew was still back at the leaving.

"Why?"

She looked at him with a mixture of pity and disgust. "You really don't have a clue, do you?"

His forehead furrowed, as if he was puzzling out a design problem.

"I'm sorry; no, I don't." And he didn't.

"I can't believe I have to spell this out for you."

He stared at her, and what went through his head was that he thought being her husband warranted at least an explanation. Then she unloaded.

"Look, I want to spend my life with a man who wants to make a mark on the world. You call yourself an architect. But what do you actually do? You sit in your tidy, minimalist university studio and develop abstract notions about shape and form and space. You lecture to your doting students. You write papers for scholarly journals. I used to think it was great to be 'Mrs. Professor Stratton,' until I realized how dull your life is. *Our* life is. Tell me something, Mr. Architect: Where are your clients? Where are your buildings? Where are your muddy construction sites? Not to mention that you could be making ten times as much as they pay you at that damned university."

"I guess I'm just not that interested in money," he'd said. "And I don't see what this has to do with money, anyway."

"Everything has to do with money, but that's not even the point. The point is, you have no passion; it's like you have ice in your veins instead of blood."

"That's not true; I love working with my students—"

"And here's the saddest thing." She was on a roll now. "You don't even know this is a lousy way to live! You don't even know you're only half alive. You know what being half alive means? That you're also half *dead!* And I'm dying being here with you. *That's* why I'm leaving!"

Andrew had heard some of this before, but never delivered with such fury. He didn't understand how, suddenly, his profession had become a reason for leaving. He didn't understand how being good at what he did was now a fault. He didn't understand how the Ice Queen could tell him he was passionless. He listened stoically, as he sometimes did at faculty meetings when one of his more "artistic" colleagues went on a rant. He breathed slowly to calm himself in the face of Kat's verbal flame throwing.

"Have you arranged someplace to stay?" he asked when Katerina finally flared out.

She stared at him in disbelief, then abruptly stood.

"I am so out of here," she said.

And then she was.

Andrew and Kat lived in an early-nineteenth-century brick row house—three windows across, three stories high—on Delancey Street. Andrew had spent years renovating the old house, turning its stacked warren of dark, cramped rooms into a flowing, light-filled, contemporary space. An inventive cook, he'd built himself a sleek commercial-grade kitchen on the ground floor—an oasis of stainless steel and marble that opened to a dining room overlooking an urban garden. A blackened steel staircase with maple treads rose to the second-floor living room and library; a second stair climbed to the master bedroom, bath, and guest room on the top floor. Skylights opened the master bedroom to the stars. To warm up what would otherwise have been a visually cold interior, he had collected a number of primitive pine antiques, most from the Pennsylvania Dutch country west of the city: a stripped pine dining table; a large, hand-painted cabinet originally made for storing bread dough; a wormwood side table to stand by his favorite reading chair; a thick and worn cobbler's workbench, cut down to serve as a coffee table.

An hour after Katerina left—an hour spent staring blankly out at the garden and replaying the scene on a continuous loop in his head—Andrew got up from the dining table at which he'd been sitting since her departure. He left the house and walked across Rittenhouse Square, picked up a couple of bottles of Australian Shiraz at the state liquor store, then went on to the Italian delicatessen on South Nineteenth Street, where he'd shopped for years. He felt scorched. Blistered. Charred. Part of him wondered why no one on the street noticed and called an ambulance.

"Buongiorno, Professore!" Mario, the deli owner, roared above the heads of the shoppers crowding the store. "The usual?"

Andrew nodded. The usual was a selection of cured meats—dry salami, prosciutto, thinly sliced bresaola—and a plastic container each of oil-cured black olives with thyme and green picholine olives in brine. These latter were from the south of France, and Mario always gave him a hard time about his preference for them over the fat Sicilian green olives. Andrew's response was always "If you don't want me to buy them, why do you sell them?" Mario's response was always a shrug and a smile. In fact, he carried them especially for *"il Professore."*

Andrew had always been fond of Mario; they'd known each other now for almost a decade, ever since Andrew started coming into the store. It had taken a couple of years before he realized the source of the fondness: He wanted to be Mario. He longed to come from a big Italian family. A noisy family with a multitude of brothers and sisters and aunts and uncles. A family that yelled a lot. And laughed a lot. And talked and fought and loved. A family whose members were inseparable, no matter who wasn't talking to whom that week. A family, in short, awash in emotion.

Instead, he'd grown up as the third member of a pathologically peaceful triad: a father who embraced his English heritage by wearing tweed and being a man of few words (and those mostly platitudes), and a mother who knew her husband could have married someone more beautiful, more vivacious, more sophisticated, but didn't. The war threw people together and made them think they'd better grab whomever they could, as soon as they could. She'd become pregnant within a month of meeting Andrew's father and, times being what they were, Graham Stratton and Sheila O'Leary married immediately. The child, a daughter, died hours after being born. It was quite a few years before Andrew came along, and, looking back, it seemed to him his parents had run out of child-rearing energy by then. He'd been left pretty much to his own devices as he'd grown up.

As he was ringing up Andrew's order, Mario said, "So, some nice antipasti, olives, wine . . . a party tonight, eh, my friend?"

Andrew looked blankly at his old friend and suddenly Mario knew something was wrong.

"Ah, no; trouble with a woman, I think." He tapped a pudgy forefinger on the side of his nose and nodded, the universal Italian gesture of confidentiality and understanding.

Andrew gave him a thin smile.

On the walk back across the square, he paused at the play area. The day was warm and fragrant from the flowers in the formal plantings at the park's four corners. All around him, children of privilege dashed about in absurdly expensive spring outfits. Their sleek young mothers, in equally stylish clothes, lounged on the dark-green benches lining the walkway, skirts hiked up a few inches so their long, lithe legs could catch the sun.

At the corner, while he waited for the light, a hand touched his elbow and a silky voice purred, "Hey, handsome."

The voice belonged to a rather Rubenesque beauty called Phyllis Lieberman, a colleague in the art and architecture school who lived a few blocks away. Single, roughly the same age as he, Phyllis never missed an opportunity to flirt with him. Andrew liked her: liked her irreverent take on modern art, about which she was an expert; liked her cavalier attitude toward the university bureaucracy; liked the easy rapport she had with her students—"her children," as she called them. He also liked her flirting. Much as he loved her, Katerina didn't have a seductive bone in her entire elegantly trim body. Phyllis was a walking embodiment of eroticism, squeezed into a small but lush package.

The light changed, but he didn't cross. He thought briefly of giving Phyllis a jaunty, deflecting response. Instead, he turned toward his friend and said, "Kat's left me."

The woman hesitated a moment, then slid her arms around him and gave him a warm, full-body hug. Then she stood back, shook her mane of henna-tinted hair, flashed him a dazzling smile, and said, "Well now, this *is* my lucky day!"

Andrew laughed in spite of himself, and they crossed the street.

Phyllis slipped her arm in his and said, "How about we two go for a walk?"

"Sure," Andrew replied, but without much enthusiasm.

She steered him east toward the river. They walked slowly, Phyllis, in her customary three-inch heels, gracefully picking her way along the uneven brick sidewalk. They'd reached Washington Square and were taking a turn around

Independence Hall when she said, "You might as well hear this from me, ducks: not many people are going to be surprised by your news." She hugged his arm.

"No, apparently I haven't been a particularly satisfactory husband. That's what Katerina says, anyway."

"That's bullshit, for starters. For Christ's sake, Stratton, you're a first-class gent; and anyway, the affair's been going on for months. She hasn't exactly been discreet about it."

Andrew stopped dead in the middle of the street and stared at her.

"Affair?"

Phyllis blanched and clapped a hand over her mouth.

"Oh my God! You don't know, do you?" She sounded like someone being strangled.

In a moment, she recovered and tugged him to a bench. There were tourists everywhere.

"Look, it's a guy she met at the climbing gym," she whispered, "a fat-cat lawyer. That's what I hear, anyway. Somebody saw them playing kissy-face outside the art museum a few weeks ago."

She took one of his hands in both of hers. "Oh, ducks, I'm so sorry. . . ."

He looked around the square. He'd always loved the old colonial part of Philadelphia—the brick, the stone, the history. But none of it gave him comfort on this day.

Phyllis leaned across the bench and kissed him on the cheek, then pulled him to his feet. "Come on, you; I have an idea. I see you've got goodies, most notably wine, in that shopping bag. We're going to my place."

Andrew didn't resist. Like an automaton, he followed the rhythmic click of her heels on the bricks. He glanced behind him and was surprised he wasn't trailing blood.

Phyllis Lieberman's elegant apartment on Spruce Street had the same sensual warmth as the woman herself. The walls in the foyer and the living room were painted the color of antique gold leaf. The plush upholstered couch and chairs were covered in thick, ivory linen and scattered with ornate pillows in black, chocolate, and leopard-skin prints. Gauzy white linen drapes pooled on the polished pine floors like trains on bridal gowns. A fan of the American Impressionists, she had a limpid Childe Hassam seascape in a thick gold frame above the black marble Victorian mantel opposite the couch. He couldn't imagine how she'd afforded it. The only primary color in the place was a huge vase of scarlet-tipped lilies on a glass-topped coffee table, so thick with fragrance you almost felt drugged. There was a zebra-skin rug beneath the coffee table.

She led him into an all-white kitchen.

"Sit," Phyllis commanded, gesturing to a stool beneath a marble counter. She laid out the smoked meats, added a sliced baguette and some cheese, then pulled the cork on the first bottle of Shiraz. She filled two big balloon glasses almost to the lip, and then leaned across the counter, deliberately displaying the very generous cleavage revealed by her scoop-necked, black silk T-shirt. "Here is how we are going to spend the afternoon, mister. I am going to feed you with your own food and ply you with your own wine and you will become happy. There will be no arguing about this. You will remember this day as one filled with love, not loss." She flashed him an utterly lascivious smile. Andrew just shook his head in disbelief and accepted the first of what were to be many glasses of wine. They clinked glasses.

"L'chaim!" Phyllis said.

"What's that mean?"

"To life, you idiot; yours has just begun again."

But why did it feel like it had just ended?

ANDREW CLIMBED HIGH up the west slope of the Valency valley. A side stream cut across the footpath he'd been following as it raced downhill. He picked his way across stepping-stones and then stopped to take in the view. Over the eons, the almost infinitesimal friction of water slipping over stone had cut a winding channel deep into the surrounding plateau. At the outer edge of the sharpest curves, he could see where seasonal floods had chewed away at the friable slate bedrock, creating bluffs. Away to the east, the hills were patterned with neat, green fields. Here and there a cluster of stone farm buildings laid claim to the land. A distant single-lane macadam road with occasional wider passing places—looking a bit like an anaconda that had swallowed several pigs—wound down the opposite side of the valley, plunged right through the shallow river at the bottom, and slithered up the other side. And for as far as he could see, the fields were defined by ancient stone walls, some ramrod straight, others sinuous. It was as if the landscape had been stitched, the walls the warp and weft knitting the disparate parts into a coherent whole. There wasn't a single square foot of the world before him, he realized, that hadn't been shaped by the hand of man. But here, unlike so much of the landscape back home, that hand had brought beauty, not blight, to the land.

He was thinking that Phyllis would like this world, with its sensuous hills and valleys. When he'd let himself out of her apartment late that evening, months ago, she was fast asleep on the couch. There had been kissing. There had been caressing. There had been sweet words of caring and solace. But while Andrew had a prodigious ability to absorb alcohol without getting drunk, Phyllis did not; she'd passed out. He'd put a pillow under her head, covered her with a cashmere throw, and gone home. He had been sober enough to know he had no business having sex with anyone that day—maybe ever—especially a colleague from the university. He felt radioactive. He felt that in the dark, he would blink on and off—LOUSY HUSBAND—like a neon sign in the window of some disreputable corner bar.

Andrew had had no idea, not the faintest inkling, how to respond to Katerina's attack the day she left. He should have said something, he thought—and yet it was clear she really wasn't interested in a response. It was as if she was that famous plane in World War II, the *Enola Gay:* Drop the atomic bomb on Hiroshima and fly home. Don't look back at the destruction.

Even if she had stayed, though, he had to admit he wouldn't have known what to say. In his stiff-upper-lip New England Presbyterian family, feelings were neither expressed nor discussed—not in his presence, anyway. He couldn't remember a single display of emotion—either affection or anger—between his parents. He'd read enough as an adult to know that feeling pain was natural and that expressing emotion was only human, and yet he'd had no practice in either.

If he hurt himself as a child, his father would check him for damage, brush him off, pat his shoulder, and shoo him away with a hearty "You're fine, lad; off you go." His mother's perennial response to any of his personal tragedies was "Don't worry; it'll be better before you're married" or, if her Irish Catholic roots were in the

70

ascendant that day and overcame her Presbyterian reserve, "Offer it up, son"—as in, offer up the pain to God and get on with it.

So that's what he did after Kat left: He offered it up and got on with things.

Except that things didn't go well. It wasn't just that he felt shell-shocked by the breakup; that would have been handicap enough. But his work seemed to have hit a brick wall as well. He had been researching what he believed would be an important contribution to his field: a book he was calling "The Anatomy of Livable Places." One summer when he was in grad school, he'd hitch-hiked across Europe and been captivated by the way hill towns in Italy or Spain, or fishing communities in Greece, or villages in rural England, seemed to possess a kind of wholeness, a certain harmony of form and material, the result of which was that they made you feel "at home," even if you didn't live there. These places settled into him, into his bones, and years later, while he was wrestling with the problem of the increasing soullessness of American communities, the comforting livability of those places came back to him. And an idea grew.

Andrew was convinced that if you could decon-struct that feeling of livability, of "home-ness," if you could identify its component parts and under-stand how they worked together, you could design new communities with the same comforting character. The older he got and the more he observed the built environment around him, the more convinced he became. The subject had become his passion. He'd already written and published several papers on it.

There were certain components of livability he thought were obvious. Most places that felt livable seldom had a building more than three or four stories high, so the scale wasn't dehumanizing the way it was in many American cities, where builders seemed to think bigger and higher was synonymous with better. Also, the buildings in livable communities tended to be clustered together companionably, with breathing space provided by small squares or plazas. They also tended to have what Andrew called "public living rooms"—coffee shops, outdoor cafés, or pubs, for example, where people gathered to chat or simply watch the world go by. He noticed that livable places had a sort of structural honesty, too. Typically, they were constructed of local materials—stucco-coated stone in Spain or Italy; granite, limestone, local brick, or slate in England; native wood in Scandinavia or New England. As a result, such places looked as if they had grown organically from the ground, rather than having been imposed upon it.

It was characteristics such as these, Andrew believed, that created that evanescent sense of rightness, of feeling at home, of welcome, of belonging. And it was the absence of these same characteristics that made many American neighborhoods, subdivisions, and entire communities so cold and uninviting. "Placeless" was the word he used.

But his editor at the University of Pennsylvania Press didn't get it. "If you're trying to define what 'home' means, why are you looking in Europe, for God's sake? You're an American!" To Andrew, the answer was personal and visceral: He'd never felt at home in America. Growing up in the suburbs of Boston, he'd known few of his family's neighbors. And to do anything—shop, go out to eat, see a movie—you had to get into a car. There weren't even sidewalks in some of the subdivisions around him, as if, in the real-estate developers' theory of evolution, they'd become as vestigial as the tails we lost when we evolved away from monkeys. The result, for Andrew at least, was a profound sense of alienation, a sense of not belonging to the place he was from.

But there was another problem with his project, too: His department chairman didn't think the subject of his research was sufficiently "professional"—which meant it flirted with the real concerns of everyday people. In academia, that was the kiss of death. The more he argued with his editor and his chairman, the more he felt like he was banging his head against a wall. His gut told him he was onto something, but Andrew had very little experience in trusting his gut.

Still, he had his champions, and steadfast, candid Phyllis was one of them. When Andrew hit bottom, both emotionally and intellectually, on the first anniversary of Katerina's departure, it was she who suggested he get away, do something different.

"Go someplace where the landscape speaks to you, and just become a part of it, if only for a few weeks. Don't think; just find out how the place *feels*. Figure out why later."

The idea both intrigued and unsettled him. It had always been his nature to study the world from a distance. It was easier, and safer, to be an observer than a participant. Being a superb observer was what had made him an expert in his branch of architectural theory in the first place: He studied, he took notes, he analyzed, and then he presented theories. It was a formula that had led him to prominence in his field.

A few weeks later, after the summer break had begun, he'd been taking a walk through the colonial part of Philadelphia. Not far from Independence Hall, two men were restoring the pavement of a plaza. The new pavement was being made with large rectangular blocks of blue-gray granite—Belgian blocks, he knew they were called. Roughly four inches wide, ten inches long, and six inches deep, they had originally been ships' ballast during the age of sail. The surplus stones had been used as street pavers back then, but in the 1950s they'd been resurfaced with asphalt. Now the whole plaza was being torn up again and the men were restoring the original stone pavers. The two men had laid down a bed of gravel and leveled sand and now were setting the granite blocks in a handsome herringbone pattern.

Andrew sat on a bench—the same bench, he later realized, he'd sat on with Phyllis the day his wife had left—and watched the men work. It was a muggy afternoon, and both workers were stripped to the waist, their tanned backs glistening with sweat. One man, wearing rubber knee pads, laid a zigzag course of blocks, each individual stone rectangle separated from the next by a gap of perhaps a quarter inch. He gave each a tap with a rubber mallet to set the stone, and then, a few moments later, his colleague—younger, an apprentice, perhaps—followed behind with a broom, sweeping a mix of fine sand and dry mortar into the gaps to stabilize the blocks. The stonelayer's hands were raw from working with the granite, and it was obvious the stones themselves were heavy. Still, each man worked with consummate care. Every so often, the man on his knees would pause, lean back on his haunches, look at the pattern developing, and smile. The result of their work—nothing more than stone and sand—was breathtaking in its artistry and simplicity.

So it was that Andrew Stratton decided it was time he got his hands dirty. And in that strange way events sometimes transpire, the opportunity presented itself. As part of his research, Andrew had contacted several organizations in Europe devoted to historic preservation and sustainable building techniques, and they regularly e-mailed him their electronic newsletters. The day after he'd sat watching the workmen setting the stone pavers, he heard from the Southwest Council for Sustainable Building, in England. Among other bits of news, he noticed that a course on mortarless stone-wall building was being offered by the Guild of Cornish Hedgers, in partnership with the National Trust, a land-protection organization. The weeklong course would be held in August in Boscastle, on Cornwall's wild Atlantic coast. Andrew looked at a map and discovered Boscastle was not far from the town from which his father never tired of telling him his ancestors had come: Stratton, in North Cornwall.

Normally, Andrew was not a superstitious man; he knew too much about probabilities and statistics for that. But he took the course announcement as a kind of sign: a chance to do something tangible and physical, to create something real and lasting from local materials, and in a place where he had ancient connections. On impulse—in itself a breakthrough for him—he e-mailed back to register for the course. A few hours of Internet searching later, he'd also found Shepherd's Cottage, and e-mailed the owners. Anne Trelissick had written back that the cottage normally would have been booked at least a year in advance, but they'd had a cancellation and he was in luck. He reserved the eighteenth-century stone cottage for two weeks.

As Philadelphia slouched into the dog days of August, he escaped, flying first to London's Gatwick Airport, then to Newquay, in Cornwall. There, he hired a taxi for the ride down the coast to Boscastle, arriving on a clear, warm afternoon just after a brief sun shower that left the air freshly laundered and the narrow, wet streets shimmering. He was immediately entranced. He didn't believe in ancestral memory or past lives, but he could not deny that he felt as if he'd just come home.

AT THE TOP of the Valency valley, Andrew climbed over a stile in a stone wall, walked through the cemetery of St. Juliot's church, with its lichen-encrusted headstones leaning this way and that like old men, and ducked under its fifteenth-century porch. He'd been looking forward to this moment; he wanted to see what Hardy had done during the restoration of the church in the late 1800s. But when he pushed open the church's heavy oak door, he found a small clutch of parishioners, Lee and Anne included. A female priest—the one Lee had been telling him about, he guessed—stood at a raised pulpit.

He mumbled an apology and took a seat in a pew at the rear.

Boscastle (SX098909) is located on the north Atlantic coast of Cornwall. Cornwall's most distinguishing feature is its long and thin peninsular character which influences the region's weather. This peninsula is one of the warmest and wettest regions in the country, and there is significant variation within the area largely influenced by proximity to the coast and topography . . . with the effects of altitude having a clear influence with Dartmoor, Exmoor and Bodmin Moor all receiving on average 1231–2584 mm of rain a year.

Special Boscastle Flood Issue,
Journal of Meteorology 29, no. 293

Heads turned to regard the stranger who had joined them. Lee grinned at him and waved. The priest looked across the tiny congregation and smiled.

"Welcome," she said, in a voice that was gentle as a breeze but nonetheless carried the length of the vaulted nave. "I was just about to tell one of my favorite stories."

The priest's informality—so unlike the sour, doctrinaire Presbyterian minister of his childhood—won him over immediately. Andrew smiled back and nodded. She began.

"I'm sure you've all heard variations of this joke: A mountain climber loses his footing and begins to fall from a cliff—perhaps a cliff like those along the coast path here in Boscastle. He grabs the branch of a shrub growing from the cliff face—perhaps it's gorse, or heather—and it arrests his fall. But the branch is slender and brittle and he knows it will not hold him long.

" 'Help!' he cries. 'Is anyone up there? Help!'

"And a deep voice answers, 'I am the Lord, your God. I can save you if you believe in me. Do you believe?'

" 'Oh yes, Lord, I do—with all my heart, and especially right now!'

" 'Good,' says the Lord. 'Let go of the branch.'

"The climber hesitates.

" 'Is there anyone *else* up there?' he asks."

There was a faint titter of laughter in the congregation. Lee, Andrew saw, had her hand over her mouth to disguise her giggles.

"The Bible tells a similar story," the priest continued. "Actually," she said, with what Andrew thought was almost a wink, "I think we get a lot of good jokes from the Bible.

"In this case, Jesus has just performed the miracle of feeding the multitudes. Five thousand people gather to hear him preach. Afterward, he tells his disciples to feed them. They reply that they have only two fish and five small loaves of bread, and it is impossible.

"But Jesus takes this meager larder and somehow manages not only to extend it to the entire crowd, but to have leftovers as well!

"Now, I don't know about you, but I think that would have made me a believer for life. But apparently some of the disciples were slow learners. When the crowd disperses, Jesus tells his disciples to get into their boat and set across the sea. He stays behind to pray and reflect, and tells them he will join them soon.

"That night a storm rakes the sea and the disciples' boat is tossed for hours. Finally, as Matthew tells us, on the fourth watch, early in the morning, they see Jesus walking toward them on the surface of the water. They cry out in fear, 'It is a ghost!'

But Jesus says, 'Take heart; it is I. Be not afraid.' Then Peter jumps up and says, 'Lord, if it is you, command me to come to you over the water.'

"And here's where I think Jesus shows us his sense of humor—in a way not all that different from the joke we began with. What does he do? He says, simply, 'Come.' And so, Peter clambers out of the boat. He lets go with one hand. He lets go with the other. And he walks across the water toward his Lord.

"So here is Peter, striding across the surface of the sea, when he sort of wakes up and looks around. He sees that the sea is rough and the sky is stormy. And suddenly he is afraid. He has, to put it simply, a crisis of faith. He fears that the branch of salvation, like the branch our climber was clutching, is slender and brittle.

"What happens next? Well, it's useful to remember that the name 'Peter' means rock . . . which is exactly what he begins sinking like."

" 'Lord, save me!' Peter cries.

"And Jesus reaches out, pulls him up, and returns him to the safety of the boat. 'O ye of little faith, why did you doubt?' Jesus asks. And the rest of the disciples, in awe, declare, 'Truly, you are the son of God.' "

The priest paused and rested her eyes on the clutch of villagers before her.

"We are only human," she said. "We are not made to be unwaveringly faithful. Our day-to-day lives test our faith repeatedly—in ourselves, in those we love, and in God. And sometimes we sink. What does Matthew's account of this episode in the life of Jesus and his disciples tell us? That faith can buoy us up. That faith can calm the storm. That faith can produce miracles—big ones, little ones, it hardly matters. Faith can enable each and every one of us to 'walk upon the water' of our lives. Faith can still our doubts. Faith can be our salvation. This is what Matthew wants us to understand when he tells us Peter's story.

"Now, let us pray . . ."

The service continued, but Andrew was still thinking about the vicar's sermon. Though he had gone to church dutifully every Sunday with his parents as he was growing up, Andrew had never had much faith in faith. He had even less faith in organized religion. The Bible seemed to him a patchwork of contradictions, not a reliable guide for human souls; you could find scriptural justification for any belief or action, however tender or brutal. You didn't have to be an historian to know that the armies on both sides in any battle believed God was with them and would speed their victory. The sheer devastation wrought by those who believed this over the course of human history was staggering. Religious organizations seemed to him little more than businesses aimed at protecting and expanding their market share, lining their pockets, and stifling dissent. He'd experienced this part of religion firsthand. As a teenager, he'd admired—almost idolized—the assistant minister at his church, a young man passionate about helping poor people in disadvantaged neighborhoods in Boston. He was doing what Andrew believed was the true work of the church, living the values of Christianity and leading by his example. But his social activism annoyed the wealthy and conservative members of the church's board of trustees, and, soon enough, the assistant minister was forced out. Andrew's father had said, "It's for the best," and Andrew wondered, *The best for whom?*

That was the end of Andrew's churchgoing. Anything less than a total boycott seemed to him immoral. How could you remain a member of the flock in the face of such injustice and hypocrisy?

As he matured, Andrew found a new faith: a faith in the power of rational thought. He believed that the universe was explainable. He believed that the mysteries of religious faith were nothing more than natural phenomena awaiting logical explanation. Andrew had faith in science, in the rigorous process of examining and analyzing the world.

But he had faith, too, in the essential goodness of human beings. He *believed* in people, in their potential for grace. He believed most people were good and the rest wanted to be good, and either didn't know how, had no experience of goodness, or somehow had been led astray. The reasons they failed at goodness, he believed, were sociological, not theological.

Andrew had also had faith in himself, in the importance of his work, and in the security and fullness of his love for his wife. But now his marriage was shattered and the value of his work was in question. In the year since Kat dropped her bomb, Andrew had felt his belief in himself, even his belief and trust in others, seeping away. It was as if his soul had sprung a leak. He imagined himself shrinking until all that was left was a puddle of clothing on the ground. *O ye of little faith,* Jesus had said. Yes, precisely.

Lee yanked him out of his bleak meditation.

"Come on," she said, tugging at his pocket, "You have to meet Janet!"

"This is Drew," Lee announced, dragging him over to the priest. "He's living with us." Andrew felt like the farm's new dog.

The vicar smiled and offered Andrew her hand. "Janet Stevenson. It was nice you could join us this morning," she said.

"Yes, well, I apologize for barging in like that. Look, I'm sorry to be so ignorant, but what does one call an Anglican priest?"

She chuckled. "Technically, I suppose it's 'the Reverend Janet Stevenson of Davidstow, Forrabury, St. Juliot, Lesnewth, Minster, Otterham, and Trevalga parishes.' But most people just call me 'Janet.'"

"Thank goodness," Andrew said. The Reverend Janet was a tall, angular woman with shoulder-length, rather severely cut brown hair shot through here and there with strands of gray. But her eyes were gentle and her smile was warm and genuine—not simply part of her professional wardrobe.

"Your sermon's given me something to think about," Andrew confessed.

"Yes, I noticed you seemed to have drifted away afterward." The priest leaned a bit closer and spoke quietly: "If there's something you'd like to discuss, the rectory's next to St. Symphorian's, at the top of the village, by Forrabury Common."

Andrew wondered whether clairvoyance was an essential skill among priests. "Thank you," he replied.

Lee was tugging at his pocket again. "Come *on,* Drew, or you'll be late at the Cobweb, too!"

"The Cobweb?"

"The pub," Janet explained. "Nearly everyone goes there for Sunday lunch, there or the Wellington—you know, roast lamb and the works."

"And if you don't get moving," Lee chided, "there'll be none left!"

"You seem to have a friend," the priest said.

Andrew laughed. "It feels more like I've been adopted. Or maybe kidnapped. Will I see you there?"

"I usually put in an appearance; have a pint at least. Professional responsibility, you see."

Andrew smiled and gave her a wave as Lee tugged him across the churchyard toward Anne's car. He never did get to look around at Thomas Hardy's handiwork.

ANDREW DUCKED THROUGH the low door of Boscastle's Cobweb Inn and thought he'd gone blind. After the shimmering brilliance of the midday August sun outside, the interior of the Cobweb was as black as the bottom of a well. He waited for his eyes to adjust; what emerged from the gloom was a pub unlike any he'd ever been in before. It had the same soft, warm lighting around the room and cheerful, backlit bottle glitter behind the bar as any other pub, and that ineffable sense of welcome that seems unique to pubs in the English countryside. But that was where the resemblance ended. The Cobweb occupied the first two floors of a massive four-story, eighteenth-century stone warehouse built deep into the black slate hillside across the road from the Visitor Centre. A formal dining room and function room occupied the upper floor, but the heart of the pub was two large, low-beamed, stone-walled, virtually windowless, cryptlike adjoining rooms on the ground floor. There were big stone fireplaces in each room, along with an eclectic collection of tables, chairs, antique high-backed settles, and miscellaneous artwork and wall ornaments. Andrew could imagine how warm and comforting it would be to step into the Cobweb on a winter afternoon to find all of the fireplaces ablaze. Mercifully, on this muggy Sunday, the hearths were cold and the pub was cool. From the thick beams overhead in the room nearest the door hung hundreds of antique beer bottles, along with all manner of other detritus. Andrew, who was only just over six feet tall, felt as if he needed to duck to move through the place.

On this Sunday, however, moving toward the bar in the back was like trying to swim through mud; the room was packed with tourists and locals alike, all intent on tucking into one of the great bargains of British pubs, the Sunday roast lunch. Three waitresses moved through the throng with the grace of ballet dancers, balancing platters laden with potatoes, vegetables, and either roast lamb, beef, or turkey with all the trimmings.

Andrew had finally reached the long bar that spanned the two rooms and was about to order a pint of St. Austell's Doom Bar ale when a woman's voice rang out.

"Well, if it isn't the sheep whisperer. Flora! It's that bloke I was telling you about!"

Andrew turned to his right and saw a darkly beautiful woman perched on a high stool at the end of the bar. She had on a black, paint-splattered, ribbed cotton sleeveless tank top that left little to the imagination, and a pair of faded cutoff jeans.

One very long, very tan leg crossed the other at the knee. From the suspended foot dangled a hot pink flip-flop. Her dark brown hair was long and gathered to one side, rather than to the back, in a ponytail held by a rolled and knotted kerchief. Her pupils were jet-black jewels surrounded by searchlight white. She smiled.

"Um . . . I'm sorry," Andrew stuttered, "I don't think we've . . . wait—you must be that woman on the cliff. With the dog."

"And you're the savior of stranded sheep, the Ovine Ranger."

An older, plump, rosy-cheeked woman—Flora, presumably—bustled up behind the bar and gave him a smile as broad and bright as a crescent of beach on a tropical island.

She ignored the others with empty glasses in their hands and said, "Pay no attention to her; she's just takin' the piss."

"The what?"

"You know, havin' you on a bit. What'll it be, me 'an 'sum?"

"A pint of Doom, please."

"On me, Flora," the woman on the stool said, and the barmaid lifted an eyebrow as she pulled down the long-handled vacuum pump to draw the fresh ale up from the cellar casks.

"Best order two," Flora said to Andrew with a wink. "You're on a roll here."

"One will do, I think."

"How's that sheep, then?" the woman in the cut-offs teased, bouncing her crossed leg rhythmically. Andrew watched the pink flip-flop dance.

"No idea." He took a long slug of his pint. He loved British ales: amber, creamy, almost no fizz. "Thanks for the drink."

"I was a little worried, frankly, about whether you'd get yourself up from that ledge."

"But not worried enough to stick around to help."

"Oh, no. I know too well how fragile is the male ego." She tilted her head to one side and gave him a crooked, amused smile.

"So this," he said, lifting his glass, "is guilt?"

"I don't think so; I believe you ordered Doom Bar. Good choice, by the way."

Suddenly, Andrew remembered the sermon. "I could have fallen," he said.

"That would have been Darwin at work again. But you didn't, did you?"

"Actually, I did. Fell nearly a hundred feet toward the knife-edged rocks and boiling surf, but arrested the fall by grabbing the branch of a bushy shrub growing from the cliff face. Unfortunately, it was gorse, so my hand was impaled by the thorns. Still, it held long enough for me to find a route back to the top, no thanks to you."

He was about to reach for his pint again, but she grabbed his hand, flipped it over to see his palm, which was unscarred, wiped her own palm over his, then let it go.

"Liar."

Andrew was trying to recover from the galvanic jolt of her touch. He'd never experienced anything like it in his life; his blood sizzled.

"I used the other hand," he said.

"Liar twice," she said. "You're right-handed; that's the hand you use to lift your glass."

"How's your dog?" Andrew asked, trying to buy time, trying to recover.

"Randi!" the woman shouted—which seemed to Andrew a somewhat unseemly answer to an innocent question. But then a big, furry dog that looked for all the world like a wolf appeared from the crowd, trailing several small children, including Lee.

"So *there* you are!" Lee called out amid the din of voices in the pub, as if Andrew were a wayward puppy wandering, lost, amid the forest of legs and ankles.

"Guess what, Drew? This is Randi, and he's the bestest dog in the world." The dog sat on his haunches beside the woman on the stool and regarded her with helpless adoration, tongue lolling.

"And Nicki!" Lee cried, noticing the woman on the stool. "Drew! Drew!" She was hopping with delight. "This is my best friend, Nicki!"

Andrew looked at the woman across from him, then back to Lee.

"Wait . . . I thought Nicki was one of your girlfriends."

"She is, silly!"

"No, I mean a girl like you . . . not a . . . a grown-up!"

"Not an old crone, you mean," the woman said, with something less than her former feistiness. Andrew glanced at her and wondered how old she actually was. Midthirties; forty, tops. Pretty young as crones go. Pretty, period. Something lush, slightly exotic about her. He was still buzzing inside from her touch.

Lee bailed him out.

"Nicki's not like other grown-ups. She's like me. A 'free spirit.' That's what Mum says, anyway."

Nicola slid off her stool and swept the girl into a bear hug, thinking just how wrong Lee was, but loving her for believing it. Lee giggled, squirmed away, and disappeared into the crowd, her introductions apparently now completed.

The woman stood facing Andrew, squinting, thoughtful.

"So you're Drew . . . I should have guessed."

Andrew smiled. "Why? Is my fame so widespread?"

"It is when Lee's your publicity agent, and yes, thank you, I'd love another drink."

Andrew laughed and signaled Flora.

"My treat this time," he said to the barmaid when she arrived.

Flora fairly leered at him. "Aren't *we* becomin' chummy! Same again, Nicki?"

"Sure, but as long as he's buying, make it a double."

"So what do you do when you're not cadging free drinks at the Cobweb?" Andrew asked.

"Oh, that's so American: *What do you do?* As if that defined you! You're in Europe, my friend. Here we inquire about your family, about life, about truth, about beauty . . ."

"Okay, then, tell me about your family."

"Don't have any; at least not here."

"Your life, then?"

"Checkered."

"Is that the truth?"

"Truth enough."

"Okay then, beauty? Besides your own, which is perfectly obvious to anyone with at least one functioning eye."

This seemed genuinely to have taken the woman aback. She turned to the tall gin and tonic Flora had left her and downed a third of it in one go. She stared at the glass for a moment, then turned toward him.

"Thank you," she muttered. Then she smiled. "Liar."

"You're right, I'm lying. I spend my days photographing gorgeous, scantily clad models for fashion magazines, and I've just gotten used to telling women they're beautiful. Apart from you, most of them seem willing to accept the compliment."

"You're a fashion photographer?"

"No. That's the 'liar' part."

She smacked his arm playfully and laughed, then raised her glass and clinked his. "You win this round."

"I didn't know it was a competition." This, too, was a lie; he felt as if he'd been fencing ever since he arrived.

"It's always a competition."

"What is?"

"Flirting."

"Is that what we're doing?"

"Isn't it?"

"Wait. This is making my head hurt. I asked first."

"And I dodged the question."

"You certainly did."

Andrew felt weirdly off balance with this lovely but curious woman. And he realized this whole business of interacting with someone new was a little scary. It had been years. How do you behave? What do you say? Especially when the woman in question seemed armed to the teeth, at least verbally. Even more especially when you found yourself powerfully attracted to her.

For her part, Nicola was rather enjoying Andrew's struggle. Although he stayed right with her in their quick-witted parry and thrust, she sensed she had the upper hand. She liked that.

Andrew did a verbal feint. "Look, I'm told the

reason to be here on Sunday afternoon is the roast dinners. Are you eating?"

"Heavens, no; far too much food for midday. I'd be asleep by three."

"So why are you here?"

"You mean, apart from the gin?"

"Apart from the gin."

She scanned the packed pub. "For the company, I guess. It's better in winter, without the tourists. But I don't mind the crowds." *They fill up the emptiness,* she thought. She waved at the Reverend Janet, who was working the crowd, a judicious half pint of ale in her free hand. "My work is pretty solitary."

As if he'd been given a peek through a keyhole, Andrew saw through Nicola's wall. But he was too much of a gentleman to pursue it.

"Ah," he said, "we're back to what you do."

"Clever how you did that."

"You brought it up, actually, but as long as you did, let me guess: You're either an exceptionally messy interior decorator or an artist."

"Aren't you observant!"

"You're an artist?"

"No. I'm an exceptionally messy decorator, and I'd better get back to my paint cans."

She drained her glass and slung a canvas purse over her shoulder.

"Nice meeting you, Drew. Thanks for the drink."

She had started to turn away from him but

stopped. "Lee was right about what she said about you."

"Which was?"

Nicki smiled a conspirator's smile. "Oh, that's just between us girls."

"Do you have a name, besides Nicki?" Andrew felt like he was trying to lasso Nicola and pull her back.

"Nicola Rhys-Jones, formerly DeLucca."

"Married then?"

"Not anymore."

Andrew smiled. She didn't.

"And you're called . . . ?" she asked.

"Stratton, like the village up the coast. Andrew Stratton."

"Married?"

"Not anymore."

This time Nicki did smile.

Then she was gone. She slipped through the crowd like water through rocks, disturbing nothing. Andrew fought his way to the door, just in time to see her disappear across the narrow bridge over the river. She was swinging her purse and Randi was dancing around her again.

The village of Boscastle lies within a conservation area amongst some of the most beautiful countryside within the British Isles, and is one of the very few unspoilt harbor villages in Cornwall. Designated an Area of Outstanding Beauty (AOB), the National Trust own and care for the surrounding coastline including the cliffs of Penally Point and Willapark which guard the Elizabethan harbor (built in 1584).

Boscastle Flood Special Issue,
Journal of Meteorology 29, no. 293

It was still too early for the sun to have crested the steep hills to the east as Andrew made his way down through Minster Wood to the footpath along the river on Monday morning. The valley was cool and misty, the grass laden with dew, the soft earth moistly fragrant. Mercifully, it was also too early for the tourist throngs. The street through Quay Town was nearly deserted, most of the shops still closed. He had a sudden glimpse of the peace that must descend here in the fall, when the only sounds were the stream clattering over its slate shelves and the raucous complaints of seagulls, when the air held the tang of smoke from coal fires in cottage hearths, when the only people along the pavements knew one another by their given name.

The coastal fog was beginning to break up; it promised to be another fair day. He stood at the edge of the car park where he was to meet his instructor, watched the river race past, and thought about Nicola. She intrigued him. Yes, she was right; they had been flirting. But there was an awfully sharp edge to her flirtation. It wasn't that she was caustic, really, or even sarcastic. But her teasing was prickly. She reminded him of the blackberry bramble bushes that overran empty lots in Philadelphia in the summer: the berries were irresistibly plump, sweet, and juicy, but the thorns lacerated you when you collected them. You could learn a lot about desire from a blackberry bramble.

Desire. He hadn't felt any for months. But Nicola had resurrected it. It wasn't even the flirty banter, though that had been fun, in a vaguely dangerous way. After all, it had been a very long time since he'd had a date. He didn't even know how to go about starting and wasn't even sure he could. Or should. It wasn't that he still loved Kat; she'd made sure he wouldn't. No, it was that he kept replaying in his head the charges she'd leveled against him; they swirled around in there like harpies. Was he too intellectual? Too controlled? Did he lack ambition, or was he simply happy teaching? Or were all those charges just the weapons she used to justify her affair and defection? In the year since she'd left, Andrew had felt as if he'd been treading water. Or just marking time. Maybe he'd become self-absorbed. Or maybe he was just so badly flayed by Kat's leaving that he was bleeding still.

But there was that galvanic shock when Nicola touched his hand. It amazed him. It confused him. It nagged at him. What was that about?

A few cars had turned into the nearly empty car park and a little knot of men was gathering by the slate-stone Visitor Centre. Andrew wandered over to join them.

"Morning! We all waiting for the teacher?" he said.

He received two curt nods and one "I reckon." Men of few words.

"Where're *you* from?" asked the talkative one, a wiry, balding fellow of perhaps thirty-five with a sharp, ferretlike face. Andrew's accent had given him away.

"Philadelphia," he answered.

Three pairs of eyes widened. Finally, another of the men, a tall, heavily built fellow in manure-splattered green rubber wellies and blue coveralls, looked him over.

"Bettur fit yew staid 'ome, lad; no 'oliday, this. This be 'ard lowster."

Andrew stared at the man for a moment, smiling what he was sure was an idiot's smile, while he waited for his brain to translate. He thought he got the gist.

"Yeah, reckon it will be," he answered, shrugging to suggest hard work was nothing new to him.

Now the third gent spoke up; it was becoming a real gabfest. "There's a lot of fine stonework around Philadelphia; it was the Pennsylvania Dutch, was it not?"

Andrew looked at this fellow in frank amazement. How would he know that? The man seemed overdressed for the task ahead: neatly pressed denim shirt with a button-down collar, sharply creased khaki trousers, and what looked like brand-new work boots. He looked like a

Bostonian, sounded like a Londoner, and was certainly no Cornishman. He extended his hand to Andrew.

"Ralph Newsome; I studied engineering at Drexel for a year."

"Andrew Stratton; I teach architecture at Penn."

"Small world," Newsome said.

The ferret didn't want to be left out. "Jacob Casehill," he said, taking Andrew's hand. "Stonemason. Everyone calls me Case."

The three of them turned to the big fellow, who suddenly seemed as shy as a child.

"Burt. Pencarrow. Farmin' out Holsworthy way." He kept his hands in the pockets of his coveralls.

It was at this point that a beat-up white van lurched into the car park. On the side of the van was written THE STONE ACADEMY.

The teacher's name was Jamie Boden, and Andrew had expected, given the diminutive first name, a young spark of a fellow. But the man who climbed down out of the van was, Andrew guessed, at least sixty, his face weathered, freckled, and deeply creased, his head crowned with a wild tangle of wispy ginger hair going white. He wore stiff canvas trousers with long patches from knee to thigh and a collarless blue shirt, both of which seemed impregnated with fine, gray dust.

"Coffee!" he said by way of greeting.

Casehill—*Case*—jerked his head to the left. "Bakery's open. Few doors down from the village shop."

"Excellent," the man responded, and promptly took his leave. "One more coming," he said over his shoulder. "Gel, thank the good Lord."

Burt lumbered after the instructor, big and slow as a draft horse.

Andrew mumbled, "Gel?"

"A woman," Newsome explained. "And, like all women, late."

As if to prove him instantaneously wrong, a dark-green Land Rover with NATIONAL TRUST stenciled on its doors roared into the car park and whipped smartly into a space. The driver's door snapped open and a young woman who looked to be in her midtwenties fairly exploded from the car and strode toward them. She was stocky, had broad shoulders, and sported a deep tan set off dramatically by a helmet of close-cropped platinum-blonde hair. She was wearing olive-drab hiking shorts, and her calves looked carved from stone.

"This it? Just the three of you?" she said without introduction.

"Lovely to meet you, too," Newsome answered with a broad grin. Andrew gathered this was not the sort of "gel" he'd anticipated.

Her manners caught up with her and she thrust out her hand. "Sorry. Becky Coombs. Got stuck

101

behind a bloody charabanc full of tourists." She shook hands all around. "Where's Jamie?"

"You know him, then?" Andrew asked.

"Oh, yes. Jamie's by way of being a god around here. Figured it was time I took one of his classes, especially since the project's on my patch. Volunteers will join us next week."

"You're at the National Trust office downstream from the first bridge?" Andrew ventured.

"That's the place. In the old forge. When I'm not out in the field, that is."

"Must be great to have a job that takes you out into countryside this beautiful," Andrew said.

"It is that . . . except maybe in the winter. Rains constantly and the wind never lets up. Storms take a toll, especially along the coast path; we've a lot of stonework needs doing."

Andrew liked Becky Coombs, her energy, her straight-ahead attitude.

Case had been quiet. Now he gave the girl a sly look and said, "Reckon you can hoist all the stone we'll be shiftin'?"

Becky smiled at Case.

"No, not all of it; just my share."

Andrew glanced at the sturdily built "gel" and then the wiry little man and figured Becky Coombs could take the ferret out in maybe twenty seconds, no contest. He chuckled.

Jamie Boden was back, big Burt close behind, both of them clutching Styrofoam coffee cups.

They gathered in a circle, and Boden looked each of them over like they were rocks he was sizing up before lifting them.

"Right then, what're you chaps driving?"

"Thought we was workin' right here, by the car park," Case said.

"Will be," Boden said. "That's our remit: Build a barrier between the verge and the river. But not this morning. This is a course, not a work party—not yet, anyways—so today we learn things. And to do that we go to my place, up on the moor. But it's rough going. Becky's got her Land Rover, so that's good. The rest of you?"

Burt rumbled that he had a Toyota pickup. Case was driving a beat-up Ford Fiesta. Newsome had a BMW 3 Series.

"Well, that's out," Boden said. "Fiesta, too, most likely."

"You?" he said to Andrew.

"I walked here."

"You'll be the American then. You ride with me in the van. Becky, you take Mr. BMW here. Burt, can you take Mr. Casehill? Right, then, stick close or you'll never find it."

A LITTLE AFTER eight-thirty, Randi dragged Nicola out for his morning walk. She didn't mind; it was a splendid day, and she wasn't scheduled to work at the Museum of Witchcraft until ten. She smiled at the thought of her "job." She'd been volunteering at the museum—"the world's largest collection of witchcraft-related artifacts"—for more than two years now. She often wondered what her very Catholic mother, dead not long before her divorce from Jeremy, would have thought. But it was really all Randi's fault. He'd belonged to an elderly woman in a nearby village—a practicing witch known only as Joan—and Colin Grant, the museum's owner, had taken the dog in after she died. Nicola met Colin while out walking along the cliffs just after sunrise one morning. He was sitting atop a ledge on Penally Point, meditating so quietly that Nicola hadn't noticed him. When he wished her a soft-spoken good morning, she'd nearly jumped out of her skin. She recognized the fellow—the museum was just across the lower bridge over the Valency, directly opposite her own cottage. She'd often thought him rather sweetly gnomish: small in stature, shy in speech, with a slightly too-large head aswirl with gray curls, and a curious aura of peacefulness that wreathed him like a cloud. He climbed down from his perch and joined her on the coast path.

"You're up early," he'd observed.

"As are you," she'd noted.

"Oh, I'm here most mornings, communing," he'd said.

He'd asked if she took walks every day and, when she said she did, mentioned he'd inherited a lovely dog that needed walking and that given the press of work at the museum during tourist season, he didn't have enough time to do it himself. Somehow she'd agreed to walk the animal, and she and Colin arranged a time later that day to meet.

The dog's name was Randi. It seemed Joan the witch had a sense of humor. She'd named her companion—her "familiar," as witches called their special animals—after a famous magician and debunker of psychic phenomena. Be that as it may, Colin explained, Joan claimed the dog had extraordinary powers, most notably knowing instantly whether anyone who came to their door was friend or potential foe.

Looking back, her first meeting with Randi still seemed like something of a miracle. The dog, who was three at the time, took one look and immediately began running joyous circles around her, bouncing on all fours like a lamb, his long, white-tipped tail wagging furiously. But he didn't let out a single bark. Colin stood there with his mouth agape.

"That's exactly what he used to do with Joan," he said finally, shaking his head in astonishment. "He connects the two of you. You're not a witch, perchance?"

Nicola laughed. "Not to the best of my knowledge!"

"Well, *he* seems to think you are. Perhaps you should reconsider."

"What, taking him for walks?"

"No. Whether you have the gift."

"The only gift I have is being a sucker for a sweet dog, and you'd already sussed that out, hadn't you?"

"Actually," Colin said with a mischievous smile, "yes."

"You're not a witch, too, are you?"

"Um . . . yes. I thought you knew that."

"Look, I didn't even know men could *be* witches, but it doesn't mean a damned thing to me. I'll take the dog."

"I only wanted you to walk him."

"The hell you did . . ."

"Are you sure you're not a witch?"

"Why?"

"Because you're a dab hand at reading minds."

And so Randi came home with Nicola, and the two of them had been inseparable ever since. He was a stunningly handsome animal. His lush coat, thick as a woman's fox-fur coat, was tan and black on his back, but snow-white on his belly. His legs and paws, too, were white, as were his muzzle and chest, the mask around his eyes, and his eyelashes. His perpetually upright ears were edged with black, as if with kohl, and soft as a lamb's. But his most distinctive feature was a dark charcoal widow's peak on his forehead with a lightning slash of white in its center.

Best of all, as fearsome as he sometimes looked, the dog had a sweet, gentle soul. Strangers fawned on him, children pawed him, and all he did was pant happily, his curled tail wagging madly. And what Colin had told her was true: Randi instantly knew friend from foe, not that foes were thick upon the ground in this little village she had come to love.

Randi usually chose the route for their morning walks, and on this day he turned right out of their front door, trotted up to the main road, crossed the road bridge, and headed up hill, past the Visitor Centre, the Cobweb, and the newsagent's shop, finally turning right onto the footpath heading up the Valency valley. Nicola wondered, not for the first time, why she needed to accompany him at all. And he never needed a leash.

They'd passed the wide part of the stream behind the weir that once had shunted water to the mill down by the bridge when Randi stopped and looked up into one of the trees. He looked at Nicola, looked up at the tree, and looked at Nicola again. Lost in a reverie of her own having vaguely to do with the American, she kept walking. But Randi didn't follow, and eventually he barked once. This was unusual. She walked back to the tree by the river and the dog looked up again.

"What?" Nicola said, exasperated.

The dog barked again, but kept looking up.

That was when she heard the giggling. She recognized it immediately.

"Lilly Trelissick! What are you up to?"

"I'm up to about half the whole tree," Lee said, giggling louder now.

"Well, you're driving Randi around the twist, so come on down and walk with us."

There was a scuffle of boots on bark, a shaking of leafy branches, and then a pair of skinny, tan legs emerged from the canopy. Nicola caught Lee as she dropped the last few feet to the ground and gave her a hug.

"Listen here, you ragamuffin; you'll break your neck one of these days."

"Uh-*uh!*"

"Uh-*huh!*"

"Will not."

"Will too!"

"Will not, 'cause that's my special tree and we have an agreement."

"An agreement?"

"Yup. If I climb it carefully, it won't let me fall."

Nicola looked at the girl and realized there was no rebuttal to such an argument. So she changed the subject.

"So tell me about this Andrew Stratton."

"I told you."

"What?"

"He's a nice man. We're chums. That's all. Why? *Wait!* You like him, don't you!"

"That's ridiculous."

"You *do,* you *do!* Nicki and Drew, Nicki and Drew!"

"Stop that! What's he doing here? That's what I want to know."

"Goin' to school is what."

"School?"

"Yup. Stone-wall school. Told him we already had plenty, but he wouldn't listen. Figures."

"Why?"

"He's a guy. Guy's don't listen. That's what *you* said, anyway."

"What are you talking about?"

" 'Member that guy? The one with the gallery in St. Ives who wanted to show your paintings and you said no and he wouldn't listen?"

"Oh, yeah."

"That's when you said it: Guys don't listen."

"Do you remember everything I say?"

"Mostly."

"Good Lord."

Randi, evidently bored, barked. And they set off up the valley.

A little way upstream of the footbridge, at a point where a tributary stream plunged over a rock shelf and joined the river, they stopped to chuck stones. Randi was off rummaging around in the under-growth on one of the slopes, following enticing smells.

"Why's an American going to stone-wall-building school?" Nicola muttered, as much to her-self as to Lee.

"I think it's to do with his work," Lee ventured.

"Which is?"

"He's an *art*-something."

"An artist?"

"No. An art . . ." Lee was searching. "Art-*tech*."
Nicola stared at the girl blankly for a moment
until the penny dropped.

"An *architect?*"

"Yeah, ar-chi-tec. Means he builds stuff, he said.
Like walls, I guess."

"Hmmm."

"Is that a good thing?" Lee asked.

"Well, let's just say it makes him interesting.
Maybe he understands something about beauty."

"He thinks *you're* beautiful."

"You're making that up."

"Uh-*uh!* Said so yesterday."

"When?"

"Coming back from the Cobweb. Mum and
Daddy drove, but we walked back, up Dunn and
Fore streets."

"And what did he say?"

" 'Bout what?"

"About me!"

"Just that you're pretty, which is pretty obvious,
if you ask me. And difficult."

"What's that supposed to mean?"

"I dunno. Just something he said. I told him you
were a witch."

"You *what?* "

"Well you are, right? You work at the museum."

Nicola hung her head in her hands: "I don't believe this . . ."

The fact was, Nicola had indeed become intrigued by witchcraft, at least the gentle form of it that had been a part of Cornish culture for centuries, even eons. Nicola wasn't sure when it was, exactly, that she'd fallen away from the Catholicism she'd been raised in. Maybe it was in Italy, when she struggled to rationalize the obscene opulence of the Roman church with the poverty of Jesus and the noble simplicity of Mary. Maybe it was when the vows she'd spoken during her marriage ceremony turned to bitter blood the first time her husband had hit her. Maybe the rot had set in long before any of that, when despite her white-dress confirmation, despite going to mass every Sunday, despite going to confession, bad things kept happening to her in Boston when she was a girl scarcely older than Lee.

But somewhere along the way of volunteering at the witchcraft museum, collecting the entry fees from the tourists, listening to the stories of pilgrims who'd come to look at the artifacts and relics in the collection, and being in the company of other volunteers who quietly confessed they were believers, Nicola had begun to embrace the earthy honesty of Cornwall's benign history of witchcraft. Cornwall's remoteness and its Celtic heritage had kept ancient traditions and practices alive long after religious zealots had stamped them out elsewhere in England. Well into the last century, the Cornish routinely sought the help of "cunning folk," "wise women," or "pellars"—people who repelled evil spirits. They provided charms to break spells, cures to heal ills, and magic to address more common needs such as identifying thieves, telling fortunes, finding water, or finding love. Witches, like doctors, were guided by a simple rule: Do what you will, but do no harm.

Modern witchcraft, she'd learned, was simply a religion that reveres nature. God is represented in both the form of the Mother Goddess and the Horned God, her consort. The fertile goddess is believed to rule during the growing season, from spring till autumn, while her consort rules during late autumn and winter. It was a system of beliefs and practices she found deeply comforting. It didn't promise salvation or threaten damnation; it simply offered a way of fitting oneself into the complex web of the universe. And here, in a landscape littered with prehistoric stone circles, enigmatic standing stones, hilltop burial quoits, sacred wells, and remote hermit's cells, a place so steeped in prehistory, witchcraft just seemed, well, natural.

"So what did he say when you told him I was a witch?"

"Not much."

"What's that mean?"

"He said you had a funny way of casting spells, but I didn't understand."

But Nicola did. She'd done what she always did: flirted and fled, leaving behind little but the sting of her barbed tongue.

THEY HAD DRIVEN through the market town of Camelford and were climbing east out of the valley of the River Camel when Jamie Boden said to Andrew, "Notice anything different?"

"It's getting steeper?"

"True enough, and that's part of the answer. Let me ask you this: When you look at buildings and walls in Boscastle, what do you see?"

"A lot of black slate, at least where it hasn't been painted over."

"Right. Now look around again."

"Granite!"

"Good lad."

"I hadn't even noticed the change."

"That's the thing about this country; the underlying geology is so complex that it seems like it changes every dozen miles or so. That's why neighboring villages can look so different sometimes. They're built of whatever material was close at hand. Granite up here on Bodmin Moor; slate down in Boscastle. Mind you, the granite's fairly new, geologically speaking. It's the result of volcanic activity only three hundred million years ago. Slate's much older."

"*Only* three hundred million years. I like that."

"Around here, you get used to thinking about

time differently. Show you what I mean in a moment."

They turned from a narrow, winding road hemmed by hedgerows to a rutted dirt track. Ahead on the horizon, the moorland was barren, virtually treeless, almost otherworldly. The summits of the hills were stacks of wind-carved granite, fractured and layered like giant wedding cakes. The slopes were littered with scree broken off by frost. Jamie's van lurched to a stop beside a rocky field. That's what it looked like to Andrew, but he would soon learn he was wrong. The other two cars pulled up behind them and everyone got out and followed Jamie across the springy turf.

"The fields hereabout are all part of my land, but I feel more like a museum curator than a landowner," Jamie commented. They stood on the edge of what Andrew now realized was a wide, circular stone wall, the remnants of a rampart of some sort. And within the circumference of the circle, which had a diameter of perhaps fifty yards, there were eight or ten smaller circles.

"This was a settlement," Newsome said quietly.

"Right you are. Round about four, maybe five thousand years ago."

Andrew tried to get his mind wrapped around such antiquity. "And it's still here" was all he could say.

"That's the thing I want you lot to understand," Jamie said. "Stone is the nearest thing we have to eternity. Building with stone is the nearest we get to immortality. When you build a stone hedge—drystone, mind, no concrete—you're building for all time."

"What's wrong with concrete?" Case, the mason, asked. He sounded defensive.

"Just that it won't last. It weathers fast. How often you reckon you have to repoint a chimney?"

Case hesitated, looked at the hut circles. "Often enough," he said.

"Stone *hedge?*" Andrew asked.

"Aye, lad. You're in Cornwall now, and in Cornwall we call 'em hedges. Doesn't matter if it's all stone, or all earth and turf, or a Cornish hedge, which is a bit of both. They're all hedges here, not walls."

"So those hedges we've been driving by that are all shrubbery," Andrew said. "What are they called?"

Andrew heard a rumble of laughter from behind him. It was Burt. "Best check avore yew lam in't wan!"

Jamie chuckled and translated. "Burt's warning you not to expect a soft landing if you run your motorcar into a leafy hedge. There's stone behind that foliage, at least here in the southwest. Upcountry, the hedges are more likely to be thickets of hawthorn, beech, and hazel, but not here. You'll understand soon.

"Right, then. To the classroom!" Jamie hoisted

himself into the van, Andrew followed, and they roared off, the others following more carefully up the potholed track.

Another hundred yards or so later, they pulled up in a cleared parking area and walked through a gate in an old stone hedge that led to Jamie's house, an ancient—medieval, Andrew guessed—gable-ended, two-story, slate-roof granite cottage with multiple ells and dormers and two massive chimneys. A sturdy stone barn stood some distance from, and perpendicular to, the house. The complex of buildings, hunched into the landscape, looked to Andrew as if they'd emerged spontaneously from the surrounding rock, without benefit of the hand of man.

"Thirteenth-century, some of it," Jamie replied to their unspoken question. "With various later bits. Come in and I'll put on some tea. Then we'll get to it."

The students milled about the ground-floor rooms. Burt, who was easily six-foot-four, had to duck beneath the beams, and everyone but Case hunched as they went through doors. Case himself prowled around scrutinizing the stonework, clearly impressed. From time to time, he would make small *huh* sounds of mason's admiration. Ralph Newsome played contentedly with a ghost-white cat that materialized from nowhere. And Becky, to Andrew's surprise, slipped into the kitchen to help Boden with the tea making. Andrew stood at the bookshelf beside one of the two massive hearths on the ground floor and thumbed through one volume after another on wall- and hedge-building styles and techniques. He'd had no idea the subject was so diverse, and it pleased him in a way that architectural theory never had. It had a rich vernacular history. It was form and function inseparable. It was real in the most elemental sense. It was stone made into art, art given timeless utility. He felt his heart expanding outward, into the immortality of it, as Jamie had said so simply and elegantly.

They took their mugs of tea outside to the front yard, which was rimmed with stone hedges. Andrew glanced around and realized the hedges varied in style every few yards; it was a display area for the craft of hedge building.

"There's something like thirty thousand miles of hedges here in Cornwall," Jamie said. "Some of them are even older than that settlement I showed you. Back in the Neolithic, maybe six or seven thousand years ago, you could say stone was the first harvest of the people creating fields here. Farmers have been clearing fields ever since."

Andrew looked at the bleak landscape around him and said, "It's a wonder they were able to raise anything *but* stone."

"Ah, well; 'twas warmer here then, y'see. We know that now from pollen studies and such," Jamie explained.

"How the devil did they move them?" Newsome asked.

"Not bloody easily, I promise you. Remember, we're talking about people scraping dirt away with antler picks and shovels fashioned from some dead animal's shoulder blade, levering the rock from the ground, rolling it on sections of log maybe, or end over end. When you figure there's roughly a ton of stone in every cubic meter of hedge, the scale of their accomplishment is staggering. And they didn't just pile the stones in rows. Even then, long before the Romans ever arrived, they had the skill to fashion hedges that'd last.

"Since then, as you can see with these demonstration hedges here, different styles evolved, driven mostly by what rock was available and, later, what tools could be used to shape the stone."

Andrew looked around. There were hedges built of raw fieldstone; hedges with regular, alternating courses of shaped granite; hedges with horizontal layers of slate and shale that looked almost like the sedimentary beds they had been wrestled from. There were slate hedges with herring-bone patterns, hedges with steps built in so you could cross from one side to the other, and hedges that incorporated slots and holes that allowed small animals and wildlife through, but not cows or sheep. There were hedges with stones on end at the top—coping stones, Jamie called them—and hedges with luxurious, flower-dappled turf tops.

"Normally, we'd stay right here and I'd teach you how to build a proper Cornish hedge on-site, but we've got a real job to do, or at least to get started, down in Boscastle. I thought we'd get the fundamentals over with here, though. I've got a hedge half built from a previous class."

The group walked around the back of the big stone barn to a sort of outdoor workroom. Jamie took them to the unfinished end of a new stone hedge.

"So, what do you notice?"

"No mortar," Case said with mock disgust, and everyone laughed.

"It's tapered and curves inward from the base," Becky commented.

"Right. That centralizes the weight and pushes the hedge into the ground."

"It's hollow in between the two sides," Andrew noted. "Well, not hollow, but filled with dirt."

"That's part of the traditional Cornish hedge design. Other hedges could be all stone. But that's not dirt. I call it 'neutral earth.' Dirt is part organic, and over time it breaks down and sinks, creating weakness. Soon enough, the stone faces will collapse inward. Neutral earth's inorganic. Around here, for example, there's a lot of rotted granite that breaks down to something like sand. We call it 'growan.' When I'm building a granite hedge, I look for a deposit of that stuff to fill the center—which is called the 'heart,' by the way. Down

Boscastle way there's usually a layer of shillet—broken-up bits of slate—just below the turf. We'll be using that, plus quarry chips, I expect.

"Speaking of which, we'd best be getting back down there. Time to get to work. Oh, by the way, a couple of reminders. Burt, when you come tomorrow, no rubber wellies. Heavy boots is what you want. Don't want those dainty toes of yours crushed. And Becky—no shorts. Proper trousers."

"Right you are, gov'nor," she said. Burt nodded his big head slowly.

When their little caravan got back to the Visitor Centre car park they drove to the far end. The county council had hauled in several loads of stone, all slate but in an earthy array of colors, from sandy brown through charcoal to blue-black. They'd left a small Bobcat front loader as well. The crew had lunch, and then Jamie gave them the bad news.

"First job's the nastiest, by my lights. We need to excavate a bed for the grounders."

"Grounders?" Newsome asked.

"The stones that make up the footin'," Case said. "They need to be set into the ground, which means diggin' a trench."

"Not bad, for a mortar man," Jamie teased. "Come on, then; tools in the van."

Jamie had an impressive array of shovels, spades, picks, and something that looked like a combination pick and spade, called a mattock. He passed them out, and then ran two twenty-foot parallel lines of twine between stakes at the edge of the macadam, each about five feet apart.

"Why so wide?" Newsome asked. "We're not trying to stop tanks!"

Jamie laughed and gathered the crew by the two parallel guide lines.

"The gentleman wishes to know why I'm having you dig such a wide trench. Contrary to rumor, it isn't because I'm sadistic. There are rules of proportion in hedge laying. The first is that the base must be as wide as the hedge is to be tall. The standard height of a hedge is five feet, including the turf, or cope, on top. Also, the width of the top should be roughly half the width of the base. It's not that we're 'trying to stop tanks,' in Mr. Newsome's words; it's that we're trying to stop gravity from pulling the hedge down once it's laid."

The five students set to work while Jamie wandered among the piles of stone the council had left. Case took his shovel and began to cut a line in the turf along the boundary Jamie had set. Becky watched him for a few moments, then grabbed a mattock and asked him to step aside.

"That'll take forever," she said. She swung the mattock above her head, then, her strong shoulders arching, brought the broad blade down and, in one smooth stroke, peeled back a one-inch-thick strip of sod as wide as the mattock blade. She moved her feet slightly to one side and repeated the movement. Working like a machine, she'd stripped the five-foot-wide trench surface to a length of ten feet in a matter of a few minutes. She stopped, drenched with sweat, stepped aside, smiled, and said, "All yours now, gents."

Andrew shook his head. "Wow, Becky."

"We do a lot of footpath maintenance at the trust; I'm well acquainted with this fellow," she said, hefting the heavy mattock.

Even silent Burt was moved to observe, with characteristic opacity, "Lass doaes a fitty job, she doaes."

Case said nothing.

They set the sod aside to be used eventually on the top of the hedge, and the men began digging. It wasn't long before they ran into trouble. After shoveling up and setting aside the layer of shillet, which, as Jamie had predicted, lay just beneath the turf, they found only a scrim of subsoil and, beneath that, solid shelves of slate. They called Jamie over.

"Figured as much," he said. "We want the hedge growing out of the ground from its footing, not perched on top of it, but we work with what we've got. One bright spot: You won't have to dig so much. Let's dig where we can and clear the ledges smooth where we find them."

They continued like this, Becky peeling sod and the rest of them clearing subsoil, while Jamie, working alone, maneuvered the biggest stones into the bucket of the Bobcat and dumped them along the edge of the car park, a couple of yards from the new trench. It soon became clear that Andrew and Ralph Newsome were in nothing like the shape Burt and the wiry Case were. They huffed and puffed while the other two shoveled and slung gravel and dirt without apparent strain. Becky, sweating just as much as the men in the muggy August heat, kept swinging her mattock, several yards ahead of them. They only stopped for water, which Jamie provided from a big blue insulated plastic barrel with a spigot.

By midafternoon, they'd begun laying the grounders. Jamie explained that the big footing stones had to tilt downward so that gravity would pull the higher levels of the hedge inward to the center.

"How much tilt?" Case asked him.

Jamie took a long-handled shovel and laid it on the ground with the blade facedown, the pointed tip facing toward the center of the trench. "Same angle as that blade."

"Fair enough," Case said. "But what about where we're laying directly on bedrock?"

"Then you'll have to find grounders that have a wedge shape that does the same thing."

"Why can't we just shim them up to that angle?" Becky asked.

"Might have to in a few places," Jamie

answered. "But as much as possible, we want the grounders in contact with the ground. More stable that way."

And so they began, using pry bars and planks to move the big stones to the edge of the trench.

"If you can move a stone a quarter inch, you can move it anywhere," Jamie explained. "It's all in the leverage. We can roll a big stone end-to-end along its edge, or 'walk' it, once we've got it up high enough that we're at the center of its gravity."

Once they had a footing stone poised at the edge, Jamie studied it closely for a moment, pivoting it so that its longest axis faced in toward the center. Then he let it drop. As they added new grounders, they used pry bars to lock the stones together and filled the spaces between with shillet for drainage, ramming it hard with a long iron ramming tool. Meanwhile, Jamie ran the Bobcat back and forth, bringing new grounder stones.

At about four-thirty, Jamie killed the Bobcat's engine and yelled, "All right, you lot, we'll leave it there till the morrow. First round at the Cobweb's on me!"

Andrew was thankful the Cobweb Inn was just on the other side of the car park. As they dragged themselves across the shimmering macadam, Jamie chattered on about the next day's lesson, but Andrew guessed the students weren't retaining much of it. They were all sweat-drenched, filthy, and weary.

Jamie, Burt, and Case, who had the farthest to drive, left after their first pint, Newsome and Becky after their second.

"Reck'n ah'll be orf t'me 'oosbund," Becky said, mimicking Burt's thick Cornish accent. Andrew had had no idea she was married; she wore no ring. She clapped him on the back and strode out the door.

Flora had just come on duty and she made a bee-line for Andrew.

"Don't you be flirtin' with yon Becky, me 'an'sum," she whispered with a wink. "That husband of hers is a right terror."

"I should think 'yon Becky' would be terror enough, but we're only working together."

"On the new hedge, I heard."

"How'd you hear about that?"

"From Nicki. Saw her on the way t'work."

"How'd *she* find out?"

"A little bird, I expect," Flora said, smiling.

"Lee."

Andrew was beginning to think the girl was the town crier.

"Thick as thieves, those two," Flora said, with what to Andrew seemed just a touch of envy. He wasn't sure how old Flora was; late fifties, maybe. Unmarried. Never married? Hard to know. Loved children; probably never had any. Did everyone covet Lee?

"Another pint of Doom Bar, Drew?"

"Sure, but I need to eat, Flora. Too beat to go home and cook for myself. What do you recommend?"

"His nibs, the chef," she said, nodding heavenward, for the kitchen was on the upper floor, "does all sorts of fancy things, but I'm thinkin' what you need is a big plate of sausage and mash, smothered with caramelized onions. Just the ticket for a workin' man. And the sausages are local-made, not store-bought."

Andrew thought about this recommendation for perhaps one second, and said, "Done. Bring it on, m'dear."

Flora came close to blushing, scribbled on her pad, and scurried to the dumbwaiter to send up the order.

And the meal was perfect: the grilled sausages herb-infused and savory, the mashed potatoes creamy, and the onions soft, brown, melt-in-your mouth sweet. There were peas and carrots, too, but they seemed an afterthought.

Later, walking along the footpath in the waning midsummer evening light, Andrew was visited by several small epiphanies. In a matter of days, and despite the English reputation for standoffishness, he had already made friends in this village, friends who meant something important he couldn't quite identify but knew he had not felt before. It had to do with honesty, the absence of pretense, something that did not—and probably could not—exist in the competitive university community he'd lived in for so long. What's more, he felt enfolded and comforted, not just by the tender green hills surrounding the valley and the tiny port, but also by the thick cloak of history that seemed draped over the entire landscape. And the landscape itself—lush in the valley, bleak on the hilltops, wild and windblown on the coast—centered him in a way he'd never experienced before. His ancestors were from nearby, his father said; maybe there was something to heritage after all. And then there was this Nicola—Nicola with the electric touch.

Andrew Stratton crossed the footbridge over the river, climbed up through Minster Wood, passed the tiny Minster church huddled in a remote notch in the valley out of the wind and away from the eyes of marauding infidels, crossed the fields, let himself into Shepherd's Cottage, and was asleep in seconds.

The traditional basis for estimating the actual rainfall accumulation has been to collect it in a suitable container and to measure the collected water at suitable intervals. The measurement process is laborious and requires care. For more frequent and less laborious measurements, automatic rain gauges are widely used which record the amount of rain collected and periodically empty themselves . . . In a standard rain gauge, rain is collected at the orifice and fed through a funnel to the collecting bucket. From there it is periodically emptied into a measuring device.

Brian Golding, ed., "Numerical Weather Prediction," Forecasting Research Technical Report No. 459, Met Office

A diffuse light, cool and bright as a breeze, flooded through the nearly seven-foot-tall multipane window on the north wall of the studio. It had once been the door through which fishing nets were winched up from the quayside below. The thick oak winch arm still hung out high over the pavement. The ceiling of the upper floor of Nicola's cottage was open to the roof peak, and on the south side two permanent skylights had been fitted in between the rafters.

Nicola stood at her easel, working quickly, adding confident bursts of a dusky yellow the color of Dijon mustard to a canvas already awash in pigment. She was working on one of her "tranquillity panels," part of a series of large, loosely impressionistic abstract paintings commissioned by a private hospital in London. The idea was that they helped people heal.

The Dave Brubeck Quartet was on the CD player and Paul Desmond had just slipped into his characteristically smoky solo in "Strange Meadow Lark." Brubeck's classic 1959 album, *Time Out,* was her all-time favorite. She never tired of the quartet's odd-meter compositions, so revolutionary when first recorded and still, almost half a century on, thrillingly experimental. Listening to the album when she painted reminded her that art could soar beyond its accustomed boundaries and still please. Miles Davis had the same effect.

Jazz had been another of Sir Michael's gifts to her. Jeremy's idea of music ran to head-banging groups like the Sex Pistols. Maybe that should have been a clue, but if it was she'd missed it, thinking him interestingly anarchic instead. Another mistake.

When she was growing up in Boston, the air in the cramped DeLucca apartment on Prince Street had seemed perpetually filled with the Italian operas her mother listened to with tears rolling down her cheeks, as if she, herself, were the dying diva. Nicola had never been able to suspend disbelief long enough to appreciate the form; if someone simply burst into song on the street, she kept thinking, they'd be put away. Nicki's own taste ran to British progressive rock: Jethro Tull, Genesis, Cream, the Police, solo work by Peter Gabriel.

But Sir Michael had introduced her to Brubeck and Davis; to Django Reinhardt and Stéphane Grappelli; to sax greats like Charlie Parker and Coleman Hawkins; to piano pioneers like Fats Waller and Thelonious Monk; and to vocalists like Ella Fitzgerald, Sarah Vaughan, and Billie Holiday. She found it too wrenching to listen to Holiday, though; her drug-slurred voice reminded Nicola too much of her older brother. Lately, she'd developed a fondness for the blues as well.

It was comical, really. Her youthful music pref-erences ran to British rock groups; then Sir Michael had introduced her to American jazz. Just as coming to England had felt to her like coming home, her father-in-law had brought her home to the signature sounds of her native land. She swayed as she painted. The hiss and clatter of the river ghosted through the studio window and slipped seamlessly into Joe Morello's drum riffs.

Randi was in his usual place, on a throw blanket atop the Victorian "fainting couch" she'd rescued from a jumble sale and had reupholstered in wine-red velvet.

Brubeck had just picked up the unevenly synco-pated beat of Morello's snare drum in "Take Five" when Randi looked up, barked once, and dashed downstairs. One sharp, happy bark meant a friend; a low growl meant uncertainty. Repeated angry barks meant trouble. It was magical how he seemed to know; as if he received wireless signals through the walls. This wasn't trouble, not with just the one bark, so Nicola chose to ignore the dog. There was a light knock, the creak of the front door opening, then a thin voice.

"Nicki?" the voice called.

It was Lee, Nicki knew. She decided to pretend she wasn't there, and tiptoed behind the sailcloth scrim that served as the wall of her bedroom area. Lee closed the door, mumbled something to Randi, and climbed the stairs to the studio.

131

"Nicki?" the girl repeated.

She stood before the easel and could tell by the smell of the oil paint and the spirit medium that it was fresh.

Before she could call her name again, Nicola swept out of her hiding place and snatched the girl up in her arms.

"Oof! You're getting too big for me to ambush you anymore!" she cried.

"Why didn't you answer the door?"

"The truth?"

"Yeah!"

"Because, sweetie, sometimes when I'm working I don't want to be interrupted, and . . ."

"Sometimes you do?"

"By you? Anytime."

Lee looked at the canvas on the easel. She didn't have the etiquette training yet to inquire politely, "Tell me about your painting." Instead, she said, "What's this?"

Nicola laughed. "You tell me."

Lee stood in front of the painting again.

"Pretty colors?" she said, tentatively.

"Well, thank you, but what else?"

"I dunno. Seems like you put a lot of different colors together in little dibs and dabs, but I can't make out what they are."

"Okay, stand back a bit," Nicola suggested. "Now what do you see?"

"Same thing: different kinds of blues and greens

and pinks and lavender . . . and kinda sandy colors, too."

"And what's that remind you of?"

"I dunno."

"Okay, come to the window." She placed Lee before the tall window overlooking the harbor, and stood behind her. It was late Tuesday afternoon. The tide was in. The summer sun was still high in the west and winked off the wind-fretted surface of the harbor, except where the cliffs cast a purple shadow.

"Look at the water," Nicola said.

Lee did.

"What color is it?" Nicola asked.

"Blue, silly!" Lee said.

"Are you sure?"

"Sure! Everyone knows water is blue."

"Okay, but what shade of blue? Look closely. Is blue all you see?"

Lee was quiet for a moment. She turned to Nicola's painting and then back to the window.

"No! There are lots of colors! Blue and green and pink and lavender and gray from the cliffs and red and yellow from the fishing boat."

"Okay, now look at the canvas."

"It's the same!" Lee exclaimed. "But then it's not."

"Right," Nicola said. "How is it different?"

Lee stood before the easel, her head cocked to one side.

133

"It's . . . softer."

"How does it make you feel?"

"What do you mean?"

"When you look at the painting, do you feel anything, sort of inside of you?"

Lee plopped down on the paint-splattered drop cloth that covered the polished wood floor. Randi joined her. The two of them studied the canvas.

The painting was large, and taller than it was wide, almost as tall as Lee. Its principal colors were an almost Mediterranean blue, a rosy pink, and a pale green the color of spring leaves. But there were also dozens of shades in between, punctuated by slashes of mauve, lavender, violet, and yellow, with occasional flashes of orange and red.

After a while, Lee heaved a sighed and said, "It feels peaceful."

"What's that supposed to mean?" Nicola asked, probing.

"It's like being in my tree. I get all calm, and I feel like I could be in that place, in that feeling, forever."

Nicola stole up behind her little friend and gave her a quick hug.

"That's what the painting's about," she said.

"Like being in my tree?" Lee asked, eyes wide.

"No, like feeling calm," Nicola answered. "This painting's going to a hospital in London, where it's supposed to make sick people feel more comfortable."

Lee was quiet for a moment.

"I think it will," she said finally, sagely nodding her head.

"Meanwhile," Nicola said, "what are you doing down here at this hour? Isn't it time for your supper?"

Lee grinned. "I was watching Drew and those other people building the new hedge up by the car park. They've all gone to the Cobweb now. They looked knackered."

"I'll bet they are. How's the wall coming?"

"Well, it's only the second day; they're laying grounders."

"Grounders?" Nicola flashed to her younger brother listening to the Red Sox game on the radio in his room.

"They're the big bottom stones. First Jamie moves them with the Bobcat, then they use levers and pry bars to get them set just right."

"Who's Jamie?"

"The teacher."

"Sounds like you're taking this course, too!"

"Nah; Drew 'splained. I think it'll be a good hedge. You should see."

"Perhaps I will."

"Drew would like it if you did."

"What?"

"You know. If you took an interest . . ."

Nicola shot her a look: "Lee?"

"He's a really nice man, Nicki."

"That's as may be. But you're not my match-maker."

"Well, *someone* should be!"

Nicola could not believe she was getting advice from a nine-year-old. "Listen," she said gently, "I love you, and I appreciate that you care about me. But being Cupid's not your job."

Lee looked at the painting for a while.

"Whose job is it, then?" she asked.

"Nobody I know," Nicola answered. "Now, I think it's time you headed up to the farm. Do you want me to call ahead and let your mum know you're okay?"

"No," Lee answered, getting up from the floor and giving Randi a whole-body hug. Then: "Yeah, maybe. Don't want to give Mum fits."

Nicola stood outside her door, in the lane between her house and the river, and watched Lee cross the bridge and head past the Cobweb toward the path up the Valency. She called Anne, cleaned the paint off her fingers, changed quickly, and walked over to the Cobweb. This time, she left Randi behind.

ANDREW WAS STANDING at the bar, nursing his pint and chatting with Flora.

"First it's hoisting sheep, then it's hoisting rocks," Nicola said as she stepped up beside him. "I can't say that's much of an improvement!" She winked at Flora.

"You're telling me," Andrew said wearily.

Nicola eyed his dirty clothes. "Love your ensemble."

"Love your perfume," he countered. "What is that, *eau du turpentine?* "

"Touché," she said, laughing.

"Can I get you somethin', Nicki," said Flora, "or are you just going to talk dirty to each other in French?"

"A G and T, please, Flora," she answered. This time, she paid for her own. Then she said to Andrew, "So how are your grounders?"

"Grinding. Did you know there's a ton of stone in every three cubic feet of hedge? I'm sure I lifted that much already today."

"You mean wall?"

"No, I mean hedge. That's what they're called in Cornwall. I thought you were local."

"Me? Hardly."

"Yeah, I guess your accent's a little soft for this area. What part of the country are you from?"

"The Boston part."

"Up in Lincolnshire?"

"No, up in Massachusetts."

"You're joking."

"Can't be; you're not laughing."

"I'm just surprised; that's where I'm from. Originally, at least."

"You're from Boston? What neighborhood?"

"Well, outside of Boston, actually: Lexington."

"Ooh, the ritzy side of the tracks. No wonder."

"No wonder what?"

"No wonder no accent."

"And you?"

"The North End."

"Hmm. You've lost your accent, too . . . and adopted a faux British one, I see."

"Fee, fi, *faux,* fum; I smell marriage to an English-mun," Nicola sang. "Thankfully, the only thing that survived that debacle was the accent."

"Sore subject, I gather."

"Dead subject."

"Your husband?"

"Ha! I wish! No, just the marriage."

"I'm sorry."

"I'm not. Couldn't be happier."

Andrew glanced at Nicola for a moment, then turned away. "I'm not sure I believe that."

"I was referring to the divorce."

"Want to talk about it?"

This was so un-British it took her by surprise. The only people in Boscastle who knew about her divorce were Flora and Anne. Even her landlady didn't know. The British would never dare ask, and she never said anything about it. Was there something about American directness, about "letting it all hang out," that she missed? Was this a form of homesickness? Or was it actually something she wanted to talk about, maybe needed to talk about. She wondered. Her answer was indirect: "No more than you'd like to talk about yours, I suspect."

"Oh, I talked about mine constantly, incessantly, to any and everyone. Then I stopped."

"Stopped, or just ran out of listeners?"

Andrew laughed. "Just got bored with the subject, I guess." He clinked the lip of his glass to hers and said, "Fuck the past!"

"I'll drink to that," Nicola replied.

The two of them stood looking at each other for a moment. It was as if each could suddenly see into the other, through the curtain of bravado and the wisecracks, back behind the wings of the stage they each acted on, doing their respective song-and-dance routines, to the dark place where there was no audience at all, only echoes and one's own secrets.

Andrew turned back to the bar and searched for a menu. "I gotta eat something; I'm gonna pass out from hunger."

"Please don't; Flora so hates scenes."

Andrew looked at Nicola, took a breath, and said, "Would you care to join me?"

Her eyes widened, but she shook her head. "On my income, I can afford to eat here or drink here, but not both."

"You've chosen wisely, I see."

"It's a lovely offer, though."

"Play your cards right and I might treat," Andrew teased.

"Only if I get to see the cards first."

"Where's your sense of adventure?"

"Can't afford that, either."

Neither of them said anything for a moment. Then Nicola surprised herself. "Look, I've probably got enough wilted lettuce and moldy vegetables at home to put together a passable salad for two. Interested?"

"With that mouthwatering description, how could one fail to be? But I'm filthy."

"I know things seem a little primitive here, compared to your Philadelphia, but believe it or not my cottage has hot water. Even soap. But the wine's on you, and if you hurry you can get something lovely and expensive before the Rock Shop across the street closes."

"I don't even know if I can move, much less hurry."

"You run the risk of having me pick it out, then." She swung her purse on to her shoulder. "See you there."

Andrew stood looking at the door, dumbfounded. He was having a date.

Flora was back. "Ordering supper, Andy-boy?"

"I guess not. I have a dinner invitation, sort of," he answered.

"What, with Nicki?"

"So it would seem."

Flora's forehead furrowed. "Careful how you go, then, me 'an'sum."

The comment took him by surprise. Was it a warning? If it was, who was Flora protecting?

"What do you mean?"

"Don't get me wrong, now; Nicki's a good soul. But she blows hot and cold when it comes to men . . . stormy, like. Not that she ever lets 'em get too near. Scares 'em off. Bit of a loner is our Nicki. Lot of artists like that, I reckon."

"I thought she was an interior decorator."

"That what she told you? That's her all over. Nope. Artist. Damn fine one, too, if you ask me."

"Thanks, Flora; careful is how I'll go."

The Rock Shop, it transpired, did not sell rocks. It took its name from the rock candy it had sold to visitors for years—along with fancy tins of cookies, boxes of handmade chocolates, a selection of local beers and hard ciders, and wine. There was an ice cream counter at the rear.

"You should call this place 'Guilty Pleasures,'" Andrew said to the attractive, prematurely gray, middle-aged woman at the till. Nicola was nowhere to be seen.

"You'd be Andrew, I'm guessing. Nicki said you'd be along. I'm Sandy."

Andrew was momentarily stunned by the woman's eyes, which were an arresting shade of bright blue with a hint of lavender. Andrew took her extended hand and introduced himself.

Sandy pushed a bottle of wine across the counter. "She chose this," she said.

Andrew studied the bottle, an inexpensive Beaujolais-Villages.

"Hmmm," he said, looking at the shelves of wine bottles behind Sandy. "Let's see if we can't choose something a little better than this, something with a bit more backbone. Ah!" He pulled down a bottle of Moulin-à-Vent. Then another.

"Good choice," the woman said. "That's one of Nicki's favorites, actually."

"Then why'd she choose the Villages, I wonder?"

"Maybe because the Beaujolais-Villages is simpler, a bit safer?"

"I don't think of Nicola as the simple, safe type," Andrew commented. "Do you?"

The woman behind the counter had a giggle the sound of a silver bell. She blushed. "I'm sure I couldn't say," she said.

Andrew didn't believe her for a minute, and he was pretty sure Sandy didn't expect him to. He paid for the wine, thanked her, stepped out the door, then turned and reentered.

"Um, this is sort of embarrassing, but I've just realized I have no idea where she lives."

The silver bell again, then: "Over the bridge, right into the lane down the south bank of the river, carry on to the bottom, where the quay begins. Hers is 'the Loft.' Can't miss it. Enjoy the wine!"

Andrew thanked her again and backed out the door. He felt like an idiot. He stopped in at the

Cornish Stores, a little convenience shop, and rescued the last remaining bunch of carnations, which were languishing, like huddled orphans, in a nearly dry bucket outside the door.

"How am I supposed to impress a woman with this?" he complained good-naturedly to André LeSeur, the French shopkeeper who met his wife, Trisha, years earlier on a hiking holiday in Cornwall and stayed on. André, whom Andrew knew well since he did much of his shopping here, gave him the classic Gallic shrug and said simply, "Delivery's tomorrow."

Andrew slid the money across the counter: "You should be paying me to take these sad things away so as not to sully your reputation!"

André gave him another shrug, then a smile.

"WHAT THE HELL have I got myself into, Randi?"

The dog barked, then resumed panting happily.

Nicola was shredding romaine with a vengeance, as if she was tearing her hair out—which, it now occurred to her, was maybe what she should have been doing. An egg was boiling in a small pot on the hob, along with four small new potatoes. She had some limp green beans refreshing in a bowl of ice water.

She had no idea why she'd invited this man to dinner. She'd never had a man in her cottage, much less one she'd known for only a couple of days— no, that was a lie: a couple of hours over a couple of days, over a couple of drinks. What was he *really* doing in Boscastle? Nobody comes to Cornwall from America to build stone hedges— nobody sane, anyway. Maybe he was on the run from someplace or something or someone. At a minimum, she should have done a Google search on him first—Andrew Stratton + architect + Philadelphia. Jesus, the man's sole character reference was a nine-year-old girl! Oh, and a sheep!

Okay, he was pretty good-looking, and neither too young nor too old. Tall enough, too; in heels, she could probably look him straight in the eye. Cute, curly, dark-brown hair salted with gray. And his eyes—good Lord, she didn't even know what color they were; they'd spent all their time together in the dimness of the Cobweb.

Plus, in a week he'd be gone.

This last thought nagged at her—not that she might never see him again, but because that was part of the attraction: He was safe. Not much chance of getting "involved." Not much chance to screw up, either. But mostly, not much chance of risking her heart. She'd done that once, with Jeremy, and he'd brutalized it. In the few years she'd lived in Boscastle, she'd seen two or three men socially. But these dates had never got much beyond dinner at the pub, and the truth was, that had suited her just fine. Single men her age were scarce in the village, and those there often turned out to be single for a good reason: They were irresponsible, or irregularly employed, or drunks, or abusers, or all four. The best men—men like Anne's Roger—were all taken. Flora told her she should broaden her "catchment area." She had laughed, because she'd thought Flora had said "catch men area." Same thing, really. Besides, no one she met seemed able or willing to keep up with her. She used her sharp wit as a sort of entrance exam, and most men failed. They either went all quiet or got nasty, as if they didn't know how to play well with others.

But this Stratton chap gave as good as he got. That took courage. She liked that.

THERE WAS A small slate sign with the name of the cottage attached to the whitewashed wall, beside the door. Just before Andrew knocked, he heard the dog bark, just once.

"Door's open!" he heard Nicola yell.

He stepped directly into a low-beamed room that ran the full width of the house. The floor was made of massive slabs of slate, rounded and worn by centuries of heavy use. There was a small dining table at one end of the room and a shallow fireplace surrounded by comfortable-looking furniture at the other. The overall color scheme was white and nautical blue, with accents of lemon yellow here and there. There was an expensively framed oil painting over the mantel, but the rest of the artwork was posters and prints suitable to a seaside

145

cottage. He wondered if the house belonged to Nicola or was a rental.

Randi sat in a bright doorway at the back and barked a second time. A summons. Andrew went through to a long, narrow kitchen that ran across the back of the house. It was brightly lit, but the only window, over the deep porcelain sink, looked out onto the cliff face not two feet away. Maybe six feet wide and three times as long, the kitchen reminded him of the galley in a railroad dining car, without the moving scenery. Nicola was squeezing lemon juice into a small bowl with olive oil in it. The tiny room was tangy with citrus.

He held out the carnations. "Wilted flowers to go with the wilted lettuce," he said.

She laughed. "Screw the flowers; did you get the wine?"

"No."

"What?"

"Got something better. You have lousy taste in wine. Unsophisticated. Here."

She pulled a bottle out of the bag and beamed. "Sandy told you."

"No, it was my choice. I may look like a mere laborer, madam, but in fact I am a connoisseur of fine wines."

"And what else, I might wonder? Okay, mister common-sewer of wine, are you equally expert at operating a tin opener?"

"I think I could cope."

"Good. There's a tin of very expensive Italian tuna just there, and the opener is in that top drawer. Avail yourself. We're having *salade niçoise.*"

"Ah, I understand now," he said as he cranked the tin opener. "Romaine lasts forever without wilting, and most of the other ingredients are tinned, preserved in salt or brine, or, like the hard-boiled egg, in a protective shell. So it doesn't matter how old they are. It's like the wine: a vintage salad."

"Hey! Beggars can't be choosers, and you, my friend, look every inch the beggar."

Andrew looked down at his clothes.

"Good point. Where can I wash?"

"Out back. With the hose."

Andrew scanned the room for a door.

Nicola laughed again. "Okay, there's no 'out back,' and no hose either, come to that. The loo's upstairs, beyond the bedroom. But first open the wine."

Andrew found a corkscrew, opened the first bottle, poured her a glass, delivered it with a flourish, and departed, picking his way up the narrow stairs, with Randi leading the way.

The painting on the easel at the top of the stairs stopped him in his tracks. He'd never seen anything like it. Outside, the light was fading, and yet the canvas seemed to glow from within, almost shimmer, the colors radiant. There was nothing representational about the piece but it reminded him of a watery sunrise, or perhaps water at sunrise. Andrew had always liked the way the French Impressionists brought out the play of light on common objects and scenes. Now he realized that Nicola's painting reminded him slightly of Monet's *Water Lilies*. But it was as if she'd focused a telephoto lens on a tiny patch of pond surface and pushed the color and light to a higher level of abstraction. Flora was right; Nicola was a fine painter.

He looked around. The upper story was a big, airy space. The walls and the cathedral ceiling were painted white and the exposed crossbeams were bare, lime-washed timbers. He didn't know any other painters, but somehow he'd always expected their studios to be chaotic. Not this one. Tubes of paint were arrayed neatly in open trays. He peered at them: cadmium yellow, lemon yellow, cadmium red, alizarin crimson, ultramarine, cobalt blue, viridian, and many more. Brushes of many types stood clean and fresh in clear glass jars. A palette board with dabs of the same colors she'd been using on the canvas lay on a table, covered with plastic wrap—to inhibit evaporation, he guessed. The studio had a wonderfully earthy smell of linseed oil.

He stepped behind the billowy canvas curtain and into Nicola's "bedroom," which was simply a section of the loft space. It was sparely furnished: a wrought-iron double bed that stood atop a multicolored rag rug; a dresser; a tall Victorian wardrobe, its door slightly ajar with an ivory silk robe hanging from the corner. A few books were stacked on a side table with a lamp. That was it: no television, no other decoration. Almost a hermit's cell. Suddenly feeling a bit like a voyeur, he went through to the bathroom and washed up.

THE SALAD WAS nearly gone and they were well into the second bottle of wine when Nicola asked Andrew how long he planned to stay in Boscastle. They'd got past the basics: family, school, career—at least the parts each was willing to share.

"Just a couple of weeks. I signed on to the hedge project for a week and came a few days early to beat the jet lag. Then, I thought I'd spend a few more days poking around Cornwall before I leave."

"Why are you really here?" Nicola asked.

He smiled. "For the salad—which was pretty terrific, by the way, despite your negative advertising."

She made a face. "You know what I mean; why are you here, in Boscastle, three thousand miles from home . . . building a stone wall for God's sake."

"Hedge," he corrected.

"You're hedging, all right."

Andrew ran his fingers through his hair and looked past her to the window that opened onto the lane and the river, both now in darkness. He listened to the music of the river tumbling over its rocky bed as it hurried to the harbor. Finally, he returned his gaze to Nicola. In the light of the curious collection of candles she'd set on the simple pine dining table—some short and squat, some slender and tall, all of them white—her eyes shone like freshly mined anthracite. The coppery highlights in her long, wavy brown hair flashed in the changing light of the candle flames.

"It seemed like a good idea at the time. Still does, actually."

"Is that supposed to be an answer?"

"It's all I have; you ask as if you suspect I'm an escaped felon."

"Are you?"

He laughed and drank some wine. "No. Though it feels that way sometimes."

"Because you left your wife?"

He looked up at her sharply. "I didn't; she . . . we . . . separated."

"How many years ago?"

He took a breath. "One."

Nicola blanched. "Bloody hell. I'm so sorry; I had no idea it was that recent. What an incredibly rude question."

"Nonsense; how could you know?"

"It's just you seem so . . . I don't know . . . calm. Under the circumstances."

"Do I?"

"On the outside, anyway."

"Yes, well, I suppose I do."

"And are you?"

A surge of emotion took him by surprise, a kind of panic. The truth was, he didn't know. He looked around the room, as if the answer were hidden there—on a shelf, under a chair, on the mantel. Had he, during the course of the past year, reached a certain state of calm, of peace? Or had he simply stuffed away his anger and fear? He knew there was at least some truth to Katerina's charges. It was true, for example, that some part of him cringed at expressing strong emotion, as if it were unseemly. Or simply a sign of weakness. But he had loved Kat, and he had expressed it often, in little and big ways—in part to earn her affection, which she rationed. He also knew he was over Kat; her affair had made that easier. But the sense of failure still dogged him. Maybe his calm was just resignation, a kind of giving up.

And the funny thing was that during the last year, no one—least of all himself—had really taken the time to consider or ask how he was, how he felt, or to wait long enough for an answer. Now Nicola waited.

He brought her face back into focus and shook his head. "Probably not."

She reached across the table and touched his hand.

"Good," she said, smiling. "You'd be a freak if you were."

"Thank you . . . I think."

"No, really. Look, I'm not even sure why I asked; it's none of my business. But now that I have, I'll just say that I didn't tell you the whole truth when I said I couldn't be happier about my divorce. I was shattered for months—and I was the one who left! Somehow that didn't make it any easier."

She paused and regarded him silently for a moment, her eyes soft as a doe's.

"She left you, didn't she?"

Andrew sighed. "Is my inadequacy that obvious? Yes, she left me. We didn't separate. I lied about that."

"She was a fool, whoever she was."

"I don't know . . ."

"Andrew, please." Nicola made a face. "I've only known you for a few days, but it doesn't take a clairvoyant to see that you are a good man. For Christ's sake, you try to save sheep!"

"But I couldn't save the marriage."

"None of us can do that single-handedly." Then a thought occurred to her. "Did you beat her?"

"What? Of course not!"

"My husband did."

Andrew looked at the woman across the table, speechless. He couldn't imagine anyone wanting to mar that beauty.

"Your husband *beat* you? Jesus."

"I don't think Jesus had much to do with it,

frankly," she said, flashing a smile still fraught with pain.

"I . . . I don't know what to say. I can't imagine . . ."

"You know what? I believe you. I believe you can't imagine doing harm to anyone, much less a woman. I suspect you're cursed."

"Cursed?"

"With being a gentleman."

"I never thought of it as a handicap."

Nicola winked at him: "Don't you know that good girls like bad boys?"

Andrew laughed. "I guess I'll never have a chance with good girls."

Nicola seemed to study him for a moment, then said, "She left you for someone else, didn't she?"

She didn't know why she knew this; the knowledge came to her as if through her pores. There was an ache in this man, the ache of betrayal. It was palpable.

Andrew looked away.

"Maybe Lee's right; maybe you are a witch. Or a mind reader."

"I'm so sorry. I shouldn't have—"

"Yes. She left me. For a lawyer, someone who earns a lot more than a university professor."

He stared at his empty plate, then looked up again. "And now, Nicola, I think it's time I trundled home to bed."

Nicola suddenly felt like a vampire who had sucked the life out of this lovely man.

"Andrew, please don't; I'm sorry. I didn't mean—"

"I know, Nicki. I'm still a little raw is all, like some reptile that's shed its skin and is still waiting for the layer underneath to toughen up."

"I remember how that feels," she said.

Randi had been resting his chin on one of Andrew's dusty boots and was asleep. Andrew slipped his foot out as gently as he could and stood. The dog looked up, then put its head down on the floor with a sigh.

"Look," Andrew continued, "dinner was wonderful—almost as wonderful as your company, but not quite. I've got a big day tomorrow; we start building the rest of the hedge, now that the foundation is laid."

She rose and stood by the table. "Thank you for the flowers, Andrew."

"Sorry they weren't a bit more, um . . . lush. You deserve better." Andrew stood at the door for a moment, waiting for Nicola to open it. She seemed riveted to the floor. He lifted the latch, stepped out into the warm evening, then turned and smiled.

"Good night, Nicola," he said quietly, "and thank you."

Nicola managed to smile. "Good night, Andrew."

She watched him walk up the lane and turn into Dunn Street. Then she closed the door.

"Shit!" she said.

Information on the storms of 16th August 2004 comes mainly from 5 tipping bucket rain gauges in the area: at Slaughterbridge in the River Camel catchment, at Woolstone Mill, Tamarstone and Crowford Bridge in the Bude catchment, and at Lesnewth/Trevalec in the Valency catchment. All use 0.2 mm buckets. The first four record the number of tips at fixed time intervals, giving 15 minute rainfall accumulations, while the last records individual tip times with a precision of 10 seconds.

Brian Golding, ed., "Numerical Weather Prediction," Forecasting Research Technical Report No. 459, Met Office

"How many of those stones you reckon you'll pick up and put down before you find one you fancy?" Jamie had walked up behind Andrew and was smiling.

They were working on the "filler" level, laying stone atop the uneven grounders to create a level base on which to build the rest of the hedge. Earlier Wednesday morning, Jamie and Becky had gone through the rock pile and sorted the stones in rows, placing the largest closest to the wall. Jamie explained that you always lay the biggest stones first, so you don't have to lift them very high.

Andrew studied the rock he'd just lifted. "I'm searching for one that fits."

"Makes sense, but for one thing."

"What's that?"

"You're doubling your work every time you lift one and put it back. Soon be exhausted and have little to show for your sweat."

"So what's your solution?"

"You don't search for the right stone, lad; you discover it."

"Huh?"

Jamie laughed and patted him on the shoulder. "I'm being a bit unfair to you; it takes years. Lads! Becky! Over here for a moment."

156

The crew gathered around the area where Andrew was working.

"You've all got the physics down pretty good," Jamie said to his crew. He'd taught them how to lift big stones safely and how to find the right side for the face of the hedge. He'd taught them to lay "one on two and two on one"—that is, to make sure the middle of the stone in the upper layer sits above the joint of the two stones beneath it, and vice versa.

"Now it's time for the metaphysics," he said.

They all looked at him like pilgrims at the oracle.

"If a stone was a perfect cube," he explained, "it would have six faces. That's six faces with four rotation possibilities, or twenty-four ways of being presented. It's no wonder you struggle to find one that fits, eh? But there's a trick to make this easier. When you look at the hedge face you're working on, I want you to remember this: You can find a stone to fit the space in front of you, or you can find a space to fit the stone. You have two choices, not one. See?

"The way I think about it, a hedge exists even before it's built. It's a space within space that wants to be filled. Stone is just the filling for the space. So when you're working the face, I want you to think about both the space you're working and the stone you're working with. Hedge building's like doing a jigsaw puzzle without a picture: You have pieces and spaces, and you just match them up. The difference here is that the pieces are bloody heavy. So never pick up a stone twice. As you make your rows, try to keep several of its spaces in your mind's eye; then pick up a stone that fits one of those spaces. In a sense, it's simple: You just put the stone where it goes. The learning is in understanding where it's going even before you lift it. So spend more time looking at your stones, but leave them on the ground. You'll soon learn to discover what fills the spaces, just by looking and rotating the stone in your head. Get the picture?"

They all nodded, though tentatively.

"Plus there's the practical problem: If you keep picking up stones and putting them down again, we'll never get to the pub."

They laughed and went back to work, but at a less-frantic pace now, each of them doing a lot more staring than lifting, moving more slowly but, increasingly, with more confidence. Soon, there were more "ahs!" than "uhs" as they discovered the stone they were looking for.

As disparate a group as they were, they worked together well, each addressing the hedge face at his own pace and with his own rhythm. Andrew found the work deeply, almost primitively satisfying: moving stone, making hedge. It also gave him time to think, and what he thought about mostly was dinner at Nicola's.

He'd said too much. He didn't fault Nicola for

asking about his divorce; he just wished now he'd been more circumspect. It wasn't the same as going on and on about the breakup, the way he'd done in the first few months. It wasn't like him to be so open, so undefended. And yet—despite her sharp tongue—something about Nicola made it safe. Though they traded verbal sword thrusts like adversaries, it only seemed to draw them closer. And he liked getting closer to Nicola. He liked that a lot.

At one point, Burt hoisted a large stone and dropped it into place with a hollow *thwok*.

"You hear that, Burt?" Jamie called from a few yards away. He looked at the rest of the crew. "You all hear that sound? That's the sound of a bad fit."

He walked to where Burt was standing like a boy caught misbehaving. The others joined them.

"See, this looks like a good join, from the front and the top, anyway. It's touching everywhere. But that hollow sound tells you that some part of the stone isn't in contact with its neighbors."

Burt moved to lift the stone off the hedge face.

"Leave it be, big guy," Jamie said, placing a hand on Burt's thick arm. "Remember the rule: Never pick up a stone twice. When you get a bad fit, you fix it with the next stone."

Jamie peered at Burt's stone in its place. He put pressure on the inside edge and the big stone rocked slightly.

"There's your weak spot, Burt. All it needs is trigging."

"Triggin'?" Burt said. None of them had a clue what Jamie was talking about.

"A trig's a small stone you use as a shim, almost always on the inside of the face, like here." Jamie poked around the stone yard and found a shard. He lifted the inside edge of Burt's stone, slipped the smaller stone beneath it, and then dropped the big one with a loud *thwack.*

"That's what we want to hear! Like the clack of two snooker balls when they collide. See, you have to listen to the stone. Stone will tell you when it's happy."

Andrew saw Case lift a skeptical eyebrow. Listen to the stone. Don't look for a stone; discover it. A hedge is a space within space that wants to be filled. It was like sitting at the feet of a Zen master, Andrew thought to himself. What he'd thought would be a course about developing a new set of mechanical skills was turning into a lesson in contemplation, in the use of all your senses, not just the application of brute force.

After lunch, Jamie hauled a five-foot-tall piece of plywood out of his truck and carried it to the slowly rising hedge. It was cut in the shape of a shallow D, except that the curve of the D didn't join the vertical at the top.

"Right now, lads . . . and lady," he said, bowing to Becky with exaggerated formality, "let's talk geology. Back at my place, as you saw, I've got granite wherever I look. But here on the coast, we're in a different geologic province, an older one. Here we've got slate. Slate is a metamorphic rock, which means that pressure and heat have turned it from what it was originally into something else—'morphed it,' as the computer types might say. Slate started out as shale, which started out as fine grains of clay and other minerals washed down from the hills into muddy deltas eons ago. As the sediments deepened, the weight exerted tremendous pressure on the layers below and changed them, hardened them. The heat and weight of the volcanic rock that came later—the granites we see up on Bodmin Moor—hardened the slates even more.

"A lot of the slate and shale in the buildings and hedges along this coast was mining waste: rock blasted loose by the old tin-mining industry hereabouts. The Delabole quarry just over the hills there, a bit west of Camelford, produces high-quality slate, for roofing tiles and such. Been operating since Elizabethan times, they have. But here we're working with rougher stuff.

"Now, there's good news and bad news in hedging with slate. The bad news is you don't get big pieces. The good news is that slate has nice, smooth parallel faces, and, if a piece is irregular, it's easy to split and dress. Slate has an obvious grain and flat cleavage planes. Of course, that's also why it busts up."

161

"Stacks real good, though," Case commented.

Jamie nodded. "As our colleague, Mr. Casehill here, knows well, it's easy to build walls and houses from slate; you just slap them and stack them, like flapjacks, and mortar them together."

Case smirked.

"But out in the fields, where most hedges get laid, you can't be fussing around with mortar. You have to come up with some other way to make the stones hold together. And that other way is called gravity."

"Is this where the herringbone thing comes in?" Becky asked.

"Top prize to the lady!" Jamie said.

"But it's so dainty-looking," she said.

"That's how it looks, but not how it works. How it works is like interlocking teeth, like a zipper. Tight and strong. It's all about the batter."

"Is that like mortar?" Case asked. Burt and Newsome laughed. It was getting to be a running gag with Case.

Jamie didn't even respond. Instead, he grabbed the big piece of plywood.

"See that curve? That's what we call the 'batter.' A Cornish hedge curves inward, gently, and that curve creates stability. It focuses the weight of each stone toward the center. It puts gravity to work holding the whole structure in place.

"See, stones are lazy buggers," Jamie continued. "You may have noticed this already: They don't like to be lifted. They don't like to be moved. They don't like to be stood on end. They want to lie down as soon as possible. It's not surprising; they're elderly. Their natural disposition is to be at rest, like your old granny. So your job, as a hedger, is to make them comfortable. How do you do that? By finding them a nice bed, and tucking them in.

"That's what the herringbone pattern's all about. We call it 'Jack-and-Jill,' or 'Darby-and-Joan,' or—no offense, Becky—'John-upon-Joan.' Whatever the name, the idea is that each stone in one row is slanted to the left at an angle of fifty to seventy degrees, and to the right in the row above, and so on. And each stone has to lock into the one below and above."

"So where's the plywood come in?" Newsome asked.

Jamie smiled. "What's the biggest contribution the Romans ever made to the world?"

"Wine?" said Newsome.

"Paved roads," said Case, with authority.

Burt shrugged.

"Hot baths!" said Becky, and everyone laughed.

Finally, Andrew mumbled, "The arch."

"Thank you, Mr. *Arch*-itect!" Jamie crowed. "The arch indeed! A curve of stones suspended in the air, something that ought to collapse but doesn't, because gravity itself holds the pieces in place, forces them tighter together, continuously."

He held the curved piece of plywood over his

163

head and made an arch. Then he put it back down on its bottom corner, the curve facing in toward the center of the still-imaginary hedge.

"The batter of a Cornish hedge is an inward curve that nearly straightens out at the top; it's like a Roman arch set on its side, and it has the same purpose: It confers strength. Oh, and one other thing . . ."

"Sheep," Burt grunted.

"Right," Jamie said. "It keeps the bloody sheep from scaling the hedge. As we say around here, 'a good hedge will put a sheep on its back.'"

"I'll be damned," Newsome said.

Jamie laughed. "Might be you will," he said, "but not till this here job's done. Till then, you're just in Purgatory. Back to work, you lot."

"I THINK YOU'RE round the twist," Nicola said.

Anne Trelissick looked up from her drawing board, where she'd been putting the final touches on a pen-and-ink illustration of a rather endearing-looking rat dressed in corduroy breeches and a plaid waistcoat. It was part of a series she was doing for a new edition of Kenneth Grahame's children's classic, *The Wind in the Willows*. Nicola had been looking over her shoulder as Anne worked. She had taken drawing classes in Boston, of course, but she still marveled at Anne's anatomical precision and her ability to give character to animals.

"No, you don't," Anne said, taking a sip from a mug of tea. "You know I'm telling you the truth, and it scares you."

"Bullshit."

"I am immune to your coarse Americanisms."

"Oh, bugger!"

"That's better. Now, about this American chap—"

"Look," Nicola exploded. "Don't be daft; his wife left him!"

"And you left your husband."

"He was a violent asshole!"

"Excuse you?"

"Okay, 'cad.' That better? You've been spending too much time in the world of Victorian English . . . and animals. But how do I know Andrew isn't violent, too?"

"You said yourself you didn't think he could be. May I remind you that this is a guy who tried to save a bloody sheep? Okay, that makes him really stupid, but nothing more. Besides, Lee really likes him, and one thing I've learned about my daughter, bless her quirky heart, is that she's a good judge of character. The evidence stands before me: You're her best friend."

"We all have our blind spots."

"Oh, stop."

"Okay, okay. I'll give you this: There's something . . . I don't know . . . tender about him."

Anne laughed. "You'd probably be tender, too—though perhaps *tenderized* is a better word—if

165

your wife walked out on you a year ago for another, richer fellow. But I'll tell you something: I think that man's got strength."

"Oh, and now you're a witch, too?"

Anne tilted her head to one side and regarded her friend with a long-suffering look. "Want to know how I know that, or do you want to just keep up this verbal tennis match?"

Nicola let out a resigned sigh.

"I know it because of the way he comports himself with everyone he's met here. He's a listener. His interest is real. He doesn't need to be the center of attention. How many men do you know like that?"

"Besides your Roger?"

"Yes, besides my Roger. And I see it in the way he treats Lilly. Most people need a lot of patience with that girl. Not him. He doesn't need patience because he respects her. He attends to her. He's exactly like you in that regard.

"And then there's the matter of the hedge building. At first, I didn't get it. Why he'd come all this way just to build a wall? And then it came to me: It's not about the hedge. It's about something inside him trying to get out. It's like he's doing this work as if it were a sort of quest. As if he was searching for something in the stone that he's determined to find, and maybe it's himself. I was down to the Visitor Centre to deliver something to Elizabeth yesterday, and I watched him awhile with Jamie. And I had the strangest thought: It was as if with every stone he lifted and fit into the hedge, he was taking one down from the wall around himself. Know what I mean? What's that word they use now? *Deconstructing,* that's it! He's deconstructing himself. And I think that takes strength."

"Well, those stones are bloody heavy," Nicola cracked.

Anne made a face. "I don't know why I bother talking to you shallow Americans."

Nicola looked at her friend for several long moments.

"Thank you, Anne," she said finally. "But there's the other point, the obvious one . . ."

"Which is?"

"He'll be gone in—what—a week? I'm not about to fall in love with him."

"Well, you're right there. You're not *about to,* you already have. You're not immune, you know, just because you got stung once."

"Nonsense. And besides, you make it sound like a disease."

"It is. It's chronic, if you're lucky."

"Like you and Roger?"

"Yes. Like me and Roger. You don't recover, and you don't want to. Even after all these years, it still feels feverish. You know what?"

"What?"

"I feel like an idiot advising a forty-year-old

woman about love. Hell, I'm six years younger than you are!"

"You probably *are* an idiot advising a forty-year-old woman about love . . . but a very sweet idiot."

"Nicki?"

"What?"

"What do you want?"

Nicola looked at the floor, her lush hair hiding her face.

"I don't know, Anne. For a long time I just wanted to be left alone. Now, I don't know; maybe I'm tired of being alone. I'm certainly tired of being afraid."

"Afraid? Of Jeremy?"

"No."

"What then?"

She raised her head, pushed her hair back, and smiled—a weary smile, full of sadness.

"You know. I told you."

Anne nodded. "That part, I guess I understand."

Nicola stood and gave Anne a hug. "Thanks, luv," she said.

Anne shrugged. "Damned if I know what for."

She walked Nicola to the door and watched her pick her way across the farmyard to her car.

"Hey, wait!" Anne called after her. "You going to the Welly tonight?"

"Of course! Wouldn't miss it for the world."

"Tonight then, luv."

"Thanks again, Anne."

Anne Trelissick shook her head and returned to the endearing rat.

LEE TRELISSICK WAS lying in wait. She'd seen the hedgers go into the Cobweb and sat on the wall opposite, waiting for Andrew to emerge. After only one pint, he did. He stood outside the door, blinking in the bright light, and considered whether to take the road home (the long but easy way), or the valley path (the short but hard way). He chose the road and had taken only a few steps before he heard the familiar greeting: "Guess what, Drew?!"

He swiveled his head and there she was. It lifted his spirits immediately.

"I don't know; *what,* Lee?"

"Today's Wednesday!"

"So I gathered. Thankfully, it's nearly over."

"No, it isn't." She was skipping along at his side now, like an eager puppy.

"Listen, kid. By my reckoning, it's coming up on five-thirty. I've been here since eight this morning. Wednesday's over."

"Uh-uh," she sang.

He stopped on the bridge over the river.

"Okay, what?"

"Wednesday's Welly night."

"Huh?"

"The singing."

"I have no idea what you're talking about, and, just between you and me, I'm too tired to care."

"The *singing!* Don't you know?"

Andrew started laughing. He couldn't help it. Lee was facing him with her hands on her hips, like a schoolmarm lecturing to the class dunce . . . which was him. She positively vibrated with impatience. He took the diplomatic route.

"Why don't you tell me about it as we walk home, Lee?"

"Okay, here's the deal. Every Wednesday night, there's singing at the Welly."

They had just passed the Wellington, Boscastle's oldest hotel, on their way up Dunn Street. It dated back to the age of horse-drawn transport, when it had been a staging post. It was a compact, handsome construction, several stories high and vaguely Victorian-looking now, its street-side corner anchored by a round, castellated turret. It had the unusual distinction of having been built directly over the little River Jordan, the main tributary of the River Valency. Just as you stepped up to the threshold of the hotel's entrance, there was a steel grating beneath which you could hear the stream rushing through an ancient stone culvert.

"What, karaoke?"

"No, silly! Old-timey songs. Some people bring instruments, too. There's been singin' at the Welly for ages and ages," Lee continued. "At least since the war."

"The war?"

"You know. The big one. Before I was born."

"World War Two?"

"Yeah, I guess. I think. Anyway . . . people just show up and, after a while, they just start singing . . . though Jack's the one who gets it going."

"Jack?"

"Jack! The Boscastle Busker! You know . . . the guy with the big hat who walks around town singing?"

Andrew, focused as he was on hedge building, had missed this bit of local color.

"He sings and people give him money. For the hospital."

"What hospital?"

"I dunno. A hosp-something, anyway. Maybe not a hospital."

"A hospice?"

"Yes! That's what!"

Andrew felt as if he was speaking to someone through an interpreter.

"Mount-something; I don't remember. Anyways, he has loads of songs in him. But absolutely *everyone* goes and sings along!"

"And that includes you?"

"Yup. Mum and Dad take me, but I can't sit in the bar. I sit in a corner and no one complains."

"So you have a pint of ale and just hang with the crowd?"

"Ugh! Dad gave me a taste once. I stick to apple-mango juice."

"Very wise, I'm sure."

"So you'll be there, right?"

Andrew sighed. He'd planned a bath, a bowl of spaghetti Bolognese, and bed, but there was no denying Miss "Guess What?!"

"Sure, Lee. When's it start?"

She had started hopping with delight, but she quickly stopped, frowning. "I dunno. After supper, I know that."

"Very helpful."

"Well, how'm I supposed to know? I'm a kid!"

"I'm sorry. You're right. I forget that sometimes."

This seemed to please Lee to no end.

"WHAT'LL IT BE, friend?"

Andrew was standing at the Wellington's famous Long Bar. Before him was an array of hand pumps, each with a name more bewildering than the next: Cornish Knocker, Betty Stogs, Keel Over (that one sounded lethal), Cornish Blonde, Figgy's Brew—all from a local brewery called Skinner's.

He looked at the barkeep and shook his head. "A pint of something, but I've no idea what."

The nattily dressed fellow behind the bar laughed. "Common problem; embarrassed for choice is what we are here at the Welly. What do you like?"

"Amber ale. Smooth, not too hoppy."

"That'll be Figgy's Brew, that will. Here, have a

taste." The barman pulled a short measure into a small tumbler and handed it to him.

Andrew tasted and nodded. "Perfect."

"Strong ale, that one," an older fellow standing next to him commented. "Four point five."

"Alcohol percentage? That doesn't sound strong to me," Andrew said.

"Nah. 'Specific gravity's' what that is."

"What's that?"

The man leaned toward him, conspiratorially. "Haven't a clue, mate; more chemistry than I ever had." He winked.

Andrew liked the place already. You were never a stranger in an English pub. He scanned the room. The place was packed. He felt a hand on his shoulder.

"Come for the singing, lad?"

"Jamie! I thought you'd gone back up to Bodmin Moor."

"Not on a Wednesday; not when Jack's in town."

"What are you drinking, Jamie? My treat."

"Well, thank you, son. Same as yours; a pint of Figgy would suit me fine."

His drink came, and Andrew clinked Jamie's glass with his. "To the fine art and craft of Cornish hedging," he said.

"I'll always drink to that. And to you as well. Been watching you. You've a head for it, hedging, now you've got the spaces notion down. Expect that's partly from your training."

"We didn't have courses in hedge building in architecture school, Jamie."

"Not what I mean. You've a good spatial sense. I think you see the hedge as a whole, in your mind, not just the stones and the spaces between them."

"Yes. I guess I do. Probably why I'm an architect. That comes easily to me."

"One thing I don't ken, though, lad."

"What's that?"

"What you're doing here—building hedges when you could be making buildings. Odd sort of holiday, if you take my meaning."

Andrew smiled at his stone master, signaled to the chap behind the bar, and ordered another round.

"I've never made a building, Jamie." He could hear Katerina's tirade and shook it out of his head. "I teach architectural theory; that's different."

"Not much theory in hedging."

"That's not true, Jamie, and you know it. You don't teach hedge building, anyway."

"Meaning?"

"Oh, sure, you teach us the technique; but that's not what turns you on. What you really teach is a reverence for the stone. You want us to listen to the stone: not just the sound it makes when it smacks into place, but the story it wants to tell—how it was formed, what it's been through since, what it can do and can't do, what it wants to be."

"Seems like somebody's been paying attention."

"I have, Jamie, and it's partly because I've been trying to puzzle out something that's vaguely related." Andrew told Jamie about his ideas about livable places, about the almost organic integrity of such places, about the honesty of simple vernacular buildings, about the beauty of working with local materials, about building to human scale, and about how this art, this way of being in the world, was disappearing in America.

When Andrew stopped long enough to take a pull from his pint, Jamie said, "Seems to me you're living in the wrong country, lad. Around here, that stuff still matters. There was a while there we almost lost it, like the Cornish language, but we found it again and it's getting stronger. I'm not sure people like Casehill will ever get it. He's a 'quick-and-dirty' bloke; cement it together and move on. But Burt does—knew his dad, I did. And this Newsome fella. He's got loads of lolly, but he wants to do the right thing on his land. I respect that. But what're *you* gonna do, build Cornish hedges in Philadelphia?"

Andrew laughed. They both did. The ale helped.

"I don't know, Jamie," Andrew said. "I didn't even really know I was searching for something until I got here. It's like you told us this morning: *You can find a stone to fit the space, or you can find a space to fit the stone.* I used to think I was the stone. Now I think maybe I'm the space that needs filling."

Jamie's face crinkled like a piece of brown paper. "That's a step toward enlightenment, lad."

"Are you a Buddhist, Jamie?"

"Nah. But I'd like to be." His face crinkled again, and Andrew threw his arm around the wiry old fellow.

"You're already there, Jamie; trust me."

"Drew!"

Andrew turned to find Lee at his side. Anne and Roger were weaving though the crowd. The bartender, whose name was Brian, and who seemed to know everyone, came around the end of the bar and bent at the waist.

"Now, missy, I'll need you to be movin' toward the family area, you know," he said gently.

"It's not *missy,* it's Lee, as you well know, Brian Shaheen!" Lee said, her chin stuck out like the prow of a ship.

"An apple and mango for the lady, please, Brian," Andrew said. "I shall escort her."

Brian grinned. "Only doin' my job, gov'nor."

"Are you buying my daughter drinks, sir?" Anne said as she reached the bar.

"I am indeed, and her patient and lovely mother as well, if I may be so bold."

"A pint of Cornish Blonde would be very welcome, I'm sure," she replied with a mock curtsy.

"Was there ever a more comely Cornish blonde than thee," Andrew countered with a bow, for Anne Trelissick was by way of being a "looker."

"You flirtin' with milady?" Roger asked, appearing at Andrew's shoulder.

"Sir! You malign my character!" Andrew replied with theatrical formality. "I am merely articulating the obvious"—he swept his arm in a circle encompassing the room—"as anyone here may vouchsafe." Heads nearby nodded appreciatively.

"Can I have my apple-mango now?" Lee demanded. Those within earshot dissolved into laughter. Lee got her drink and vanished. Andrew introduced Anne and Roger to Jamie, only to learn they knew him already.

Then, apropos of nothing, an unaccompanied baritone voice rang out from the rear of the long room.

Come all jolly fellows, that love to be mellow,
Attend unto me and set easy;
A pint when it's quiet, come lads let us try it,
For thinking can drive a man crazy.

By plowing and sowing, and reaping and mowing . . .

Andrew moved away from the bar, following Jamie, and was amazed as voices around the room picked up the tune. By the time the leader got to the chorus, it seemed to Andrew half the crowd had chimed in.

I have lawns, I have bowers, I have fields,
I have flowers,
And the lark is my morning alarmer;
So you jolly boys now, here's health to the
plow,
Long life and success to the farmer . . .

Jack Vaughan was a slender, handsome man of about sixty, with a shiny, balding pate, a short, neatly trimmed, graying beard, brilliant blue eyes, and an almost beatific face when he sang. His voice was splendid; the song flowed out of him, sweet and clear, like a breeze freshening the air in the crowded room. And his friends and neighbors joined him. Beside him, singing alto harmony, was an apple-cheeked woman Andrew took to be Jack's wife. Opposite them at their table was a stockier fellow who occasionally played guitar with a deft touch and filled in the tenor harmonies. The crowd, some thirty strong, fell into two groups: those who sang all the stanzas along with Jack, whom Andrew took to be locals; and those who only chimed in at the chorus, whom Andrew figured were visitors, like him. Some distance away, he could see Lee singing, too. He wondered what happy bit of magic, what curious throwback to another decade, made her want to be here, with adults, singing old folk songs and sea shanties.

Andrew was well into his third pint, and singing the chorus of "John Barleycorn," when a voice in an upper register joined him. He knew the voice even though it had never sung for him before. The song ended.

"Hello, sailor," Nicola said. She was wearing a simple but flattering raw linen wrap dress tied at the hip, and heels.

"Not me; I get seasick," Andrew said with a grin.

"When you're sailing, or when you're drinking?"

"Yes."

She punched his shoulder, and suddenly he was reminded of the way adolescents poked and shoved in their awkward early attempts at physical intimacy. Was that what he and Nicola were— middle-aged adolescents?

"Do you always sing harmony?" Nicola asked.

"Guess so. Used to drive my mother nuts. We'd be riding in the car, listening to the radio, and she'd ask why I didn't sing the melody like everyone else. I just sing what I hear, which is usually the bass harmony line."

"You could be a regular here, with that voice."

Andrew feigned shock. "I believe that was a compliment!"

"Christ, I think you're right; I must be slipping."

"Careful; you have a reputation to protect."

"A reputation?"

"You know: prickly, pugnacious."

"I prefer to think of it as proactive."

"Get 'em before they get you?"

"Something like that."

"Is it so unsafe out there?"

"You have no idea."

"No. I suppose I don't. Then again, I'm not a woman."

"Yes, I noticed that."

"Did you, indeed? What was the clue? The fact that I'm a monosyllabic mouth breather? The way I slope along, hairy knuckles dragging, drool dripping from the corner of my mouth? Maybe it was the club in my hand? Like those Neanderthals you warned Lee about?"

She looked down at her drink. "I'm pretty sure you're not one of them."

"Ah, but you can't be sure, can you? My wife left me, after all."

"Look," Nicola said, looking directly at him. "I'm sorry about last night."

"Sorry for what? Sorry for sharing a lovely meal with me? Sorry for giving me the gift of your company? Sorry for being so pleasing to the eye?"

"You know what I mean."

"If I do, I don't remember."

"Okay, I give up. I'm sorry I drank so much of the wine. That's what I meant, of course."

"Speaking of which, how about another drink?"

Nicola smiled. "I wouldn't say no."

Andrew slipped through the crowd to get their drinks. Nicola waved across the room to Lee, who was sitting on the steps to the upstairs sitting room.

I wouldn't say no, Nicola repeated to herself. Freudian slip? She'd been saying "No" for years now. "No" was her armor. "No" was her stockade, her weapon against . . . what? Her fears? If it was, it wasn't working; they still shimmered in the air around her, like an aura. And what was it about this Andrew fellow that suddenly made her wall feel as permeable as mesh netting?

When he returned with her gin and tonic, she was nodding her head to the music, but not singing. She looked far away.

"You okay?" he asked.

"What? Oh yes, fine! Just enjoying the scene. Thanks for the drink."

"You said last night you've only been here a few years, but you seem very at home."

"Yes . . . yes, I suppose I am."

"You hesitated there for a moment."

"You're right. I do love it here, truly, and people have been so sweet to me. But if I'm honest, I have to say I miss St. Ives—and Trevega House, too, for that matter. Partly, it's just the light in that part of Cornwall, but light means a lot to me. Someday some scientist is going to figure out what it is about the light in St. Ives, but artists have understood it intuitively for more than a century. It's just clearer, truer. And let's face it, St. Ives is a bit more cosmopolitan than Boscastle—for Cornwall, at least. Lots of galleries and shops and cafés and a community of painters that just doesn't exist here.

Plus . . . well, Jeremy's Dad made me feel more at home there than I ever felt in Boston. I suppose that sounds weird."

"Not at all. Will you ever go back?"

"No as long as Jeremy's around. Plus, it's got so expensive I couldn't afford it. I didn't have to worry about that before."

"You lost a lot more than a marriage, didn't you?"

Nicola looked at Andrew and put her free arm through his, giving it the slightest squeeze. "Yes. Thank you for understanding that."

The Valency reaches the sea at Boscastle, and its tributary, the Jordan, flows into the Valency in the centre of the village . . . Their catchment (the area they drain) is relatively small—at 20 square kilometers (km) or 7.7 square miles—and steep, rising more than 300 metres (m) or 984 feet (ft) in 6 km (3.7 miles).

Brian Golding, ed., "Numerical Weather Prediction," Forecasting Research Technical Report No. 459, Met Office

Lee was pretending she was Margaret Mead. She'd heard a program about the lady anthropologist on BBC Radio Four's *Women's Hour,* a program her mum listened to. Lee liked the idea of going to faraway places to study people. That's what she was doing now, from her own private observation perch at the Welly. She liked the fact that her mum and dad let her come. And she liked studying the grown-ups. It was like being in her special tree, spying on the walkers going by below her. She thought she should be taking notes, like Miss Mead did—that's how she thought of her, "Miss Mead," her partner in anthropology. She should bring a little notebook next time; there were so many interesting things going on.

Take Colin Grant over there, the chap who owned the witchcraft museum. She'd heard he was a witch himself, which was confusing, since she thought witches were only women. He was talking to Harriet, the woman who sat in the little booth in the museum selling tickets most days. She had on a long, clingy black dress with a scooped neckline. Was she a witch, too? Maybe her broomstick was out in the car park. She noticed that Harriet's eyes almost sparkled as she listened to whatever Colin was saying. *She likes him,* Lee concluded. *That's obvious.* But Colin didn't look at her as he talked. Instead, he looked to one side, as if he were talking to Harriet's left shoulder. From time to time, Harriet would move slightly, so as to be in Colin's line of sight, but he'd shift his head away again. Then, after a few minutes, he nodded to her shoulder and took his leave, and Harriet's eyes stopped sparkling. *Maybe he knows she likes him, but he doesn't like her. That's so sad. Or wait! Maybe he really* does *like her, but he's too shy!* She liked this explanation better. But then she thought maybe it wasn't very scientific to like one explanation more than another. Boy, this was hard work.

Jack and his wife, Mary, now, that was easy. Mary just beamed when she sang along beside Jack, and always patted his leg after they finished a song—as if she was saying, *That was fun; do another!* Lee frowned. Of course, since they're married, probably that's what she's supposed to do. Lee wasn't sure about that. She knew her dad and mum loved each other, 'cause they were always telling each other they did. Really, it was embarrassing sometimes. But how did you know someone liked you if you weren't already married to them? Like Brian and Flora down at the bar. Flora took Wednesday nights off at the Cobweb so she could come to the Welly for the singing. Leastways, that's what she *said.* But she spent all her time sitting on a stool at the Long Bar, chat-

185

ting up Brian, which he seemed to like. Maybe she had a bad voice and just liked to listen. But then about the only thing she seemed to listen to was Brian. So maybe it was Brian she came for, not the singing? Did Brian go to the Cobweb on *his* day off? This would require additional research.

She watched Drew and Nicki for a while and couldn't figure them out. Seemed to her the best thing they did was give each other a hard time, and sometimes she punched him in the arm. What was *that* about, anyway? But they laughed, too. So did that mean they liked each other? She kinda hoped they did. She liked Drew a lot and she liked Nicki at lot and she thought of course they'd like each other, too. But watching them here, and at the Cobweb last Sunday afternoon, it was hard to tell. She knew Miss Mead looked for little signs that told you what people thought of each other, and that seemed a good idea—like the way Lee looked for signs in the woods up in the valley: disturbed branches and leaves on the ground by the river that told you where deer came down to drink, or circles on the still water behind the weir that told you a fish had just eaten a bug, or rooks screeching when you got too close to one of their nest colonies, or the way the leaves on some trees will show you their silvery undersides when the wind changes just before a storm. But people signs were turning out to be a lot harder to figure out than nature signs. It was annoying, really. She wondered whether she should think about becoming a zoologist instead.

IT WAS JUST coming up on eleven when Jack's voice rang out on another song and the crowd picked right up.

> *In South Australia I was born.*
> *Heave away! Haul away!*
> *South Australia, round Cape Horn.*
> *We're bound for South Australia.*

Then the by-now-well-oiled crowd joined in on the chorus, singing out:

> *Heave away, you rolling king.*
> *Heave away! Haul away!*
> *All the way you'll hear me sing.*
> *We're bound for South Australia.*

By the middle of the song, the room was ringing, with men and women taking equal pleasure in the sea shanty's bawdier lyrics.

> *There ain't but one thing grieves my mind.*
> *Heave away! Haul away!*
> *It's to leave Miss Nancy Blair behind.*
> *We're bound for South Australia.*

I run her all night, I run her all day.
Heave away! Haul away!
Run her before we sailed away.
We're bound for South Australia.

Andrew was well into the following chorus before he remembered what Nicola had told him about the way Jeremy treated her, and his throat clenched. But she was standing right beside him singing as lustily as anyone in the throbbing room, and she sang the next stanza looking straight at him.

I shook her up, I shook her down.
Heave away! Haul away!
I shook her round and round and round.
We're bound for South Australia.

Thunderous applause and much hooting followed this song, and Andrew realized it was their traditional closing number. The crowd began milling about and drifting slowly toward the entrance; the singing was over for another week. There was much chat and shaking of hands and clapping on shoulders by the men and good-bye hugs by the women.

Lee found him and said, "See? See? I *told* you!"

Andrew laughed. Roger scooped up his daughter and Anne whispered something to Nicola. Slowly, the rowdy energy in the room dwindled to a happy sigh, like air from a leaky balloon.

Nicola asked Andrew to walk her to her door, but all the ale he'd consumed suddenly demanded attention. "Listen, Nicola," he said, "I need to make a quick stop at the gent's first."

"You do that, Mr. Stratton," she said with a slightly woozy slur that made his name come out "Sshtratton." "You can catch up with me. Think you can remember the way?" Then she winked and headed for the door, hips swinging.

Andrew stood there in the Long Bar of the Welly, astonished, until his screaming bladder brought him back to reality. When he got back from the bathroom, most of the crowd was gone and Flora circled the room collecting empty glasses for Brian. Flora intercepted him.

"Mind what I said, luv," she cautioned.

" 'Careful how you go'?"

"That's it."

Andrew felt offended and must have looked it.

"No, luv; it's not her I'm worried for, it's you," she said, giving his hand a squeeze.

Andrew crossed the hotel's car park, walked a few steps down to the end of Dunn Street, then turned left before the bridge and walked down the lane beside the river toward the harbor. He felt like an imbecile. He didn't understand Nicola's invitation, or Flora's warning. One was more mysterious than the other. Or maybe it was the beer making him stupid. No, he felt perfectly clearheaded. What, then? A woman with whom most of his previous interactions were best described as jousting matches had invited him back to her place—for what? A nightcap? The night? And one of her friends was warning him to be careful, for his own sake. It was completely bewildering. It was also exciting, a feeling he hadn't felt since . . . well, he couldn't remember when.

He knocked lightly at Nicola's door.

"Come upstairs. I've something I want to show you."

The voice was above him and he looked up. She was leaning out the studio window. The cream-colored linen dress glowed in the moonlight.

"Rapunzel, Rapunzel . . . ," he began.

"I have no golden hair to let down, in case you haven't noticed," she said, giggling. "And anyway, the door's open."

He entered Nicola's cottage. Randi greeted him with his standard single bark, then raced up the stairs. Andrew followed. Nicola was waiting for him beside her easel.

"Hi," he said, feeling suddenly awkward. "You look so lovely."

She made a teasing, and slightly unsteady, curtsy and said, "Thank you, sir. But I'm not what I wanted you to see."

"Nicola, I think you may be the only thing I want to see, ever again," he said, amazed to hear himself say the words.

She smiled, a wide, bright-eyed grin, but then said, "Stop that, you silly man, and pay attention."

Andrew realized then that her watery painting was no longer on the easel. There was something else in its place, covered with a sheet.

"Close your eyes," she ordered.

He obeyed and heard her sweep the sheet off the easel.

"Right. Open them."

Before him was a painting of a girl dancing across a flower-strewn meadow by a stream. But not just any girl. He recognized Lee instantly. And it was not just any painting. Nicola had captured not only the image but also the spirit of the girl and the world she inhabited, a world of trees and grasses and wildflowers and water that shimmered with a light he could only describe as ethereal.

He sat heavily on the edge of the chaise. "My God, it's . . . it's . . . perfect."

Nicola sat beside him. The two of them looked at the painting for a long while and said nothing. Andrew could feel the warmth of Nicola's skin radiating through the thin linen.

"You're the first person I've shown it to," she said, finally.

"Then I am deeply honored." Hesitantly, Andrew put his right arm around Nicola's shoulder and drew her gently toward him. She leaned her head on his shoulder.

"I love that little girl," she whispered.

"Me too," Andrew said. "I always wanted a kid just like her."

"But your wife didn't?"

"Right. Except now she's having a baby with my replacement."

"Christ."

"What about you and Jeremy?"

"We tried. It didn't work. Thank God."

"I think you'd have made a pretty terrific mother," he said. They were both still staring at the new painting. Andrew turned his head and placed a light kiss on Nicola's left temple.

She leaned into him a little closer. "Thanks."

"For the compliment or the kiss?" he asked.

"Yes."

Nicola turned and looked at the man beside her. His eyes were green-gray, she now knew, with a downward slope toward the outside edges that made him look perpetually wistful. It was a good and gentle face. A caring face. Genuine. She straightened and kissed his lips lightly, tentatively.

"I think you are a good man, Andrew Stratton," she said, her voice barely a whisper.

She watched his face fall.

"I used to think I was, but since Kat—"

"Shhh," she said, and kissed him again. It felt to him like forgiveness. But then he drew back.

"Wait. I need to tell you that I lied to you last night," he said. "She didn't just leave me for someone richer. I was too embarrassed to tell you the truth, partly because I think she was right. She said she was divorcing me because I was passionless. Because I have ice in my veins, she said."

Nicola looked at him, her head tilted. He wasn't sure she was focusing.

"She was wrong, you know," she said.

"Why?"

"Because your lips are warm. Very warm. And sweet."

Andrew smiled at Nicola and said, "I think one of us is drunk."

"Um-hmm. You shouldn't drink so much."

She kissed him again, harder this time. He responded in kind, his hands cupping her chin. Their tongues met and it seemed to Nicola that the studio evaporated like mist and the entirety of reality was the dark, warm, wet world of their exploring tongues. She closed her eyes and felt desire rise from somewhere subterranean. It would have astonished her had she been sober, but she wasn't, and instead it engulfed her. She swiveled to her left and straddled Andrew's lap, facing him, pressing her lips to his, running her hands beneath his shirt, her fingertips tracing the small, tensed muscles on either side of his spine. His lips moved to her ear. She heard him whisper, "Oh God, Nicola," and then felt him nibble his way down the side of her neck, burying his face in her hair, then tracing a line with his tongue downward, downward, along the lapel of her wrap dress to the point where the two sides crossed at the hollow between the tops of her breasts. Nicola groaned and arched her back, pulling his face into her. She laced her fingers through his curly hair and pressed closer, as if trying to absorb him through her pores.

Andrew Stratton could barely credit what was happening, and it was a struggle to keep his head clear. This in itself took him by surprise. When he had made love with Katerina, a part of him had always stood to one side, watching, monitoring. It wasn't that he had some bizarre need to be in control; it was that he was intent on pleasing her, on bringing her to orgasm, which was no easy task. He never permitted himself to dissolve into sex. And besides, who knew what void he might spin off into if he did? But with Nicola, he was poised at the very edge of that chasm, not so much afraid to fall as eager to leap.

The situation was almost incomprehensible: a wonderful, talented, and undeniably lovely woman was kissing him, clutching him, her breath ragged, her desire undisguised. He wasn't at all sure how it had come about. The two of them had been so busy trading snappy remarks to keep the distance, he hadn't noticed the distance had been an illusion, that he'd been falling in love for days. And Andrew suddenly also understood—the way someone struck by lightning comprehends the fragility of life in a way no one else can—that he'd never loved this way before. After Katerina left him, his heart had shriveled like a hard, infolded black raisin. But now it was plumping up again, growing fuller than it had ever been before, growing larger, it seemed, than could be accommodated within his chest.

Nicola kissed him again, urgently, and struggled to unbutton his shirt, eventually yanking it over his head. She had not said a word and her eyes were squeezed tight, as if she was in pain. He took her by the shoulders and laid her down upon the long chaise, stroking her face, then her neck, moving his hands gently. Slowly her dress fell open and he ran his palm along the perfect, G-clef outer curve of her left breast, then along its mirror image on the right. He cupped each and marveled at their weight. Her skin was silky and darkly tanned, except for two small, creamy bikini triangles from sunbathing. Her areolas were large, a dusky rose color with a coffee-tinged circumference, her nipples tall and stiff. He placed his hands atop them, lightly, barely connecting with the skin, and felt the heat radiating in both directions. Nicola made a sound somewhere in between a sigh and a moan and seemed to sink into the cushion beneath her, like someone falling through a cloud. Her muscles, so taut only moments before, softened.

Andrew lay beside her on the edge of the chaise and, with great care, as if Nicola were made of thin lead crystal, explored the supple landscape of her body using only the tips of his fingers. He was suffused with a tidal gentleness; he felt like a worshipper, a pilgrim. He wanted to tell her how full of her spirit he had become, how overwhelmed he felt by her acceptance, by her desire.

And it dawned on him at last that it wasn't that he lacked passion, it was that he had so little experience in expressing it; he did not know the vocabulary of love. For years, he'd just assumed that Katerina knew from his actions, from his constancy, from his eagerness to attend responsibly to all the details of their life together—from his *serving*—that he loved her. And he'd been very, very wrong. She did not understand that language. Or perhaps she did but did not value it. Or perhaps they had never really been in love. Certainly, he'd never felt the way he did now: amazed, entranced, transported. And, suddenly, the words were coming to him, in a flood: *wonder, enamor, ardor, cherish, head over heels*—nouns, verbs, adverbs. Out of nowhere. He felt like a thesaurus of endearments.

Yet with all these words, all these emotions, he still felt tongue-tied, so he tried to speak through his fingers, adoring this miracle beside him with touch. His fingertips glanced across her eyebrows, slipped down to the rise of her cheekbones, then followed the curve of her chin lower, to her collarbone and out to her shoulder, and then slid down her side, climbing and descending the velvet ridges of her rib cage, rising again along the hard slope of her hip, rounding the perfect curve of her rear, and floating along the surprisingly muscular length of her thigh. Moving upward again, he mapped the buttery skin along the inside of her thighs. Then, finally, his fingers reached the lush tangle of dark, silky hair foresting the cleft between her legs. Heat and perfume radiated from it as if it were tropical. The heat drove him on; the perfume intoxicated. The middle finger of his right hand skipped along the moist folds there, and found, at last, the source.

Nicola suddenly went rigid. Her eyes flew open. "No! Johnny, don't! *Please!*"

Andrew tried to hold her, but again she screamed, *"NO!"*

Her feet found purchase on the chaise and she struggled backward, pushing herself up the sloped arm of the chair till she teetered on its edge, flailing her arms in defense, yanking at her dress.

Andrew had shot to his feet and now stood beside the chaise, transfixed with shock. Nicola was staring straight ahead, eyes wild with fear, but also glazed. He suddenly understood that she was somewhere else—not with him in her studio, but off in some distant, private hell. He grasped her shoulders, as much to keep her from tumbling off the arm of the chair as anything else.

"Nicola!" he said, trying to get her to focus on his face. "It's okay."

"No! It's *not!* I'll *tell!* "

She was crying now, her arms clutched around

her stomach, her body convulsing. Andrew eased her back down the chaise, and she curled into a ball on her side. He knelt on the floor and held her close, whispering her name, telling her she was safe. Her sobs shook them both. After a while, they lessened and then ceased altogether. He realized she was asleep. He tried to rouse her but failed.

He looked around the room and saw Randi, watching from the shadows of a far corner of the studio. He was amazed that the dog had not barked. Then he understood that Randi was as frightened as he was. Or perhaps the dog had been through this before.

Andrew stood and tried to come to terms with what had just happened. Had Nicola fallen asleep as he caressed her and then awakened from a nightmare? Was she drunk and hallucinating? Had he frightened her?

What Andrew understood was that he needed to get her to bed. He slipped behind the sailcloth room divider and turned back the covers of Nicola's bed. Then he went back to the chaise, gathered her in his arms, and lifted. He was suddenly grateful for Jamie's lessons on how to lift heavy stones; Nicola was not petite. As he settled her in bed, she mumbled something anxiously, but he couldn't make it out. He pulled the covers around her, marveled again at her beauty, kissed her forehead, and turned out the light on the side table. He sat beside her for a very long time, listening to the whisper of her breathing, watching the gentle rise and fall of her chest, and wondering what the hell had just happened.

After a while, he rose and went back into the studio, where he found Randi sitting patiently in the middle of the room, panting slightly.

"Well, my friend," he said to the dog, "what do you suggest we do now?"

Andrew was troubled by the idea of spending the night in Nicola's cottage, but was also afraid of leaving her alone.

As he stood in the middle of the room, Randi got up and walked across the studio to the chaise, made a single quiet woofing sound, yawned, and lay down on the floor, his head on his front paws but his eyes still on Andrew.

"Good suggestion," Andrew said, chuckling.

He gathered a couple of drop cloths to use as blankets, and lay down on the chaise. It wasn't very comfortable, and though he was emotionally drained, he could feel the adrenaline still pumping in his ears. The whole experience had shaken him to his core, the way even the most momentary of earth tremors makes you question the solidity of the world around you for the first time. Nicola had seemed in a trance, as if she were possessed. She'd been terrified, though not, it seemed, by him. By something else. Someone else.

Andrew looked around the room for something tangible to ground him in reality and found the painting of Lee, in the meadow by the river. He wondered if Lee didn't represent Nicola's own childhood spirit—innocent, alive to the world, forever at play.

But who was "Johnny"?

The synchronized initiation of showers along the whole coast at about 1100UTC [coordinated universal time] *is consistent with friction-induced coastal convergence as the primary cause. Initially the storms developed just offshore, consistent with pure frictionally driven convergence. The subsequent move inland and then back to the coast may be associated with a response to the late morning solar heating . . .*

Brian Golding, ed., "Numerical Weather Prediction," Forecasting Research Technical Report No. 459, Met Office

Andrew was moving stone like a machine. He'd reached a nearly Zen-like state with the hedging, a zone of quiet concentration in which he had very little sense of the world around him. The choosing, the lifting, and the placing of stone and the movements of his body all seemed of a piece, as if he, the stone, and the hedge were extensions of one another, rather than discrete elements. He wasn't conscious of any single act, just of the flow, of the whole. And however solid the component parts were, the process itself had become fluid, as if the hedging mimicked the river it paralleled.

They'd completed the first section, mounded turf at the top, and moved on. Becky and Ralph had stripped the second sixteen-foot segment of topsoil and started on the third, while Jamie and Case moved stone with the Bobcat and laid grounders. It was Burt with whom Andrew worked most, the two of them placing the levelers, then stacking the rows of herringbone, and ramming the fill into the heart between the two rising faces.

Andrew had underestimated the big man. What Burt lacked in words he more than made up for in quiet artistry. While Andrew checked the batter with the plywood form from time to time, Burt never did; his batter curve rose smoothly, as if it were the most natural thing in the world. Burt often talked to the stone—"How's tha', then?" he'd ask quietly as he thwacked one in place, or "Rest easy there, mate." He'd catch Andrew watching and smile like a child caught out. They talked sometimes as they worked, and Andrew learned more about Burt's dad, who'd died a couple of years before, and about their farm. Burt said something once that Andrew found revealing. He'd mentioned that laying stone made him feel more connected to the earth than any of his regular farm chores ever had, and that he looked forward to working on his own hedges when the week was out. Andrew thought perhaps it was this task, more than any other, that would make the farm his own, now that his father was gone.

But mostly, he and Burt worked in companionable silence, and in that silence, Andrew thought about Nicola. He'd left her cottage just after dawn. He'd been awakened by the screech of seagulls arguing over a morsel of something no doubt unspeakably rank and decided he was glad his cottage was in the fields above the harbor, where the morning symphony tended to feature sparrows and little English robins—an altogether sweeter alarm.

He'd tiptoed around the edge of the sailcloth room divider and found Randi asleep at the foot of his mistress's bed, though the big dog lifted his head momentarily before dropping it again like a lead weight. Andrew could almost have sworn the good-natured beast smiled. Nicola was asleep, the cascade of her hair fanning out across the pillow, her chest rising and falling softly, her breath the faintest whisper, like wavelets kissing a powdery beach, slipping up to the tide line, hesitating there a moment, then sighing as they retreated. Her face was untroubled, almost childlike in its peacefulness. So unlike the night before.

He'd stood there for a while, thinking, marveling, and then ducked back into the studio, picked up his shoes, padded down the steep stairs, and let himself out into the moist morning. Though the air was warm, the port was thick with mist. There was ventriloquism in the air: the scrape and slap of crab traps being dragged and stacked, the *pop-pop-pop* of a diesel boat engine warming up, seemed, in the fog, as if they were beside him in the lane instead of down in the harbor. At the bridge, he hesitated, trying to decide which route to take home. He chose the river valley; it would set tongues wagging if he were to be seen walking home along the road through the upper village at this hour. Half the town knew where he'd been last night and who he'd stood beside during the singing.

In the lower village, the streets were deserted, the shops shuttered. The only human being abroad besides himself was Peter Weston, the newsagent, and he was too busy hauling in bales of *The Times, The Independent, The Telegraph, The Guardian,* and tabloids like *The Sun* to notice him passing on the pavement opposite, for which Andrew was grateful.

It was amazing, Andrew thought, how a little village like Boscastle could change your way of being in the world—even change your age; he felt like a guilty teenager sneaking back home after a clandestine assignation. It was idiotic, but no less real for being so.

As he wandered up the valley, following the riverbed and pushing the mist ahead of him with his shins, he kept replaying the stages of the evening before: the by-now expected early verbal skirmishes at the Welly; the unexpected but easily entered armistice; the growing harmony between them, like something that grew out of the music; the unorthodox invitation; the magical intimacy that followed; and then her blind fear, like a seismic fissure growing to a chasm between the here and now and the . . . what? . . . Nicola's other reality. The dark continent. The unknown.

He knew he'd left early not just because he needed to eat and change for work, but also because he did not know what to say to her about the night before. She would be embarrassed, he thought . . . that is, if she remembered anything. And what would he have said? What should he say? It was clear someone had hurt her. He knew about Jeremy; that much she'd shared. But this other thing . . . did he have any business asking her about that? Yet he cared about her. No, that wasn't true; the truth was, he was in love. It seemed as if she was, too. It amazed him. And though his head told him he was in no emotional shape to be doing so, his heart thrilled. It was as if that shock he first felt when she touched him had left his heart vibrating like a tuning fork, but with the difference that the vibrations did not diminish. And instead of protecting them, all their verbal fencing had become a strange sort of foreplay. He had a sudden vision of porcupines mating, ever so carefully.

He thought about the tranquillity panels she painted: how peaceful they were, and how apparently at odds with her soul. He wondered how, or even if, he should approach the subject of her terror. He didn't even know whether his care would be welcome.

It took until afternoon, but he thought of something. And it calmed him. When the crew knocked off for the day, Andrew took a pass on their usual pint at the Cobweb.

"Oh sure, go missing when it's your turn to stand a round, is it?" Becky teased. There was general outrage all around.

Andrew laughed. He was fond of this disparate bunch of characters. "I'll buy two rounds tomorrow, promise," he'd said, earning nothing but jeers for his trouble.

"We'll nay forget tha'," Burt called after him as Andrew struck off toward the bridge with a wave.

• • •

JANET STEVENSON ANSWERED his knock wearing blue jeans and a University of Michigan sweatshirt.

"Reverend Janet?" Andrew said, thinking, absurdly, that the priest would be in her vestments.

"It's Andrew, isn't it?" she said, smiling.

"That's some memory you have, ma'am," he replied, trying to recover from his surprise at her outfit.

"It helps in this trade," she said. "Would you like to come in?"

Andrew looked down at his dirty clothes, then smiled. "Perhaps not, given the state I'm in."

"I'm not exactly overdressed myself," she said. "It's my son's sweatshirt. I was cleaning; I'm the help as well as the vicar."

"Look, I've just barged in without an appointment, so let me begin with an apology. Do you have a moment? Maybe we could take a short walk?"

"Yes, and yes. My husband's doing dinner tonight. Let me just tell him where I'm going. Where am I going, by the way?" she said, smiling again.

Andrew looked around. The church sat on high ground, looking out to sea. "The churchyard?"

"I've been there before," she said. "But it has its charms. I'll just be a tick."

A few minutes later, they were walking up the hill.

"There may have been a church here for nearly a millennium, you know," Janet said, filling the silence. "A document from 1189 records the gift of the church to the abbey at Hartland, up in Devon, but clearly it was here earlier. There are still portions of the building that are Norman, but much of what you see is much more recent. But you'd know that; I hear you're an architect. An architect learning to build Cornish hedges, which—pardon me for saying this—sounds a bit backward to me."

Andrew paused, looked at her, and started walking again. They were strolling among the ancient, lichen-encrusted headstones that surrounded the church. He wondered if the close-cropped grass was the work of a mower or sheep. He hoped the latter: Jesus, the Good Shepherd.

"It started as a whim, I suppose; or maybe a kind of therapy. But it's become something else, something elemental."

They stopped at a gate that looked west, toward the sea and Forrabury Common, a medieval system of raised farming beds that had remained in use until only recently.

"It sounds like you're searching for something. Is that what got to you in my sermon about Peter last Sunday?" she asked.

Andrew leaned on the top of the gate. "I've certainly had my faith tested recently, Reverend Janet."

"Just 'Janet' is fine."

"Janet. . . . But that's not why I came to see you."

The priest said nothing. She had learned the value of silence.

Andrew began walking again; Janet walked with him.

"Let's say you knew someone," he began, "to whom something terrible seems to have happened. Maybe a long time ago. But it's clear it haunts the person still."

"Why do I think it's not you you're talking about? It's someone else, isn't it?"

"Yes." He wondered whether everyone in this village was a mind reader.

"How can I help?"

Andrew was impressed that she didn't ask, "Who?" He took a deep breath. "I don't know. That's what I came here to ask *you*," he said.

He stood beside a stone cross—Celtic, he thought, its edges and intricately carved pattern worn by centuries of Atlantic storms, but not yet obliterated. The permanence of stone; the impermanence of man's impressions upon it.

The priest folded her hands together before her, as she might in church. She looked at the ground.

"I have to confess, Andrew, that the Church isn't very good at this sort of thing," she said to her feet. "We're charged with looking after the faith of our 'flock,' of trying to be of comfort in crises. But it sounds as if your friend is beyond that, and we're ill-equipped to serve as either social workers or psychologists."

209

She looked at Andrew steadily for a moment and he saw a deep sadness.

"My tools are so limited," she said. "I could counsel this person about the everlasting love of God, about the redemption inherent in faith in his love. But she—may I guess it is a 'she'?—would have to embrace that love. And I suspect, given her trauma, that may be a lot to ask."

Andrew was amazed. In his experience, ministers always claimed to have all the answers. That had been part of his attraction to religion as a child: the certainty. And suddenly he felt embarrassed. What had he really expected? What did he hope to achieve? He was a searcher all right, looking for the cure to an ailment he didn't even understand.

"Janet," he said finally. "Reverend Janet of Forrabury, et cetera and so on, I'm sorry. I should have thought about this more, I guess. I'm just trying to help someone I care about."

"I know you are," she said softly, "and she is lucky to have you—*if* she will have you. I sense you are a good soul, Andrew. Others in this village think so, too. I believe you can reach her."

"I don't know that; how can you?"

"Think about Peter, Andrew. Think about the lesson of his faith. If you believe you can help, if that belief comes from a good heart—which I believe it does—then you can walk on that water, and perhaps carry her with you."

Andrew and Janet Stevenson stood looking at each other for several moments, and he understood that they were done. He nodded to the priest, and said, "Thank you. I'm sorry to have interrupted your evening."

"You did nothing of the sort."

"Good evening, Reverend Janet."

"Good evening, Andrew. And good luck."

He'd nodded and had walked just a few steps down the narrow asphalt path toward the lane when she said, "Have you thought of talking to Colin Grant?"

"The witch? I wouldn't have thought you had much in common with Mr. Grant."

"More than you might guess; it's a very small parish, after all. Besides, I'll take someone who believes in something over someone who believes in nothing any day."

"But witchcraft?"

" 'There are more things in heaven and earth, Horatio . . . ,' " she said, quoting Shakespeare.

And Andrew thought, *This is not your average priest.*

He did not go to see Colin Grant next; it was late, and he needed to think that suggestion through. He was making a dinner salad in the tiny kitchen at Shepherd's Cottage when he saw Nicola walking across the meadow from Roger and Anne's house. He met her at the door.

"Some hot date you are," she said, flashing a

grin. "You're so exciting you put me right to sleep!"

Andrew was so startled by the absurdity of this greeting, he just stared.

Then he regained his composure. "Would you like to come in?"

"No, I just walked all the way up here to give you a hard time."

Andrew stood aside and Nicola danced in and plopped herself down in the overstuffed easy chair by the stone hearth.

"So," she said, "I have two questions."

"One?"

"Do you have a decent wine in this house?"

"Yes, a chilled Pinot Grigio from the Alto Adige in Italy, by way of the Rock Shop. Will that be adequate, madam?"

"We'll see."

"And the second question?"

Nicola tilted her head to one side and smirked. "Was it good for you?"

Andrew blinked.

"Because I certainly don't remember," she added, rolling her eyes.

"I'll just get that wine, shall I?" Andrew answered, shaking his head as he disappeared into the kitchen. He was glad to have the excuse to leave the room, because he hadn't the first inkling what he should say next, if anything.

"Would you like to stay for dinner?" he called

from the kitchen. "I was just making a sort of Italian dinner salad—mixed baby greens, tomato, prosciutto, mozzarella, fennel, onion, and black olives."

"Wait!" Nicola called back. "You mean you have no fresh basil?"

Andrew walked to the door of the kitchen and leaned against the jamb. It was impossible to stay focused on the strangeness of the night before. Nicola was sitting sideways in the big chair, her back against one arm, her tanned legs over the other. She was wearing a simple, sleeveless printed cotton sundress with a deeply scooped neckline. She looked delicious. "Of course I have fresh basil," he said. "I just thought it would be wasted on you."

"Ooh, that was below the belt."

It was Andrew's turn to smirk. "I only wish . . ." He went back to the kitchen, opened the Pinot Grigio, and returned with it and two simple tumblers. "Pardon the absence of stemware; we're going peasant this evening."

He poured, and they clinked glasses. "To the ever-unpredictable Ms. Nicola Rhys-Jones, née DeLucca."

"To the phantom date," she countered. "There one moment, gone . . . well, at some point."

He smiled, but sadly. "You don't remember, do you?"

Nicola closed her eyes for a moment, and when

she opened them again, the bemused look was gone, replaced with what Andrew could only describe as self-disgust. "I'm sorry, Andrew; truly. I don't usually drink that much—well, actually, I do—but I don't usually pass out. I'm utterly embarrassed. I have no memory of last night, apart from your kissing me and my loving it."

Andrew's voice was gentle. "It's okay, Nicola; you have nothing to apologize for."

"Oh, but I do. Because I have a confession to make."

"You don't have to tell me . . ."

"Yes, I do, and here it is: I've never invited a man to my cottage since I moved here from St. Ives. In fact, I haven't been involved with another man since Jeremy."

"It sounds to me like Jeremy would put any woman off men for a very long time."

"Thank you. Yes. That's it, you see; I'm terrified of men."

"I understand."

"With one possible exception: you."

"I'm not sure that's a compliment. I think I'd like to be thought of as having an exciting, possibly dangerous edge."

She smiled, as if indulging a child. "Want to know why?" she asked.

Andrew nodded uncertainly.

"Because you *do* understand. You're not like other men."

"You can't know that," Andrew said.

"Actually, I can. Want to know how?"

"Sure."

"First, I'm a witch; I know these things."

"How come you didn't know about Jeremy?"

"I wasn't a witch then, and don't interrupt."

"Right."

"Second, Lee adores you."

"Is she a witch, too?"

"You're interrupting again, but no, she's not . . . although, I don't know, maybe she is and doesn't know it yet because, Lord knows, she's different."

Nicola waited here to see if Andrew would comment again. Instead, he smiled. He knew the game.

"And third . . ." Nicola paused and looked at him with affection. "A chap who risks his neck for a sheep is not abusive."

"Oh, thank you."

Nicola grinned. "So there you have it: my indisputable, three-point, Jesuitical proof of your goodness."

"My head is spinning, but that could be hunger. Dinner?"

She sank into her chair. "Dinner would be splendid. Thank you."

Okay, he thought to himself as he finished assembling the salad, *one of two things is going on here. Either she has no idea what happened last night, or she does and doesn't want to broach it. Either way, it's not a topic for discussion.* He whisked together a Dijon vinaigrette, dressed the salad, added torn basil, grated some pecorino Romano cheese over the top, and brought the bowl out to the tiny dining table by the window looking out toward the sea. Then he brought out plates and forks.

"You will, I'm afraid, have to bestir yourself if you wish to eat."

Nicola had simply been watching him, like someone at a sidewalk café regarding the passersby. Now she swung her legs off the chair arm and rose in one fluid motion, and he was struck again by how lovely this odd woman was. He held her chair and she slipped into it.

"Hello," he said. "My name is Andrew, and I'll be your waiter tonight. May I top off your glass?"

"You may."

He began to do so, but she added, "You should pour from the right."

"Um . . . there's a wall there."

She heaved a sigh. "It's so hard to get good help."

He set the bottle next to her. "Pour your own goddamn wine." He sat opposite her, and she reached across and poured wine into his glass.

"I hope you don't mind," she said. "We seem to have lost our waiter."

"Just as well; I'd rather we were alone."

She lifted an eyebrow. Was it skepticism? Surprise?

"Shall I serve?" she said.

"By all means, but toss the salad first."

She did so, in the process scattering lettuce leaves across the tabletop. A fugitive olive rolled off the edge and disappeared somewhere.

He smiled. "I see you've done this before."

"I lived in Italy; in Italy we do everything *con gusto!*"

"Ah, but this is England, and in England we like to get at least some of the salad on our plate."

She passed him the salad servers and took a slug from her wineglass. "Serve your own goddamn salad."

It was what they did best, this skirmishing. It was fun, and they'd each met their match. And as sharp as the exchanges sometimes were, as the dinner progressed each of them marveled privately that it never crossed the line to nastiness. Indeed, there was more affection, and more excitement, than if they'd been flirting—which is what they were doing, of course, in their own backward sort of way. They'd retreated to the way things were before she'd invited him home, retreated to safety.

In the midst of this, Nicola had the strangest thought: *This is what it would be like to have a true companion. After the craziness of courting passes, after the bonfire of passion settles to a steady glow, after real life truly begins, you could have someone to talk to, someone to play with. And it would be safe.* The thought—or was it a fantasy?—was deeply seductive. It was something she'd dreamed of since childhood. It was what she'd expected with Jeremy, until he bludgeoned it out of her mind. Could she be safe with Andrew? *Could one ever be safe?*

"Do you mind if I ask you something serious?" she heard Andrew say.

"What? No, of course not," she answered, when what she really meant was *It depends . . . what do you want?*

"How do you paint those tranquillity panels? I mean, how do you even begin? How do they become so luminous?"

She smiled at him. *Why is my first reaction always defensive?* she thought. *Why do I always assume the worst?*

"Ah, the flattery technique," she teased. "Make her think you like her work and she'll do anything for you. . . ."

"Will you?"

"No."

"I didn't think so. But really, I'd like to know a little about how you do it. It just amazes me. The architecture department is part of the School of Design at Penn, so I see a lot of painting. But I've never seen anything like that."

"So, I'm better than a college student, eh?"

"Come on; you know what I mean."

"Okay, you're right. I do. I'm just not very good at accepting compliments."

"I don't think I said I liked it; I just asked how you did it," he deadpanned.

"Bastard. Okay, I begin with a colored ground." Andrew looked blank.

"That's the base layer I cover the canvas with, usually—for those paintings, at least—a cadmium yellow, or an ocher, or perhaps a rose pink. Virtually all of it will be covered by layers of other colors eventually, but somehow the brightness still shows through and resonates, like a visual echo. Also, I find that if I begin with a canvas that only has white priming on it, the painting starts out on too light a key, since everything you apply initially looks too dark against the white."

She shot him a look. "Bored yet?"

"Keep trying."

"Right. So then I just start painting."

She shrugged, then grinned.

He slumped in his chair.

"All right; if you insist. So then it's a process of building layers of color and, in a sense, light. I like to think of it as light broken by a prism, or maybe a fractured prism. The idea is to create an almost distilled, saturated light with the pigment."

"How do you create light from paint? I don't get that."

"It's partly technique; I lay a small amount of several pigments on the palette, and when I mix my final colors, I really thin them. Sometimes they're almost transparent. And then I build up layers. I'm working with a range of colors—they would seem too powerful on their own, but when I apply them thinly, they turn out soft, almost gauzy. After many, many layers of individual brushstrokes—I never use a palette knife in these pieces—it's as if the painting begins to glow. I've left some of the ground thinly covered, so that it shows through in places, tying the composition together, but primarily it's the color layers that create that softness. And I scrumble with my finger a lot."

"I don't even want to ask what that's about," Andrew cracked.

She laughed once, hard, then swiped back. "Get your mind out of the gutter, you creep. 'Scrumbling' is a way of blending the colors you've applied next to one another; it softens the effect, makes them—I don't know—more real at the same time as it muddies them. Some people use a blunt brush, or a bit of rag. I use my middle finger."

"Do you have a clear idea of what you want to create when you begin?"

"No . . . and yes, in a sense. I'm trying to capture the grace of the natural world. I think most people have lost touch with it. They don't 'see' anymore. It's like they move through the world but aren't part of it. And don't even get me started on cell phones. Or iPods."

She paused for a moment and stared out the window. Andrew followed her gaze.

"Look. Look at the way the setting sun scatters color across the sea, and tints the slopes leading down to it. It's not just yellow on the blue-green; it's so much more. On a night like this, when there's a fog bank or a haze or something out to sea, the light is filtered, gentle. Except where the cliffs cast hard shadows, everything is softened. The world is suffused with mauves and violets. Blues like lobelia and others like Hidcote lavender. A touch of rose and apricot on the waves, where the water catches the western light. The blue-black of the cliffs, except along the western edges, where they luminesce. The way Roger's fields pick up the last light and the grass goes from green—what is green, really; so many things—the way it goes from green to gold, especially at the very tips of the blades of grass, as if each were a tiny torch, a beacon . . . the last holdouts against the night."

Andrew said nothing. He was mesmerized. He was used to seeing the world as composed of structures, not of colors. He felt as if he'd been given sight, or at least a new way of seeing.

"Anyway, in the end, all those thin layers of paint seem somehow to refract light differently, softly, a little like that haze out over the sea."

"Nicola, I can't image how you make that happen, or how long it must take."

She laughed. "It takes forever, but that's because I keep at the painting as long as it's in the studio. I keep seeing things, keep adding layers. I don't know how to let go. It isn't until the client pushes me to deliver that I do, and even then I don't want to."

"And that totally different painting of Lee?"

"That's me, too. I haven't completely abandoned figurative works."

"I guess I meant that I wondered what you'd do with that painting."

"It's meant to be an anniversary present for Anne and Roger, but I'm having trouble letting go of that one, too."

"I think I can understand that." And then he wondered how many other things Nicola had trouble letting go of—the damage Jeremy had done to her, certainly, but this other fear, this far more sinister beast that seemed to live within her.

"Hello?"

Andrew snapped into the present. "I'm sorry; I was thinking."

"And I was saying, it's getting dark and I need to get home and feed Randi."

"Okay. Right. Of course."

"Thank you for dinner, Andrew."

"Anytime." He realized, though, that he didn't have "anytime." He didn't live here. He wouldn't be here for her to just drop in on. It made his heart hurt.

"How about if I walk you back?"

"I'll be okay."

"How about if I'd like to?"

"That's okay, too." And she smiled.

· · ·

THEY WERE ALMOST to the bottom of Fore Street when Nicola slipped her arm inside his. "Do you mind if I ask you something serious?" she said, echoing his words from earlier.

"Of course not. What?"

She squeezed his arm gently. "Did we make love last night? We didn't, did we?"

"If you mean did we have intercourse, then no."

"But we were intimate."

"Yes, rather magically so, I thought."

"But I passed out."

"Yes . . . well, no, not exactly."

She laughed lightly, "What is that supposed to mean?"

"I don't know, really; maybe you could tell me."

"Tell you what? You're talking in riddles."

He took a deep breath, looked down the empty lane, then turned to her.

"Nicola, I just need to ask you this."

"What?"

"Who's Johnny?"

Nicola stiffened, halted, and slid her arm out of Andrew's.

"How do you know about Johnny?" she said, stepping away from him as if he were radio-active.

"I don't know anything about Johnny. You

screamed, *No! Johnny, don't!* when we were making love last night. It was like you were in a trance or something. Then you passed out. That's what I know. That's *all* I know."

It was as if Nicola had been turned to stone. She stood stock-still, her eyes wide and wary. Finally, frostily, she said, "Johnny does not exist." It was a warning.

Andrew didn't catch it. "Nicola, look . . . I saw you go rigid, I saw you struggling to get away. You were terrified."

"It's none of your business," she said through a clenched jaw. Then she turned on her heel and walked quickly down the street toward the harbor. Andrew jogged to catch up with her.

"Nicola, I'm just trying to help."

"Then leave me *alone!* " she snapped.

Andrew stopped. Nicola continued.

"Don't you understand how I feel about you?" he cried.

Now she stopped and spun around. Her mouth opened but no sound escaped. She turned again and ran headlong down the hill.

He did not follow. And as he stood there in the lane, watching her fleeing form dissolve into the gathering darkness, he wondered if he could even answer that question himself. How *did* he feel about her? Bewitched, or just besotted? In need of a life with this woman, or just needy? Did he care for her, or just think she needed a caretaker?

He turned and slowly retraced his steps. Halfway back up the hill, just as he passed the tiny post office in Fore Street, he realized he had never been in love before. Not with Kat. Not with anyone. But he was now.

The extreme rainfall accumulations, observed in the Valency catchment, resulted from prolonged very heavy rain over the four hour period 1200–1600UTC. The exact track of the heavy rainfall cells varied slightly during this period, but between the Camel Estuary and Bude the variation was sufficiently small to ensure that the heaviest rainfall fell into the same coast-facing catchments throughout the period.

Brian Golding, ed., "Numerical Weather Prediction," Forecasting Research Technical Report No. 459, Met Office

Nicola awoke in darkness, her body taut, her sheet pulled to her throat in two clenched fists. She had been dreaming again about Johnny, something she hadn't done for years—not since she left her husband.

Johnny. Her older brother. The handsome one, with their father's broad shoulders and sleek, black hair. The brilliant one, with the effortless straight As right into high school. The ambitious one, who started his drug dealing small in the ninth grade— a few ounces of marijuana here and there, mostly for friends—but who later developed a talent for dealing cocaine. The manipulative one, who got his little brother, who wanted more than anything else to please his big brother, to be his mule, making deliveries in their little corner of the North End, until one day Jamie—the bookworm, the altar boy—came home beaten bloody. Johnny, the cocky one, who thought he could outsmart everyone including his mother (at which he succeeded) and his drug-selling competitors, whose territory he took, incrementally, street corner by street corner, but who were not, in the end, either outsmarted or amused.

Johnny, who began feeling her up when she was only twelve, on the afternoon of her confirmation—she still in her white dress. "Be sealed with the gift of the Holy Spirit," the priest had said, anointing her. "You're a grown-up now," her brother whispered later, cornering her at the end of her party. He'd been drinking wine and smoking dope; he was fifteen. She thought it must be her fault, because she already had breasts. His hands were all over them.

A few weeks later, he began sneaking into her room at night, when their mother was cleaning offices in the State House. "I've got something for you," he'd hiss as he slipped under the covers. "A present." He made her hold it, that strange, hard, twitchy thing, made her pull it till it exploded. "I'm the man of the family now, like Ma says; you have to do what I say. If you squeal, I'll tell her it was your idea—because you're overdeveloped. Oversexed. You can't help yourself. I'll tell her you do it to Tony and Mario after school." She had a crush on Mario, and her mother knew it. Her poor, nearly illiterate, exhausted mother would believe every word.

She would pretend to be fast asleep when he appeared by her bed, her eyes squeezed shut, her hands tight as claws clutching the bedclothes. He took to slapping her face to wake her, then covering her mouth. It occurred to her that if she stopped developing, he'd leave her alone, so she simply stopped eating.

All that did was melt off her baby fat. By the time she was fourteen, Johnny was a gang leader running a neighborhood drug operation—grass, pills, cocaine, who knew what else. When rival gang members began hassling her on her way home from school—whistling, hooting, making rude gestures—she assumed it was Johnny's doing, a way to humiliate her further. But when she confronted him about it, he exploded in a kind of strange paternal fury and had his allies beat one of her tormenters so severely the kid had to be hospitalized.

Then Johnny raped her. "See, Nicki, I'm your protector now. You want me to keep protecting you, right? *Right?*"

She nodded, crying. He crouched above her, whipped on a condom, and forced himself inside her—all the while keeping one hand over her mouth. She couldn't fight him off, so she did the only thing she could: She fled. She left her body behind, under her brother, and occupied the far corner of her room, up at the ceiling, from which perch she could observe dispassionately what was happening below. It was sort of like watching a bad horror movie; what was happening was brutal, yes, but also more than a little bit ridiculous looking. She knew about sex, of course, from school and from her girlfriends, but she had somehow thought it would be more graceful, more like a slow dance with the lights low at the Catholic Community Center. Not this.

Afterward, after the grunting and thrusting, he

simply climbed off of her and said: "Here's the name of the game, slut: You take care of Papa Johnny, Papa Johnny takes care of you." Then he leaned down, as if to kiss her, but instead said, "And if you don't, I'm not gonna hurt you. Oh no, Papa Johnny would never harm his Nicki, even if she is a slut. Papa Johnny will have someone he knows hurt good little Jamie instead. I'll put the hurt on Jamie so bad you'll never forget it—never forget what *you* did to your own little brother."

There was a picture of the three of them on her bureau, a wet, happy trio holding hands as they ran out of the water at Revere Beach. She was maybe six, Jamie four, Johnny nine. It must have been taken before their father left, because they seemed so happy. Maybe this was all her father's fault, this thing her brother had become.

Angela noticed that her daughter was losing weight and made bigger meals on weekends when she was home at dinnertime. Nicola forced them down, then excused herself and threw it all up again. Angela noticed that her daughter's grades were slipping and berated her, pointing out what a good student Johnny was—Johnny, whose only purpose in school was to protect his customer base and who now hired friends to do his schoolwork. Angela never noticed anything else going on in the walk-up apartment, including the drug traffic at night. *How can she?* Nicola reasoned. *She's not here; she's working all night to feed us. It's not her fault.* But she felt desperately alone, isolated, as if she existed in a stockade to which only Johnny had the key. She never knew when he would steal into her room; that was part of the fun for him, to keep her guessing, to be in control. Only once did she try to gain the upper hand; she figured maybe if he thought she liked it, he'd leave her alone. He was slouched in front of the television, watching *Kojak,* his favorite show.

She leaned over the back of the chair and whispered: "How about it tonight, huh, stud?"

His head jerked around. "Get away from me, pig!"

"Whatsamatta, Papa Johnny can't get it up?" she sneered.

Fast as a lightning bolt, and with almost as much power, he slugged her, knocking her to the floor, her head spinning. Then he returned to the TV show, as if none of it had happened. That night, he did come to her room, and was especially vicious. She never taunted him again.

Sometimes she thought Jamie knew what his older brother was doing to her. If Johnny wasn't at home distributing, Jamie would come to her room, where she was trying to do homework, and sit beside her, just holding her hand. He never said anything, but his love was like a lifeline, like salvation itself.

Johnny stopped raping her about a year later, partly because he had no shortage of older, more experienced girls now, and partly because he was just too busy dealing to bother. Nicola had no idea where the money he made was going. It certainly wasn't going to their mother, and he wasn't spending it on drugs for himself; he was scrupulous about staying in control and seldom indulged in his own products.

He didn't want her for sex anymore, but he still found ways of using her. His "customers" came and went, up and down the stairs. An ugly, desperate parade. The traffic was especially heavy in the early evening after Angela went to work. He'd brag to his low-life pals about what a great body his sister had, and encourage them to check her out. Sometimes he'd drag her out of her room and put her on display: "Hey, slut, come meet some of my gentlemen friends!" Lots of laughter—some of it oozing lust, some of it nervous and wary. They leered at her and made disgusting noises. But no one ever touched her. They were too afraid of Johnny. It was hard for her to tell which made her feel dirtier, the rapes or the slurs.

THERE WAS A noise downstairs and Nicola shot upright. She realized she wasn't fully awake; she'd been drifting, and now she struggled to become conscious. The sound came again and she relaxed, dropping back down on her pillows. It was just Randi pushing his aluminum water bowl on the slate kitchen floor as he drank. Next came the click of his nails on the stairs, the cold, wet nose nudging her palm, and the familiar thump as he leaped up to the foot of her bed, walked in a circle a couple of times, then flopped down. Her guardian.

Outside, there was only the music of the river.

IT'S A HOT SATURDAY afternoon in August when Ricky DiCarlo, one of Johnny's preadolescent henchmen, shows up at the apartment door, drenched with sweat.

"Nicola, you gotta come. It's Johnny." Ricky is a short, wiry kid with a nose so big it precedes him by five minutes. He's got a Red Sox hat on backward, the rear-facing brim like a counterbalance to the nose. Johnny calls him "Durante." He is vibrating with fear.

"What's he done now?"

"Holy Mary, Mother of God, Nicola; they topped him!"

Nicola stares at the little thug, frozen for a moment, and notices blood spots on his shirt, like rust stains. She glances over her shoulder; her mother is taking a nap. She steps into the hall and heads down the stairs, taking them two at a time and calling over her shoulder, *"Where?"*

"Gennero's."

Nicola knows the place, a hole-in-the-wall pizza joint so narrow you felt as if you had to walk in sideways.

"We was hangin' out and Johnny, he decides he wants to go get a slice, you know?" Ricky says as they burst out into the street. "We're just standing there and these three guys elbow in—big guys, grown-ups. One pulls out a sawed-off, sticks it in Johnny's face, and *bam!* "

They're running down Hanover Street now, heading for the pizza joint. Nicola can hear sirens approaching. "What did *you* do?" she yells.

"We—none of us—did nothin'! The whole thing was, like, two seconds. Then they back out the door, get into a car, and they're gone."

They round the corner and Nicola sees there's a small crowd outside Gennero's, like maybe it's lunchtime and they're in line to order a slice.

"Who was it, Ricky?" she asks, panting.

"I dunno."

Nicola stops, grabs the kid by the shirt, and spins him against a brick wall so hard his head comes away bleeding. "Don't gimme that shit! Who *was* it?!"

"No, I *swear,* Nicola; I don't know them!"

"Yeah, like you don't know your mother, eh? You chickenshit!"

She slaps him full across the face and he doesn't even try to stop her. Then she wades through the crowd, and when old man Gennero in his stained apron yells, "Hey! No!" and tries to stop her, she bodychecks him aside and keeps going, right through the door and into the place, where the air is fragrant with pizza dough, tomato, garlic, herbs, and the lingering, acrid smell of fireworks on the Fourth of July.

The restaurant is deserted.

But Johnny is there. He's sitting on the floor in the corner beneath the niche where Gennero has a blue and white statue of the Virgin. His head is hanging down as if he's napping or something. The wall and the Virgin behind him are splattered red, like somebody had flung an institutional-size can of tomato sauce. The sirens are very close now.

She expects to be horrified, and in some corner of her brain she is, but she is oddly separate from that part of herself. It's as if she's Kojak; she's trying to make sense of the scene before her, trying to take it all in. She is about to lift Johnny's head—it's a reflex; she knows he's dead, but she wants to see his eyes—when the cops arrive and one of them grabs her.

"Come away from there, girlie; that's not for you," the cop says quietly. He's from Southie; she can tell by the Irish accent. He's trying to be gentle, assumes she's in shock, and he's correct.

"Take your fuckin' hands offa me!" she screams. "That's my *brother!*" And now she's crying and flailing punches.

In one swift, sure, graceful move, the cop scoops her off her feet, carries her out the door, and gently sets her in the backseat of a squad car, where, empty of fury now, she sits stonelike, staring, like someone waiting for a long traffic light to change. Another cop, a lady, kneels on the pavement by the open rear door and talks quietly to her, trying to get her name. Nicola suddenly folds at the waist, clutching her stomach. The lady cop sees it coming and pulls her out of the car so she can throw up in the street. The woman strokes her long hair and says soothing things to her as Nicola retches; she has no idea what the woman is saying, but it helps.

RANDI WAS SNORING. She didn't know why, but she found this endearing, only one of many sweet things about the witch's dog. She leaned over and stroked his velvet head. The snoring stopped; the dog heaved a damp sigh, shifted position, and was once again asleep.

Nicola wished she could sleep, too, but she was thinking about Andrew now—happy to be rid of Johnny, at least for a while, but no less troubled for thinking about Andrew. What the hell was wrong with the guy? *"Don't you understand how I feel about you?"* he'd yelled. Yeah, I do, but you're out of here in a few days, for Christ's sake. Probably the guy was just plain out of it; still shell-shocked by his wife's walking out on him. Either way, it was meaningless. What kind of man falls in love with you after only a few days? A lunatic, that's who.

And yet, she was almost certain there was nothing else crazy about him. Softhearted, perhaps, but not softheaded. That was it, then: He was a scheming Lothario. Maybe his wife really left him because she was tired of all his affairs. No, if that were the case, he wouldn't have seemed so surprised when she'd invited him home, and then upstairs. Surprised, and also shy. So, what then? A romantic? Lord, that might be even worse. She'd been one of those once herself, and look what it got her. *All right, then,* she said to herself, *let's look at the facts. He's a professor in Philadelphia. I'm an artist in Cornwall. And this is where I belong. Is he going to toss aside a career at a major university to build stone hedges? Not likely.* Then again, she'd overheard Jamie talking to someone at the Welly the other night about "this American" who was a "stone artist." She remembered that she'd felt secretly proud of Andrew then.

Then it struck her that the reason she was lying here in the dark trying to figure out Andrew Stratton was that she cared for him. A lot. This astonished her. What if he *did* love her? Did she love him? No, that was ridiculous. She'd fallen for Jeremy because he was handsome and charming and, as it later turned out, rather wealthy. She'd agreed to marry him before she knew anything about him, really, anything deeper than the superficial charm. And that veneer had turned out to be very thin indeed. She wasn't falling for this

Andrew chap either: far too little information upon which to base a decision.

Assuming love was something you decided upon . . .

LEE WAS HALFWAY up her favorite tree, but the climbing was slow, what with having to hook the umbrella over a branch each time she climbed higher. After having been drenched more than once by summer showers while reading in her tree, she'd had the brilliant idea of keeping her old red umbrella with the white polka dots there permanently, hooked over a limb to be used as and when necessary. The thing about summer showers was that they were short, sharp, and unpredictable. It could be sunny one minute and absolutely pelting down the next. You could stay in the tree and get soaked, or you could climb down, run home, and also get soaked, by which time the shower would have passed. With a brolly you could wait it out and keep your book dry. She thought this arrangement exceptionally clever. And besides, she considered the dotted umbrella too childish to be seen in public with anyway. A proper seat—a couple of planks nailed to two limbs, maybe— would be nice, too, but Elizabeth at the Visitor Centre had told her the valley was owned by the National Trust and she knew they'd never go for that. The trust was very strict; her Dad leased land from the trust, and they even told him what kind of cattle he could graze there. Maybe a pillow would be okay, though. She was reading the latest Harry Potter, and the branch she favored tended to get hard after a couple of chapters.

Today, however, she wasn't reading. She'd come up to have a think. The tree was a good place to think, what with the water bubbling along below and the birds and the privacy and all. It was like Harry Potter's Platform 9¾ at King's Cross station; it was her portal to a special, if not actually magical world.

Today's think was about Nicki—well, Nicki and Drew, really. Nicki had called while she and Mum were having breakfast and, after listening a bit and glancing at Lee, Mum had taken the phone out into the hall, where she talked in urgent whispers. Naturally, Lee went to the door to listen—Nicki was *her* best friend, after all. She couldn't hear what Nicki was saying, of course, and all she could catch were snatches of what her mum was saying in response: "Andrew said *what?*" and "Why'd you run away, you silly cow?" and "Sweetie, you need to let go of Johnny."

That was all Lee needed. Obviously, Nicki liked Drew but was seeing somebody named Johnny whom she needed to "let go of." In her perch high above the river, now, Lee realized she felt kind of hurt that Nicki had a boyfriend she didn't know about. After all, she told Nicki absolutely *everything* that was going on in *her* life. Why had Nicki kept this a secret? She scrunched her eyes and made her mind sail above the village, on a reconnaissance mission, like Harry on his broomstick. But she couldn't think of anybody named Johnny in Boscastle—not in the upper town, not by the harbor, not in Forrabury. Maybe he was from Camelford or Tintagel. Wherever he was from, it was clear Mum didn't think much of him.

Lee decided she needed to talk to Drew about this situation. She felt she'd sort of pushed him and Nicki together, and now she worried he might be sad about whatever had happened between them yesterday. Plus, there was the whole problem of Drew returning to America next week. If Nicki liked him, that would make her sad, too, probably. Lee had looked at the reservations book her mum kept by the kitchen phone and knew other people had reserved the cottage starting the following week, so even if Drew wanted to stay, he couldn't—at least not at Shepherd's Cottage. She didn't want Drew to leave. She liked him, liked the way he treated her like a grown-up. A lot of grown-ups treated kids as if they weren't worth wasting time on, or as if they weren't even there at all. But not Drew. He always made time for her, as if she mattered. She left the umbrella hanging from a branch, tucked her book between the waistband of her shorts and the small of her back, returned to the ground, and headed down the valley toward the harbor.

• • •

"RECKUN YON CHIELD wanna ax yew summat, Andrew," Burt said, nodding toward the distant end of the wall. The hedge-laying crew was sitting by the river, finishing lunch.

Andrew followed his gaze and saw Lee, who was standing, storklike, with one knee bent, foot resting against the opposite knee. He'd no idea how long she'd been there. The girl was capable of the kind of deep quiet that made you think she'd appeared out of thin air. When she saw he'd noticed her, she grinned and waved.

"Don't go getting snared by these local lasses, now, Andrew," Jamie teased. "We've work to do yet."

Andrew got to his feet and walked stiffly to where Lee waited, marveling that she could hold her balance on one leg. "Hiya, toots; whatcha doing down here?" Andrew said.

"Came to see you," she answered, dropping the other foot to the ground.

Andrew smiled and bowed. "Then I am honored, madam."

"We need to talk," Lee said, her pale eyebrows knit together to signal serious business.

"We do?"

"Uh-huh."

"Now?"

"Uh-huh. Can you?"

Andrew looked back at the crew, who were

tidying up and going back to work. He knew Jamie wouldn't mind. "Sure, for a bit anyway."

Lee turned and started walking toward the entrance to the car park. Andrew followed. When they were out of earshot from the others, she said, "You like Nicki, right?"

Andrew kept walking. "Well, yes, Nicola is a lovely woman, plus she's your best friend, too, and any friend of yours . . ."

Lee leveled a look at him. "Don't treat me like a kid."

Andrew was about to protest, but he caught himself. "All right, yes; I like her. I think she's pretty terrific, although a lot of the time we seem to be at daggers drawn."

"What's that supposed to mean?"

"Oh, you know, sort of teasing each other all the time."

Lee nodded, and said nothing for a few moments.

"Lee, what's troubling you? Something is, or you wouldn't have come down here when you could be in your tree."

"Nicki called Mum this morning, all upset. About something that happened between you two, I guess." She left the implicit question hanging.

"Yes, well. We . . . um . . . had a bit of a disagreement."

Lee reached the bridge and stopped. She pretended to watch the water rushing underneath. "I think Nicki's got another boyfriend, Drew. His name is Johnny. Mum told her she should let him go. I don't think Mum likes him. Mum likes you, though," she added.

Andrew leaned on the parapet beside the gangly girl. "Girl" was such an inadequate term for this wonderful little human being beside him. She was destined for an exceptional life, he was sure. For one thing, even at this age, she didn't suffer fools. She'd never "go along to get along" like other girls. She'd never hide her brains to fit in. In another five, maybe six years, she'd be dating boys, and he almost felt sorry for them. They'd be no match for this one. Five years after that, a little more, she'd be a scientist, or studying the law, or running some activist organization.

He sighed. "It must have been hard for you to come down here to tell me that," he said.

"A little," she confessed.

Andrew turned and scooped up the bony child in his arms in a giant hug. "I love you to pieces, Lee Trelissick, and if I had a daughter I'd want her to be just like you."

She wriggled away, giggling, and he let her go. He was a little surprised by his own impetuousness. Something inside him was softening, uncurling, anxiety calving off him like a glacier melting. This new gentleness was, he knew, partly a legacy of the hedge building. He didn't need to anticipate or prepare for anything, he could let things take their natural course. He could just "be." He could even admit to himself the pure joy and wonder he felt whenever he was with this solemn little girl.

They were walking back to the work site.

"What are you going to do about this Johnny?" Lee asked. She could hear the anxious note in her voice; she didn't know what happened in situations like this.

Andrew stopped and kneeled in front of her. "Look, I'm a visitor here, Lee. I'm just passing through. I have no business being involved in the troubles and cares of those who live here. It would be like someone coming to stay at the cottage for a week and telling your father how to run the farm. Know what I mean?"

Lee nodded. "Yeah. But that's a bad example. You love Nicki. That makes it different."

Andrew just stared at her. "You're right. I do. And I'm gonna take care of this Johnny guy. Thank you for telling me. But now I have to get back to work; it's our last day. That okay with you?"

Lee nodded and Andrew set off for the hedge site.

"You won't hurt him, will you?" Lee called after him.

"Who?"

"Johnny!"

He looked back at the girl, who was all angles and attitudes. "No, Lee; I don't think that will be necessary."

But, of course, he had no idea what would be necessary.

During the morning, shower clouds developed inland as temperatures rose past the trigger temperature required to start convection. . . . The approaching air would have been bodily lifted past its Level of Free Convection (LFC) allowing deep cumulonimbus clouds to develop.

Boscastle Flood Special Issue,
Journal of Meteorology 29, no. 293

eleven

Nicola had been painting furiously for hours. She'd started in the dark, before dawn, covering a fresh canvas with a ground of fiery yellow ocher mixed with a tiny bit of alizarin crimson for depth. She was working now with a palette far darker than any she'd used before, working, too, almost automatically. She did not have a vision she was trying to capture; the vision was emerging from the paint itself, as if she were simply delivering pigment to it, like fuel to a furnace.

It was as if she'd shut off the power to the left side of her brain, the side that gives names to things, and, by doing so, limits their expression. Her hand, holding broader brushes than she normally used, swept across the ocher ground, adding slashes of muddy, almost olive, brown; swirls of ivory black mixed with viridian; smudges of umber and orange; flashes of brilliant red; and, behind the violent darkness, beacons of pure cadmium yellow. There was a vaguely suggested horizon, tilted, a thin pale blue line almost engulfed in massing clouds of fire and smoke. She'd also laid in a few nearly vertical features, brush bristles creating veils of paler yellow and green plunging from the darkness at the top of the painting to the pale horizon, like approaching squall lines over the ocean—but an ocean that was aflame. On some level, this was emotion on canvas, and yet it was more accurately the case that she was, for the present, caught up in a world of pure perception. She was not painting the idea of an emotion, or even being driven by emotion, as much as she was finding the emotion through the paint. She made no attempt to correct what emerged from under the brush, though she responded constantly to what appeared—the shapes, the angles, the hues—her brush scrubbing together new colors on the palette and swirling them onto the surface of the image that was developing.

She stopped only when, a little before noon, Randi let her know she was trying his patience, and his bladder, sorely. She took him for a short walk along the harbor front, but it was as if she was in a trance, her body navigating the familiar landscape—the quay, the breakwater, the cliff path above—but her eyes seeing only the painting and feeling what it needed next. She grabbed a banana on her way back upstairs, ate half before forgetting about it, and was lost again in the work.

She felt both free in the way she was painting and oddly compelled—like a dog on a very long chain, free to move or bark as it wished, but nonetheless constrained by the limits of the chain. She suspected this storm of paint arose from her nightmare, from anger, from fear. But it also felt weirdly like a premonition, a vision not so much of the anguish of the past as of the present and future. As if a threat were cresting high above her, as if getting it on the canvas would freeze it there, perhaps. She didn't know. She wasn't trying to know. She was just painting with an intensity and at a speed she had never experienced before. As if her life depended on it.

Sometime around three o'clock, she put her brush down. It wasn't because she was tired, though she was exhausted, or that she was hungry, though she was famished. It was just done. Whatever it was, it was finished. She stared at it as if waking from a dream. She'd never painted anything this fast before, or this strange. It was as if she'd been taken over by some spirit and she was merely its instrument. She was shocked by the violence of the work, but also exhilarated. She shrugged at the work in amazement, called to Randi, and headed off to the Cobweb to celebrate. She just made it through the door when the sky opened up and fat raindrops fell like diamonds through the slanting afternoon sunshine.

JAMIE HAD SEEN it coming.

"All right, you lot," he'd called out as the first drops splattered the dusty ground, "get the tools in the van and your sorry selves to the pub; you've been reprieved!" He watched them finish their work and gather the equipment, laying it out neatly on the bed of the big van. Though there was still

248

another twenty yards or so of hedge still to be laid, what they'd built looked clean and solid. And he'd turned his crew from a group of clumsy amateurs into skilled craftspeople—proper hedge layers who, by and large, he'd be proud to work beside. It was always like this at the end; he hated to let them go. Ever since his wife of forty years died—what, five years ago now—his students had been his family. In between courses, without their company, he felt bereft, holing up in his ancient house up on the moor, drinking whisky and reading Shakespeare—the plays, not the love sonnets. The sonnets were too painful.

Now here they were, this latest lot, shambling in from the street, sweaty, dirty, smiling, their shirts pockmarked with raindrops.

"Flora, my dear, sweet lass," he called to the barmaid after they'd muscled their way through the crowd of tourists who were also sheltering from the shower, "drinks for my crew, on me." This was met with a chorus of dispute from his students, but the teacher prevailed, and when their glasses were delivered, he lifted his in a toast.

"You're ugly as sin, every last man of you—the ever-lovely Becky, of course, excepted—but you're Cornish hedgers now, by God, and damned fine ones!" He knew he was lying about Casehill. That bloke would never give up his mortar crutch, though Jamie hoped he'd appreciate the craft a bit more. But as to the rest, he knew he'd succeeded.

Especially with this American chap. The rest of them had become skilled, but this one had gained more than skill. Something about the fellow had changed, sometime during the third day. At the beginning, Andrew was a blur of excess motion. Jamie would watch him walk back and forth between the hedge face and the rock pile, lifting, carrying, and then returning stone until he found something he thought was perfect. And sometimes it was, but often it wasn't. Then, somewhere along the line, he'd got it: got that perfection, if it could be attained at all, was the product of the whole, not a requirement of each piece; got it that the essential oddity, almost the absurdity, of hedge building was endeavoring to make straight lines out of wildly irregular chunks of rock; got it that the mystical heart of the craft was visualizing the whole even as you're working with just a small part—that the stone in your hand *is* the hedge. And so is the next one, and the next. They're just waiting for you to find them, to give them a home.

NICOLA SAT ON a stool in the bar on the other side of the double fireplace wall; only the back of the bar communicated with the two rooms. She was wolfing down a delightfully sinful and messy hamburger smothered in caramelized onions and melted cheddar, along with a plateful of chips, and washing it all down with her usual gin and tonic. Flora had told her that Andrew was there in the adjoining bar with the rest of Jamie's crew, but she stayed put. She didn't want to see him. Well, actually she did, but she had no idea what to say if she did, how to begin, and, having begun, where to stop. Whatever the new painting was about, whatever it defined or resolved, it wasn't about Andrew; there was no resolution there. As good and as caring a man as he was—and she was sure all that was genuine—she could not get past her wariness. She didn't really want to continue fencing with him, but she was afraid to stop, afraid to let her guard down. Not because of what he might do if she did, but because she did not know what might emerge from herself—what fears, what ghosts, what demons. And then there was the repeated refrain, the leitmotif: He was as good as gone anyway.

The shower passed, the tourists drifted outside again, and Flora plunked herself down next to Nicola on her break, a half pint of lager in front of her. She leaned close to Nicola's ear.

"Tell you what, luv; that there Jamie: If he weren't always so bloody filthy, I could get to likin' him. Hard body, soft eyes. What's not to like, eh?" She was grinning and blushing simultaneously.

"Flora, you trollop; you shock me!" Nicola said, giggling.

"What, you think 'cause I'm old enough to be your mother I can't hanker after a good man?"

"No! It's just . . . I don't know . . . I thought you were sweet on Brian, over at the Welly."

"What, *him?* Oh, our Brian's okay as far as that goes, good for a laugh and a bit of a flirt, but I don't see him ever makin' much of hisself. Men who bartend, well, most of them are a bit short of ambition, you know? Like they're just markin' time. Unless they own the place, which Brian don't. Plus, I think he likes that bar between him and the rest o' the world—protection, like. Can't tell whether he's hidin' something or got nuthin' to hide, if you take my meanin'."

Nicola liked Flora a lot. She might be old enough to be her mother—it was hard to tell—but she was much more like the kind of aunt you could talk to about anything, without fear of being judged. She was open and dead honest; it was something the regulars admired about her.

"But is Jamie Boden that much better a prospect? I mean, the chap's a hedge builder."

Flora laughed. *"Hedge craftsman* to you, dearie. But he wasn't always, is what I hear."

"Oh?"

"No, been at that less than ten years, for all his skill. What I hear is that before that he was in finance, up in London. Worked for that billionaire currency trader, Soros. Made a pile in hedge funds, got fed up, and moved back here to live in his wife Lydia's family's place up there on the moor. Then lost her to cancer, poor soul." She went quiet for a moment and then started laughing, her ample body rippling with mirth. "Old Jamie went from hedge funds to hedge building! Just thought of that, I did; pretty good, eh?"

Nicola laughed, too, and Flora got called back behind the bar.

She liked watching Flora work, the way she moved smoothly from one task to another, the way she worked without seeming to be working. Not that it was effortless, mind you, just that it looked that way—the way a talented ballet dancer could make flying leaps look effortless. And then it struck her that Jamie worked the same way, as if he and the stone were in harmony somehow. Yes, maybe Flora and Jamie were right for each other. She wondered whether Flora would make a move. Or Jamie. Or if Jamie even had a clue. She realized she didn't know the first thing about this "courtin'" stuff. Jeremy had come along and swept her off her feet, and she'd been paying for it ever since.

And as happy as she was, painting in her attic studio, visiting with friends like Flora and Anne, adoring Lee, volunteering at the witchcraft museum, walking Randi along the cliffs, knowing most people in the village by their first name, she suddenly wondered whether perhaps she wasn't a bit more like Brian than Flora. Was she, too, simply "marking time"? Was she living in the present or just avoiding the future? Her routines gave her a certain quiet comfort, as if the patterns of a day were the meaning of the day. But were they? Okay, she knew the answer to this one. No, patterns were the rhythm, not the meaning. Meaning came from one's work and, if you were a woman, from what one gave and received from one's partner and one's children. She had neither . . . or, rather, she had both, in the form of Randi— steadfast friend and protector, and dependent child. It wasn't enough. But anything more put her at risk. And that frightened her more than her loneliness.

JAMIE KEPT BUYING rounds and the crew was full of affection for one another, Burt clapping his arm, thick and heavy as a haunch of beef, around Andrew's shoulder; Ralph becoming ever-so-mildly amorous with a tipsy Becky; Case promising in the most solemn terms that he would forswear mortar henceforth. Jamie watched them with a bemused and benevolent smile, turning occasionally to flirt with Flora.

"Flora, my sweet," he called to her at one point, "let's have us some peanuts!" He pointed to a cardboard display for Big D nuts that hung on a wall behind the bar. The display featured the face of a sultry blonde, beneath which image were clipped rows of salted peanut packets. Flora pulled down several, in the process revealing the plunging décolletage of the model pictured on the display.

"Oh, I think we'll need a few more, my dear," Jamie said to Flora with a wink. Flora gave him a jaundiced look, but obliged, revealing, as she removed the next row of packets, the model's Big Ds in all their fulsome, naked glory. This, of course, to the accompaniment of hoots from the crew, and "Oh my God, that's so disgusting," from Becky, at which point Flora leaned across the bar, her own formidable bosom perfectly evident, put her face close to Jamie's, and said, "You ain't seen nuthin', mister." There was more raucous laughter, followed by "You tell him, sister" from Becky. Jamie blushed almost as red as his hair.

After several more rounds than usual, Jamie's students began to take their leave—Burt and Ralph first, with a salute from Ralph and a standing invitation from Burt to come up to the farm for a visit anytime and an unexpected, bone-crushing hug. Andrew got a nod from Casehill, not unlike the one he'd greeted him with on the first day, and a handshake. And a luscious smooch from Becky accompanied by a boozily whispered, "Bloody bother I've already got a husband," which left Andrew speechless. She hugged Jamie and said, "See you Monday," and was gone.

"Monday?" Andrew asked his teacher.

"Got a crew of National Trust volunteers coming to continue work on the hedge. Becky's rounded them up; some experienced, some not. What're your plans next week, lad?"

Andrew sighed. "Leaving. Probably Wednesday or Thursday."

"A shame is what that is, now I got you nearly useful."

Andrew laughed. "I can't spend the rest of my life building Cornish hedges, Jamie."

"Why not? Market demand's growing, and I can't begin to keep up with it. Pay's good, too; plus, no one's your boss."

"I'm an architect, Jamie."

"You like being an architect?"

This stopped Andrew cold. It wasn't a question he'd ever consciously entertained. He'd known he wanted to be an architect almost from childhood; he'd never even considered anything else. Then he'd sort of fallen into teaching, rather than designing and building, but thought it suited him. It was what he did. It was who he was. But were you an architect if you never built anything? Did teaching count? When Kat slammed him on this the day she walked out, he'd thought it mean-spiritedness, meant to make him feel a failure—at which she'd largely succeeded. But maybe it was really truth telling. Maybe he had disappointed her. And himself.

"How old d'you reckon I am?" he heard Jamie ask.

"Sixty-something?" Andrew answered.

"Pushin' seventy. And feeling every year of it. Been lookin' for someone to pass the Stone

Academy on to for a while now, and I'm thinking you're a natural for it."

Andrew looked at his friend and took a slug from his pint. "Well, sir," he said finally, "that's as fine a compliment as I've been paid in a very long time."

"It isn't a compliment, you bloody numbskull; it's the offer of a lifetime!"

Andrew turned to his mentor. "Jamie, look. I've got a house in Philadelphia and a mortgage and a new semester of classes to teach in less than a month. I'm sorry. I can't."

"Can't or won't?" It could have been a taunt, but Andrew could see the affection in the older man's eyes. "You know what they say, don't you?"

"No, what's that?"

"No one ever said on his deathbed he wished he'd spent more time at his job."

"Very pithy, I'll admit," Andrew said. "But aren't you just offering me a different job?"

"Nay, lad, that's where you have it wrong. I'm not offering you a job; I'm offering you a life. The only question is whether you have the courage to live it."

Andrew stared at him for a moment, finally saying, "It's not that simple."

"Isn't it? Remember what you were telling me at the Welly last Wednesday? About honest, vernacular architecture, and livable communities, and local materials? That's not a scholarly pursuit, lad, that's your passion, even if you're too blind to see it. And while I'm at it—and I promise this'll be the last of it—let me tell you something else: You were born to work with stone. Never seen anyone take to it so naturally. You and the stone understand each other, is how I see it. And I think you know that."

Andrew didn't know whether this was salesmanship or just more of Jamie's Zen, but he felt honored nonetheless. "Look, I hear you, Jamie; I just think it's . . . I don't know . . . crazy. Not to mention that if I didn't show up at school next month, that would probably be the end of my career."

Jamie nodded. He'd said more already than he was used to saying to anybody. But something about the American got to him, as if perhaps he were the son Jamie'd never had.

"Right then," he said, "here's my fallback position . . ."

Andrew lifted a skeptical eyebrow.

"What're you doing Monday?"

Andrew laughed hard. He'd planned on seeing a bit of the county before he left, but the truth was, he really would prefer to work some more on the hedge. He hated unfinished business. And he could hardly turn Jamie down now.

"See you in the car park at eight," Andrew said.

"Good lad," Jamie said.

Andrew clapped an arm around his friend, gave

him an awkward, sideways guy hug, thanked him for the lessons and the drinks, and took his leave.

Flora had been watching this exchange while serving customers at the two bars, and now she sidled over to Jamie.

"What are you up to, you old rascal?" she asked.

Jamie smiled, but it was a tired smile. "Looking for a successor, Flora; looking for a successor."

"You retirin'?"

"No, luv, just thinking ahead. Plus, I like that chap. Good man, that one."

Jamie paid the bar bill and turned to leave.

"See you again Monday, Jamie?"

Jamie looked at her for several moments, as if something was dawning on him, then grinned. "If not sooner," he said.

FLORA KNEW THERE was something going on between Nicola and Andrew, and it puzzled her that the girl would stay holed up where she was, knowing the man was at the adjacent bar. When all the crew had left, she mixed an unrequested gin and tonic and slapped it down in front of her younger friend.

"My shout," she said about the drink, "but only if you tell me what the hell's going on between you and the American."

Nicola slumped. "Is my private life such public knowledge?"

"No, just to me and those who care about you,

259

which includes . . . oh, I don't know . . . maybe half the village?"

"Bloody hell."

"Hang on; gotta pull some bloke a pint."

Nicola stared at her drink, watching the condensation bead on the outside of the glass and slide down to the bar. She knew Wednesday night had gone all pear-shaped. She woke up in bed the next morning, fully dressed and alone. Andrew had asked her about Johnny. What did he know? What had she said?

Flora was back. She said nothing, but her look was a question. Nicola sighed.

"I'm just wrestling with some old ghosts, is all," she said.

"Meanwhile, I'd like to wrestle with that old goat, Jamie," Flora quipped. It was meant to be funny, to lighten the mood, but it failed. She tried again.

"Nicki, let me tell you something from my long years of romantic experience."

This, at last, made Nicola smile.

"The calendar is a bum way to measure the passage of time. Time's more like the Valency out there," she said nodding toward the door. "It just rushes by—slower some days than others, I'll grant you, but wicked fast nonetheless. And it don't give much of a damn about your history . . . or your ghosts. I'm not sayin' this because I'm so wise, luv; I'm sayin' it because I haven't been, and an awful lot of time has passed under my bridge and I've been standin' on it alone. That Andrew of yours—"

"He's not 'that Andrew of mine.' "

"That Andrew of yours," Flora continued, ignoring her, "is not the kinda man who's gonna hurt you. Ain't got it in him, for one thing. And cares for you a lot, for another. Like Jamie does me. I know he does; he just hasn't tumbled to it yet, poor sod. You been solitary so long—leastways as long as I've known you—I don't think you even remember what it's like to have a warm body beside you . . . and I'm not countin' that dog of yours, however clever he is. I'm not tellin' you this because I know so much about havin' someone to comfort me; I'm tellin' you this because I know so much about *not* havin' someone to comfort me. I'm givin' you the benefit of my experience. You live by yourself long enough, you get used to it. Live by yourself too long, and you get so set in your ways you can't abide being with someone else. And then you get to thinkin' that's just fine with you, that you like it that way . . .

"Hold your water, Harold, I'll be with you in a sec," she called to a regular at the other bar.

". . . but that's an illusion, luv. We aren't meant to live solitary. Isn't natural. Not how we're made, especially us women."

"But—" Nicola interjected.

"I know, I know; he's leavin'. That any reason why you shouldn't have a few moments of togetherness? Of happiness?"

Flora left her with that, to tend to the impatient Harold.

But, of course, it wasn't Andrew. Or even Jeremy. It was goddamned Johnny, whom she'd loved and admired so deeply as a child, and hated and feared so profoundly as an adolescent. Goddamned Johnny, who made everything ugly. Goddamned Johnny, who got himself killed before she'd ever had a chance to confront him as an adult, and demand acknowledgment, and extract apology, and confer forgiveness. Goddamned Johnny.

Nicola slapped some money on the bar, well more than she owed, and left. Randi, who'd been asleep at her feet, roused himself and followed—with a head-down, shambling gait, as if the weight upon his mistress was upon his shoulders as well.

As the south-westerly flow crossed Cornwall, surface frictional effects caused the flow to decrease and back over the land. A convergence line then developed between the moderate southwesterlies over the sea and the light southwesterlies over Cornwall. This convergence line formed almost parallel along the North Cornwall coast, and just inland at Boscastle.

Boscastle Flood Special Issue,
Journal of Meteorology 29, no. 293

Early Saturday morning, Andrew stood at the kitchen window and waited for the teakettle to boil. Roger and Anne's house was invisible, drowned in a miasma of milky white. In the meadow across the road, one of Roger's steers materialized from the fog and, just as suddenly, vanished.

Andrew welcomed the mist; he had a walk planned that would take him up along the high ridge east of the River Valency, then west to the coast and High Cliff—said to be the highest in England. The fog would keep the air cool for what he could tell from his Ordnance Survey map would be several steep climbs.

After a breakfast of fresh eggs from the farm and crusty bread, he tossed a water bottle, a rain jacket, and the map into his day pack, laced up his boots, and stepped out his door. Lee was not waiting for him on her wall, which came as a disappointment. Apparently, she drew the line at sitting on cold, damp rocks.

He struck off along a narrow, single-track road that skirted a wood in which huddled Minster church, one of the four ancient churches in the parish. The lane carried on high above the Valency valley, on this morning slumbering beneath its blanket of fog. As if to mimic the mist, the verges along the lane were frothy with the faded, hip-high heads of cow parsley, punctuated here and there by the attenuated magenta spires of fireweed. After a mile or so, the lane dipped steeply into a rocky ravine, climbed up again, and zigzagged through a tiny hamlet of slatestone cottages and barns called Treworld, then stretched out across the shoulder of the valley again. A little farther on, the road descended a second time, into a deep, bosky glen magical in the mist with lichen-encrusted trees and moss-covered rocks and outcrops. At the bottom, another tributary to the Valency clattered downhill to the river valley below. He sat on the bridge here for a while and watched a pair of pudgy, white-bibbed dippers doing their curious bobbing "curtsy" to each other and then plunging right into the fast-flowing stream to feed, using their wings to "swim" underwater.

At Lesnewth, Andrew stopped to visit the fourth ancient church in the parish, St. Michael and All Angels. The original Saxon church here had been nestled into the steep hillside beside a stream to hide it from Danish invaders. After the Norman Conquest, a new church was built on the foundations of the older one, but when he entered through its side porch, Andrew discovered yet another essentially modern interior, the decaying church having been stripped and rebuilt in 1862. All that was left of the Norman church was a tiny window set into a thick wall. The church was deserted, flowers from an earlier service wilting on the altar. He sat on one of the simple benches, wondered what had happened to the ancient carved-oak pews, and mourned the widespread "restoration" of parish churches by the Victorians. He couldn't help but think of the parallel with Henry VIII's dissolution and pillaging of the great Catholic monasteries in the mid-sixteenth century. From an architectural point of view, only the scale of the destruction was different.

He left a few coins in the donation box and drifted out of Lesnewth feeling somehow diminished, rather than uplifted, by the visit to the church. He could almost hear Jamie's voice reminding him of his own passion for protecting what was genuine in vernacular buildings. Andrew knew he wasn't a Luddite; he wasn't opposed to progress or even modernization. In fact, he'd used a lot of new technology on his own house in Philadelphia, while at the same time lovingly restoring its original nineteenth-century facade. What he was opposed to, he was learning, was the loss of architectural heritage and, even more, the departicularization of authentic places—the loss of character to what was, in effect, simply the latest architectural fad. There was an ache in his heart for the places that were still real, for the places that still seemed to function at human scale.

Just outside of Lesnewth, a signpost pointed to a footpath that cut across a meadow to another lane that led to the village of Tresparrett, where there was a pub Andrew thought he might try for lunch. He was halfway across the field when a voice called out to him. He peered downslope and there was Roger, sitting atop an open all-terrain vehicle, a knit cap pulled down over his head against the mist, surrounded by mahogany cattle. Andrew walked down the hill toward him and, at just that moment, the sun began to burn through the fog. This was a phenomenon that fascinated him; the fog didn't drift away like clouds, it evaporated, like steam from a city manhole cover in winter: there one moment, and then gone.

"Running away from home?" Roger called, climbing down from the ATV.

"It's my day off," Andrew said. "No hedge building on Saturdays; it's a rule in Cornwall, I understand."

"Not on my farm, it isn't; when are you starting?"

"Starting?"

"On my hedges, man! They need attending to!"

Andrew laughed, and then realized they were being surrounded by large, quietly chewing cattle that seemed to think the two of them were the most fascinating phenomena in Cornwall. Roger caught his momentary flash of concern.

"Needn't worry about these fellows; sweetest breed in the country."

"What are they? I have to say they're beautiful beasts."

"They are, aren't they? These are Devon Rubies. Might well be the oldest cattle breed in Britain. There are records suggesting that they date back at least to pre-Roman times. Practically prehistoric."

"How'd they survive?"

"By evolving to be naturally disease-resistant and brilliant grass feeders. Don't need grain or supplemental feeds, and yet they still produce finely marbled meat. Used to be raised as both beef cattle and as dairy cows, but now it's mostly for the meat. You go to any independent butcher in England and they'll tell you it's Devon Rubies they prize most. Most of our beef, though, we sell directly from our farm store and to a few high-class restaurants."

"How'd you come to choose them?" Andrew asked, patting the curly forehead of one of the steers.

"The National Trust gave me no choice. This is their land, see, like most of the land on either side of the Valency, and along the coast. I lease it from them. They wanted Devon Rubies because they're easy on the land. They're smaller than most other beef cattle, and they're gentle browsers, so they don't tear up the ground. Ideal for conservation, which is what the trust's all about. As far as the trust's concerned, they're basically lawn mowers. Plus, they're almost impervious to our tough winter weather. They're out in the fields nearly year-round. Wonderful animals."

Roger walked among his cattle, stroking their backs, patting their rumps, talking gently to them, even as he was inspecting them. It seemed to Andrew that cattle and farmer regarded each other with equal affection. Andrew hadn't spent a lot of time with Roger, but he respected and liked the man. There was a gentleness in Roger not unlike that of his cattle, a sweet temper matched with quiet competence. Quick to smile, rawboned and muscular, with thinning blond hair, he was like a sinewy and slightly more talkative version of Burt, and Andrew wondered if spending one's days with your animals and measuring time by the seasons didn't bring about a gentleness in men you didn't find elsewhere.

"Where you off to?" Roger asked.

"The Horseshoe in Tresparrett, for lunch."

"Want a lift?"

"Sure! Buy you a pint?"

"Sure!"

"Then I believe we have a deal, my friend," Andrew said climbing onto the back of the ATV. Roger engaged the gears and they were off, bumping across the field so ruggedly that Andrew thought he'd lose his teeth before he had a chance to use them on lunch. They reached a gate in the stone hedge bounding the field and Andrew hopped off to let the vehicle through. He closed the gate again and climbed back on, and they rocketed noisily down the lane toward the river below, with

Andrew peering over Roger's shoulder like a vigilant farm dog. At the bottom, there was no bridge over the river; the road simply plunged under the water and climbed out again on the opposite bank. Roger didn't even slow down; they plowed through the stream, which was less than a foot deep, sending curtains of water flying off to both sides.

Andrew was laughing. "What the hell was *that?*" he shouted above the motor's din.

"Cornish car wash!"

"Come on . . ."

"A ford. We call it a 'splash' around here."

"There's a surprise!"

At the top of the hill, they whipped a quick left turn and promptly entered the little hamlet of Tresparrett. The Horseshoe Inn was a low, whitewashed stone cottage just off the main road, on the left. It was just opening.

"Good day to you, Derek!" Roger shouted to the bearded fellow behind the bar as they entered.

"Tha' looks a mite dampish, there, Roger; been playing in the splash again, have you? I just finished moppin' the floor, I'll have you know."

Derek nodded to Andrew and winked. "Some folks never grow up, eh?"

"Derek, Andrew; Andrew, Derek," Roger said by way of introduction. "Him and me go back a ways."

"And it never gets any better," Derek said, smiling.

"Derek's never got over losing Anne to me, you see. Sweet on her, he was, weren't you, lad?"

"And who wouldn't have been, I ask you! How is your fine lady, then?"

"Oh, tolerable, Derek. Tolerable," said Roger. But he was grinning.

Derek shook his head and, addressing Andrew, said, "Haven't a clue why she chose him. Nor why she's stuck it out with him this long. Horrible fate for a nice girl. Horrible."

"Just a guess, mind you, Derek," Roger shot back, "but maybe she didn't want to marry a bloke whose sole ambition in life was being the landlord of a boozer like this place."

Derek drew himself to full height, which was only about five-foot-six. "I'll have you know the Horseshoe is no boozer, sir. We've live jazz on weekends and panini sandwiches at luncheon!"

Roger was loving this. He turned to Andrew and said, "Goes off on his hols to Rome, and the next thing you know it's fancy foreign names for a cheese and onion bap!"

Andrew stepped in. "Panini, is it? Let's see that menu! And in the meantime, a pint for my ill-mannered friend and me and whatever you're having as well, Derek."

Derek made a slight bow. "I see you're a gentleman, Andrew, and a generous one at that. But you might think more carefully about the company you keep." He slid a lunch menu across the bar to Andrew, and none to Roger. Andrew could tell this was a routine the two men had been running for years, perhaps since their school days. Roger had a packed lunch, he said, so Andrew ordered a bacon and Brie panini for himself. While it was being grilled in the kitchen, the two old friends caught up. He envied them their long friendship and their rootedness to this part of Cornwall. Like many Americans, Andrew had bounced around from one part of the country to the other, wherever school and work led him. When someone asked him where he was from, he never knew how to answer. Where he was born? Where he'd lived the longest? Where he'd lived last? And there was a related question, one he suspected was more important still: Where did he *belong?* What were the bits and pieces of being that gave you a sense of belonging someplace—the way Roger and Derek so clearly belonged here?

Andrew and Roger took their pints to a table and, after delivering the panini—which was excellent—Derek drifted off to tend to new arrivals.

"That's nice work you lot have been doing down there by the harbor," Roger said as Andrew ate.

"The hedge? Thanks, but it's all due to Jamie."

"Not what he tells me. Word is, you're gifted."

Andrew laughed. "Oh? And what else does the Boscastle grapevine have to say about me?"

Andrew was kidding Roger, but the other man's face became serious.

272

"I also hear there's some trouble between you and Anne's friend Nicki."

Andrew felt suddenly defensive. "Look, Roger, I don't know what you think of me, but I've done nothing that—"

The farmer interrupted, waving his free hand. "Nay, friend; not what I meant, not at all. I'm not supposed to know anything, if you follow, but it's not about you."

"Yeah; Lee says Nicola's got some guy named Johnny in her life."

"Not anymore, she don't," Roger replied. "He's dead."

"Her boyfriend died?"

"Not her boyfriend, Andrew. Her older brother. And a nasty piece of work, is what I hear. A drug dealer. Happens he also, um, fiddled her, as a kid."

Andrew looked blank.

"You know, had sex with her. Incest and all. Then got himself killed."

"Oh, Jesus."

"Look, the missus tells me Nicola's sweet on you, but scared. This dead brother, it's like he's sleeping under her bed, you know? Makes me think of those fairy tales we used to read to Lilly— the troll under the bridge and all. Way I look at it, Nicola's hiding here in Boscastle. But not from that upper-class asshole of an ex-husband of hers; I reckon she's hiding from the dead brother—and the rest of the world as well. You're the first thing she's taken notice of, besides that dog of hers, since she got here. And it's been years."

It all made sense, of course, but Andrew still struggled to take it in. He felt swept by waves of compassion for Nicola and fury about this dead, but not dead, brother. No wonder she was terrified when he touched her. No wonder she ran from him when he told her he cared for her. A part of him said, *Let it go; you're leaving in a few days, and this isn't your battle.* But that was his head talking, and he was tired of doing what his head said. His heart told him this woman mattered. It also told him this place mattered.

Roger was still talking, and Andrew dragged himself into the present moment.

"But you didn't hear it from me, right?"

"What?"

"Anne will kill me if she knows I've told you. Though, bloody hell, I don't know why."

Andrew looked at the man for a moment.

"Thank you, friend," he said finally. He put out his hand and Roger took it.

"I was daydreaming there for a moment, Roger," Andrew said. "Did you say something just now?"

"I don't think so."

"I didn't think so, either."

ANDREW REALIZED HE'D taken High Cliff the easy way, though by accident. When he parted from Roger at Tresparrett, he followed a series of minor roads and lanes across the coastal fields, rising gradually as he approached the Atlantic. When he reached the coast path at its highest point, the ocean was so far below he couldn't hear it. It wasn't a sheer cliff. He had more the sense that over the eons, the sea and wind and frost had gnawed away at the shale to create the long, steep scree slope that fell away from the summit, gradually, to the surf below. Still, it was a very long way down. Gulls wheeled above, the sunburned husks of sea thrift danced on the wind, spikes of orange montbretia thrust up from clefts in the rock, blankets of heather cloaked the ground, and here and there the gorse still bloomed, adding clusters of lemon yellow to the purple slopes.

The coast path back to Boscastle was, he decided, the opposite of Newton's law. It wasn't that "what goes up must come down," it was that "what goes down must come up again," because every quarter mile or so, streams cut into the cliffs, creating deep, narrow gorges, and necessitating arduous descents, followed by steep, stair-step climbs up the other side. Thus, he walked down from High Cliff, then up to Rusey Cliff, and then down and up to Beeny Cliff, until, finally, he circuited Pentargon Falls (noting that neither the stranded sheep nor its bones occupied the little terrace the two of them once shared) and approached the cliffs above Boscastle. Far below was the cluster of stone buildings he'd come to know so well. Just upstream from the mouth of the Valency, he could see the Museum of Witchcraft, and he made a decision.

ANDREW STOOD AT a window in the upstairs library of the museum, gazing at the little river below and waiting for Colin Grant to finish a phone conversation. He'd been immensely relieved to find someone other than Nicola at the ticket desk when he asked after Colin; Saturday was the museum's busiest day of the week, but Nicola had had the morning shift.

"My good fellow, please accept my apologies," Colin said, putting down the receiver at last. "One of my board members, a somewhat trying chap, but well intentioned, well intentioned. What can I do for you? A book, perhaps?" he added, gesturing to the shelves that lined the walls.

"A question, really," Andrew said. Not knowing quite how to begin, he stopped there. It was a bit off-putting that the museum owner didn't look directly at you when he spoke.

"Yes?" the man prompted.

"Something the vicar suggested you might be able to help with."

"Ah, yes, the Reverend Janet. It wouldn't be the first time. You have a matter she can't address?"

There was another uncomfortable pause, then, finally, Andrew nodded and dove in. "Let's say someone, a woman, was sexually abused as a child by an older brother. And let's say that brother died soon thereafter, but the memory of his abuse still haunts the woman in adulthood, so much so that it makes forming normal relationships with men extremely difficult."

"An all-too-common phenomenon, I'm afraid," Colin said, shaking his head in dismay.

"Are there practices or . . . I don't know what to call it . . . cures in witchcraft that might apply?"

"Oh yes, certainly; though perhaps nothing quite so specific." Colin went to one of the shelf units. "You're really talking about two broad categories of concerns: visitations—you used the word 'haunts,' and it is apt—by an evil spirit, in this case the dead brother, but also issues associated with love in general. There is, of course, a long history of witches applying what we might call white magic to address such problems, love and abuse hardly being new concerns. On this shelf," he said, sweeping a hand along a row of book bindings, "we have volumes associated with matters of the heart. And over there," he added, pointing across the room, "is an entire section on dealing with quieting or banishing evil or unquiet spirits. I'd be happy to lend you however many books you'd like to examine. That's why we're here."

"Mr. Grant . . ."

"Colin."

"Colin. I was thinking more along the lines of direct intervention."

"Ah . . ."

"I know there is a community of believers in and around Boscastle, though I gather it is also the case that they don't exactly advertise themselves."

"This is true; people have peculiar and rather lurid ideas about witchcraft and witches, almost all of which are wrong."

"Let's say you knew a witch who could act on this person's behalf; what might they do to intervene in such a matter?"

Colin was quiet for a moment, and Andrew felt himself being screened for safety, like a piece of luggage at the airport.

"We're speaking in purely theoretical terms, you understand."

Andrew nodded.

"Right. Well, for a start, the witch might scry in a dark mirror or an old glass fishing float."

"I'm sorry, *scry?*"

"Oh. Sorry. An old word derived from the verb *descry,* which means 'to catch sight of.' Witches sometimes use dark mirrors to see into the future, or into the world of the spirits."

"Like with a crystal ball?"

"Right, except we don't use crystal balls. They're mostly used in Hollywood and the occasional traveling carnival. You're a lot more likely to have an old, dark mirror lying about than a crystal ball."

"True."

"So she would ask the spirits, or 'old ones,' to give her advice, and might see visions in the mirror and use those visions to find a solution. She might even come in contact with the spirit of the dead brother."

Colin was gazing at the ceiling, as if a sacred text was written there and he was simply reading it off the plaster. "She would wait for a waning moon, because that's believed to be the best time for banishing terrors. Then the witch might advise the woman to tear off a bit of a photograph of her brother each night of the waning moon, then burn the pieces on the night of the dark of the moon."

"So the woman would have to be an active participant?"

"That's best, but the witch might perform this herself on behalf of the woman, with or without her knowledge. Of course, she'd have to have the picture, or something once owned by the brother."

Andrew thought about this for a moment and remembered a photograph in Nicola's bedroom, a picture of three children at a beach. "Would a photocopy of a picture work?"

"Oh yes, certainly; it's the image itself, not the medium upon which it is embedded, that matters. And if there is a new relationship involved"—here he looked briefly, though indirectly, at Andrew, then returned to the ceiling—"she would use a waxing moon to bring about a good relationship."

"How would she do that?"

"Oh, during the waxing moon, she might encourage the woman to take a potion every night to help her dream. She might be encouraged to visualize herself in a loving relationship with someone. The witch might secretly bind two sticks together, one gathered from the garden of the woman and one from the garden of a suitable man. This would encourage the relationship. She would probably gather the sticks on a full moon and bind the sticks with red thread."

Andrew listened to Colin with respect, as he might have any colleague at the university. Colin was a scholar, there was no question about that, a serious student of these arts, an expert. And yet Andrew's faith in Cartesian analysis, in dispassionate reasoning, left little breathing space for such arcane notions. Skepticism rose from him like a spiritual seasickness, but he fought it down. What choice was there, really? It did not seem there was anything in the world as he knew it—the world of logic, of philosophy, of reason—that could banish the ghost that plagued the woman he now, to his utter surprise, thought of as his beloved.

"Colin, I know you don't do this every day, and I appreciate it immensely. The next question, I suppose, is whether you can think of anyone who might perform such a ceremony?"

Andrew did not expect Colin to suggest anyone, but here the museum owner surprised him with an almost childlike grin. "You already know such a person, my dear fellow, and I would recommend her wholeheartedly, although I cannot promise she would do it."

Andrew looked at Colin, his head cocked to one side in a silent question.

"Flora Penwellan," Colin said.

"Flora at the Cobweb?"

"The very same. A gifted and gentle witch. Runs in her family. I knew her mother."

"Colin, I think she might help after all; this person's her friend."

"Well, then, I leave it to you. And welcome to our particular bit of old Cornish culture." Colin extended his hand and Andrew took it. The two nodded, and Andrew left.

From her studio, just across the narrow river from the museum, Nicola saw Andrew emerge and turn upriver toward the bridge. What was he doing there? Was he looking for her? At first, she thought she would call out to him, but she decided against it. What would she say? What could she do? And what did it matter, anyway? She threw herself onto the chaise by her easel and pounded the tufted upholstery in frustration.

Then an idea bubbled up out of her confusion, and she picked up the phone.

In places such as Boscastle, steep-sided valleys accentuate flooding by acting as huge funnels for the runoff and channel it very quickly down to the sea. Therefore, the high rainfall falling in such a short time could not be absorbed into the ground and a surge of water through the village of Boscastle estimated to have been in excess of 100 square metres per second created a 10–15 ft (3–4.5 m) high flood traveling up to 40 mph (65 km/h).

Boscastle Flood Special Issue,
Journal of Meteorology 29, no. 293

thirteen

On Sunday morning, Andrew was awakened by a peculiar, episodic crackling noise. In his dream, it was the sparking of a campfire beside which he was sleeping in a clearing in the woods near the meandering Charles River, in the gentle countryside upriver of Boston—but a Boston of a century or two ago. As he climbed up out of the dream, he understood gradually that the sound was more a rattle than a crackle. He opened his eyes, got his bearings, and saw the morning was already well advanced.

The rattle ceased, then began again, like hail against a roof. No, like gravel against a window. His kitchen window. He pulled on a pair of jeans, stumbled to the kitchen, and peered out. Sure enough, there was Lee, sitting on the stone wall. Also Nicola. Both of them were grinning.

He shook his head, as if doing so would make the apparition disperse, but it didn't change. They were still there, rocking their legs back and forth in unison and chucking gravel at the cottage. He sighed, put water in the kettle, turned it on, and opened the door.

"Ladies!" he barked. "It is barely daylight!"

"Uh-uh!" said Lee.

"Uh-uh!" said Nicola.

They seemed immensely pleased with themselves. He wandered back inside, desperate for tea. The girl and the woman skipped in behind him as if they belonged there.

"We thought you were gonna sleep *forever,* like Sleeping Beauty!" Lee chided as she hopped up to sit on the counter by the sink.

"So how come I got gravel instead of a magic kiss?" Andrew grumped.

"We couldn't find any handsome princes," Nicola said, clamping her hand over her mouth, her shoulders bouncing with suppressed laughter, in which Lee, naturally, joined, though she didn't understand the joke.

"Why aren't you getting ready for church?" Andrew asked the girl.

"Nicki and me are going to a different church, a *really old* one!"

"Older than St. Symphorian's or Minster?"

"Uh-huh," Lee said, casting a quick glance at Nicola for support. Nicola nodded.

"What's your mother think of this arrangement?" he asked. The kettle clicked off and he poured the steaming water into a teapot.

"Mum's poorly," Lee said. "Says she has a summer cold or something. She said it was fine."

"And you two needed to inform me of your devotional plans"—he glanced at the clock—"at this ungodly hour because . . . ?"

" 'Cause you're meant to come with us! Right, Nicki?"

"If you'd like," Nicola said looking at him, her eyes soft, her voice signaling a kind of apology.

"I need some breakfast," Andrew groused, now playing up the role of the put-upon victim.

Nicola came over to the counter, used her hip to push him gently aside, cut a thick hunk of crusty bread from the loaf Andrew kept under a kitchen towel, slathered it with butter, and then drizzled it with honey from the crock on the windowsill.

"Petit déjeuner, monsieur," she said, handing it to him on a paper napkin, privately admiring the thicket of curly, graying hairs that furred Andrew's chest. "Come on, you'll like it," she added, her French failing her.

Andrew slumped his shoulders in resignation and shuffled off to the bedroom to look for a shirt. Then he came back out and asked, "What's the appropriate dress for this church?"

"Oh, it's quite casual," Nicola said lightly, flashing a quick wink at Lee. "And it's a bit of a hike to get there."

Lee was wearing her usual faded khaki shorts, T-shirt, and wellies. Nicola had on hiking sandals with lugged soles, a flatteringly snug pair of black capri pants, a tailored white cotton broadcloth shirt with the collar turned up in the back, and a black-and-white-striped silk scarf tied around her forehead, Indian style, its tails trailing down to her left shoulder. Once again, he marveled at how lovely she was with so little artifice. He retreated to his room again and put on a faded blue chambray shirt, socks, and his boots. In the kitchen, he grabbed his honeyed bread, filled a lidded traveler's mug with milky tea, and followed the ladies out to Nicola's car, which turned out to be a farm vehicle: a rugged old olive-green four-wheel Land Rover Defender. Lee climbed in the back, joining a delighted Randi, who hammered the rear wheel well with his wagging tail like a maniacal conga drummer. Andrew took the passenger seat, and the moment he clicked his seat belt, Nicola rocketed up the farm track and turned right onto the main road south toward Tintagel. They were driving along the shoulder of the coastal ridge, which swept down across a broad shelf that once had been a beach at a prehistoric ocean's edge. Farther west, the shelf dropped down to the roiling sea, now far below.

At a hairpin curve in a narrow, lushly forested valley about three miles from Boscastle, Nicola pulled the car to the left shoulder, brought it to an abrupt stop, and yanked up the parking brake lever. She looked at Lee through the rearview mirror and said, "Long way or short?"

"Long way!" Lee said, bouncing in her seat as if she was attached to an elastic band.

"Good call; Randi needs the exercise," Nicola said as she climbed down from the car. Randi and Lee exited through her door and Andrew stepped out of his, by which time the others had already walked several paces back in the direction from which they'd come. He hesitated.

"Come on, then," Nicola called over her shoulder. "It won't kill you to walk a bit."

He slugged back the last of his tea and followed them up the hill to a cluster of stone cottages called Trethevey, at which point they turned right and followed a farm track uphill past an ancient well and then up to high grazing meadows. The girls chattered away and Randi raced ahead, coming back every few minutes like a child checking in with his mother. After perhaps half a mile, the lane plunged into a leafy hollow, and Andrew could hear the low rumble of falling water.

"Am I permitted to know where we're going?" Andrew finally asked.

Nicola smiled. "That's a secret, but just now we're going to St. Nectan's Kieve."

"Kieve?"

"Waterfall, silly," Lee piped up.

"Never heard of it," Andrew griped.

Lee looked at Andrew and then at Nicola, to whom she said, "He doesn't know much, does he." It wasn't a question.

Nicola laughed and gave the girl a hug. "He's not one of us, sweetie."

"One of what?" Andrew asked.

"That's a secret, too," Lee announced.

These two are thick as thieves, Andrew mused happily. He thought how lucky Lee was to have an adult friend with whom to share secrets, and once again mourned not having had children of his own. Maybe Nicki did, too.

"So who's this St. Nectan character?" he asked, knowing Lee would roll her eyes, which indeed she did.

"Fifth-century Celtic holy man," Nicola answered. "Came over from Ireland and apparently was a hermit here at some point. There's a lovely church dedicated to him in Stoke, near Hartland, up on the Devon coast. But it's believed that this glen was a place of reverence and healing much earlier, in pre-Christian times."

Andrew was going to ask how anyone could know that, but he bit his tongue. This was Cornwall, after all, a land of legend and mystery, a place where people still believed that "piskies" lived in woods like this one.

The trio continued to descend until they passed through a gate beside which were a wooden box with a coin slot and a sign announcing admission prices.

"Somebody owns the waterfall?" he asked.

"The waterfall and the hermit's cell, yes," Nicola said. "In fact, the cell is in their basement. But the owners know me from the museum, so it's all right." The path now led through a dense thicket of rhododendron and laurel, and as they advanced, the noise of the waterfall grew to a roar.

Lee pulled Nicola down toward her and whispered something in her ear. Nicola clapped her hands and said, "Oh, yes; let's!"

"Close your eyes," Nicola ordered Andrew. Lee took one of his hands and Nicola slipped behind him, pressed her body against him, and covered his eyes with her hands.

"No cheating," Lee warned.

Andrew didn't protest; he could feel the warmth and softness of Nicola's breasts against his back. He caught a faint fragrance—musky, with a touch of spice—from the inside of her left wrist. He hadn't the slightest interest in breaking free. The two frog-marched him another dozen yards or so through the damp, thundering air, until finally Nicola took away her hands, stepped back, and said, "Okay, open."

And it was a splendid sight. Ahead, a stream from somewhere high above them flung itself over a shelf of shale and dropped some six or seven stories—Andrew, the city boy, couldn't help measuring distances in blocks and stories. It fell through a series of intermediate shelved pools, launching itself again and again into the void. In the last of its leaps, it foamed beneath and through a stone arch before finally clattering to the rock-choked streambed below.

The three stood as if hypnotized by the cataract, their eyes returning repeatedly to the lip at the top and following the water as it plunged in that odd slow-motion way water does, as if it were somehow simultaneously lighter and more viscous than it actually is. Andrew marveled at how this thing so insubstantial you could not hold it in your hands for more than a moment could nonetheless carve its way down through the layers of blue-brown Paleozoic rock, slicing through ancient history, micron by micron.

Randi, however, was bored. He barked only once and then wheeled off downstream along the footpath through the shrubbery.

"I guess we're leaving," Nicola said with a chuckle. Lee took her hand and, reluctantly, Andrew followed.

St. Nectan's Glen proved to be a cool, leafy, steep-sided gorge through which the stream hastened, as if it smelled the nearby sea, much as a horse knows it's nearing its barn long before the structure is visible. They crossed a narrow footbridge and climbed up the opposite hillside and out of the valley, eventually crossing a sunny meadow sparkling with oxeye daisies and buttercups. A stile in the stone hedge on the other side led to a narrow lane that twisted steeply downhill to the main road, joining it just above the bend where they had parked.

Instead of returning to the car, however, Andrew's guides surprised him by crossing the road and continuing downstream. The trail passed a handsome old stone gristmill nestled in a sunny hollow, crossed the stream again, and then edged around a series of ever-higher rock outcrops and pillars, many hung with verdant buntings of glossy English ivy.

"What's this place called?" Andrew asked, feeling oddly rude for breaking the magical stillness of the air around them.

His question met with an incredulous look from Lee and a forgiving smile from Nicola.

"Rocky Valley," she said.

"Duh," Andrew said, grinning.

A little farther down the valley, they arrived at the ruins of two neighboring stone structures. Another mill, Andrew realized when he discovered the grindstones half buried in the rubble. He was about to ask Nicola about the place when he realized she and Lee had disappeared.

He found them bent over and staring at the face of an exposed wall of shale behind one of the ruined buildings. As he approached, he realized that with their forefingers they were tracing the circuitous outlines of a labyrinth design cut into the rock face. The carving was delicately incised and a little over a foot in diameter. As he watched, they moved on to a second, nearly identical labyrinth of connected concentric circles a few feet away. Again, they traced it with their fingers, as if performing some silent ritual. Andrew found a brass plaque attached to the rock face that said that the stone-carved labyrinths dated from the Bronze Age, between 1800 BC and 1400 BC, and were believed to have religious significance. Somewhere in the back of his brain, he heard a discordant note, but before it could fully register his attention was drawn to the rest of the cliff face.

Tucked into every nook and cranny, wedged into every crack and seam, as high as a human being could reach, there were tiny, fetishlike objects: a miniature baby shoe, a toy dog, a tiny model boat, a doll no more than an inch high, and simpler items—a button, a key, a piece of string tied in an elaborate sailor's knot, a pyramid of small shells. Nicola herself was pushing a polished cowrie shell into a cleft in the rock. She gazed at it in its niche for a few moments, then dipped her head and closed her eyes. He looked around further and realized there were bits of fabric tied to many of the branches of shrubs and trees surrounding the narrow rock grotto. Scratched into the rock face were cryptic messages: "Our little Claire is always with us," "You are not forgotten, Brian," and more. Lee stood off to one side, her hands clasped loosely below her waist, and was preternaturally quiet, as if in a trance.

Nicola lifted her head, turned to Andrew, and smiled peacefully and with unabashed affection.

"Welcome to church."

Andrew blinked.

"Here in Cornwall, the practice of witchcraft survives and thrives. It's very gentle and mostly about acknowledging the power and the blessings provided by each of the turning seasons, revering the flow of the natural world. It helps us find our place in that flow. It tries to bring us into harmony with it."

"So you really are a witch?"

Nicola laughed. "No, I'm not nearly that far along. I'm just learning about witchcraft, partly from working at the museum, but also by talking with friends of Randi's former owner."

"She was a witch?"

"Oh yes, a revered one. I'm told that many people in and around Boscastle sought her advice and help over the years. There are times when I think her spirit lives on in Randi; I don't know how else to explain how he senses things so much more acutely than other dogs."

Andrew looked again at the artifacts strewn about the area.

"And all this?"

"Offerings—prayers, if you will. This has been a holy place for millennia, as the marker next to the labyrinths explains. Believers in this area are simply carrying on a very long tradition of communing with the spirits and with nature in this special place. Labyrinths like these are common symbols of the gateway to the spirit world."

"What's with the pieces of fabric tied to all these branches?"

"They're *clouties,*" Lee piped up. "You tie them on and make a wish."

"And do the wishes come true?"

The girl shrugged. "Maybe."

Nicola took his hand. "Come on," she said. "There's more to see."

The three of them followed the dog across another footbridge and continued downstream. The little river was rushing now, cutting its way through a narrow rocky gorge. The outcroppings that had hung above the valley upstream now merged into a continuous corridor of ever-higher cliffs. The valley itself had become a constricted, twisting defile. One could almost imagine the stream elbowing the cliffs aside in its headlong rush to the sea.

Randi raced ahead and disappeared around a bend. Lee dashed after him. When Andrew and Nicola turned the corner, too, he came to an abrupt stop and said, simply, "Wow."

Nicola smiled. "I thought you might like this," she said.

Invisible until you rounded the bend, what lay before them was a wedge-shaped pocket of deep, boiling ocean into which the stream they'd been following flung itself with all the abandon of a lover meeting her long-absent mate. Charcoal-black slate cliffs rose almost vertically on both sides, creating a sharp contrast to the brilliant white surf foaming on the rocks below with each incoming surge. Gulls wheeled on the updrafts and salt spray blew back from the cleft at the base of the cove. Apparently oblivious to the lethal tumult below, black-faced sheep grazed at the very edge of the cliff face, the wind off the ocean rippling their thick, creamy coats.

Out over the ocean, the sky was busy. Vast tracts of milky blue were broken by towering cumulus cloud masses and, closer to the water, fuzzy fast-moving squall bands ruffled the water where showers met salt. Had it been afternoon, with the sun low in the west, there would have been rainbows. Even so, the colors dancing on the undulating surface of the water were myriad, and put him in mind of one of Nicola's paintings.

Nicola and Andrew had been sitting peacefully, a few feet apart, watching the seascape and keeping an eye on Lee, who clambered around on the rocks. They hardly needed to; Randi was herding the girl as if he were a border collie and she an errant ewe. Eventually, Nicola rose, put two fingers in her mouth, and startled Andrew with a piercing whistle. Both dog and girl turned and headed back.

On their way back up the narrow valley toward the car, Andrew stopped by the ruined mill to look again at the labyrinths. Something about them bothered him, and, after a few moments of studying, he grasped what it was, what had caused the soundless discord when he'd first seen them and read the plaque.

"Lovely, aren't they," Nicola said.

"Yes, and that's the problem. They're *too* lovely."

"I don't follow you."

"You see how clean and delicate these incisions are? There's no way they could be Bronze Age. The tools they had then were too primitive. To do something this precise, this sharply defined, you'd need hardened steel. But, you see, materials like that didn't exist then."

"I thought you were an architect; since when did you become an archaeologist?" There was an edge in her voice, and instinctively Lee moved off with the dog. Andrew, in his certainty, missed the signal, and drove home his point, instead.

"Okay, okay; let's forget the matter of tools. This rock is shale. Shale is sedimentary and relatively soft. It erodes when exposed to water, and it fractures and crumbles when it freezes. Hell, that's how this valley was created; with enough time, water cuts through this stuff as if it were butter. Anything carved in this rock thirty-five hundred years ago would have disappeared altogether in just a few centuries of rain, flooding, freezing, and thawing. And that's not even counting the way the roots of plants, like all this ivy, would break up the rock face."

"Um . . . guys?" Lee was back. Nicola ignored her. Randi barked twice—his warning.

"Listen, Mr. Know-it-all," Nicola said, her voice rising, "this has been a holy place for centuries;

just ask anyone around here! Who the hell are you to say it's not?! A week of stone-wall building and now you're a rock expert, too? Give me a break!"

This time, Andrew could hear the shrill edge to her voice. He softened his. "Look, Nicola; I'm not trying to insult you. It's just that, well, I don't think these labyrinths are any older than that tumbled-down mill behind you. I think they both date back about a hundred and fifty years. Tops."

"Nicki? Drew?" It was Lee, more insistent this time. "The wind's changed, and look at the sky back that way."

She pointed toward the ocean, and the two adults followed her finger. The girl had sensed what neither of them had: The sky over the cove was as black as the slate cliffs surrounding it, and the wind had picked up and was sharp with the tang of ozone. At that moment, there was a single crack of lightning, close by. Even as they stood there, drops of rain the size of marbles began hammering the ground around them, raising little puffs of dust in the dirt and splattering the stones of the old mill like gunshots. The argument instantly forgotten, the three of them ran up the path. Randi led the way.

By the time they climbed into the Land Rover, the squall had passed, but they were soaked to the skin. Skinny Lee looked like a drowned rat. Nicola's white cotton blouse had turned trans-parent, and Andrew realized she was braless. His own shirt was much the same and clung to him like skin. It should have been a moment of hilarity, a sort of impromptu wet T-shirt event. Instead, apart from the damp panting of the dog in the back, no one spoke, and the atmosphere in the car was electric as they drove back to Bottreaux Farm. Even Lee, who had romped through the downpour gleefully, was quiet, her clear blue eyes panning back and forth between the two rigid people in the front seats, trying to parse the body language of silent adults.

They lurched to a stop in front of Shepherd's Cottage and Andrew got out. He stood with the door open, leaned in, and said quietly, "I'm sorry I spoiled things."

Without turning away from the windscreen, Nicola said, "Not everything in creation is amenable to rational analysis."

Andrew nodded and closed the door. The car sped away down the track toward the farm.

AFTER SHE DROPPED off Lee, after she chatted amiably for several minutes with Roger (Anne was still in bed, still under the weather), after she got home, changed into dry clothes, brewed a pot of tea, and climbed up to her studio, Nicola was still fuming. Who the hell did he think he was—Sherlock bloody Holmes? What right did he have to question what everyone with any sensitivity at all had always understood intuitively—that Rocky

Valley was a place of magic? Why had he been so insistent, so dogmatic? Even if the stone carvings weren't Bronze Age—and, in truth, she had to admit his arguments made sense—why was it so terribly important for him to be right? What did he win by winning? For that matter, what did *she,* if she prevailed?

Nicola sipped her tea and stared out the tall window beside the chaise. The sun beat down on the quayside, and tourists wandered below licking melting ice-cream cones. If it had rained in Boscastle earlier, as it had in Rocky Valley, the sun had burned away any trace. On the other side of the river, the witchcraft museum was doing a brisk trade. Why was she drawn to these beliefs and practices? Why was it suddenly so important for her to defend them?

She understood that part of the attraction was really the effect of repulsion: Her Catholicism hadn't protected her when she was being violated by her brother. Who could she go to, her priest? Not likely! In the church of her childhood, there were only three versions of women: the virgin, the wife, and the whore. Her brother had stolen the first of these. She'd turned to the second role and found only more abuse. Where did that leave her?

This new faith she found herself embracing rose from maternal, not paternalistic roots—a reverence for the Earth Mother and her consort, not the all-powerful Father and the hapless Madonna. In this gentler, more humane faith—if "faith" was even the right term—the female was elevated, not denigrated. Accepting and embracing what now, at last, seemed to her so obvious—the timeless cycle of the seasons, the wheel of the year, the noble and graceful stages of birth, growth, ripening, decline, death, and rebirth, on and on, throughout history and beyond—made her feel an integral part of the universe, rather than a pitiful and damned speck within it. Here there was no "original" sin—a notion she rejected instinctively whenever she beheld a newborn infant. There was no heaven, no hell, no eternal damnation for simply being human. Nor was this simply her Catholic dogma turned on its head; it was not the denigration of men and the worship of a vengeful, all-powerful woman. It was simply recognition of the purest, simplest, most obvious fact of nature: that woman is the source, that man is the parallel energy, that the two of them are forever partners, like the stamen and pistil of a flower, in the work of creating the world.

As she was sorting out these thoughts, it suddenly dawned on her that Andrew hadn't actually challenged her beliefs; he'd only questioned the true age of the labyrinths. She'd somehow conflated the two things at the time, as if his analyses were intended to undermine the still-setting concrete of her new beliefs. She'd lashed out. Ridden right over him. Silenced him. Moreover, she'd flatly rejected his apology.

Nicola groaned and slid down on the chaise.

Randi trotted to her side and cocked his head, first to one side, then to the other. He blinked. He barked once. She swore he smiled.

"Oh, shut up, you idiot dog! I already know. I've screwed it up again."

Rainfall radar loops show that the shower cells initiated over the high ground of North Cornwall, at around 1330 Greenwich Mean Time (GMT) on the 16th. These grew in structure and then an almost constant "shower train" sat over the area for at least two hours.

Boscastle Flood Special Issue,
Journal of Meteorology 29, No. 293

"I don't think Nicki was very happy with you yesterday."

"Thank you, Harry; what a wise wizard you are."

Lee shot Andrew a look. She had been sitting on the wall outside his door again, reading her Harry Potter, when Andrew emerged from his cottage Monday morning. Now she had the book buried in her little forest-green knapsack. The two of them were walking through the Valency valley toward the port. Andrew had promised to help Jamie and Becky with the new hedging volunteers; he wasn't entirely sure what Lee's agenda was, other than to point out that he'd blown it the day before. It would have been annoying had he not been so fond of the kid . . . and had it not been so true.

"I'm just saying . . . ," Lee continued.

"Yeah, yeah. I know."

". . . that maybe it's not so bad to believe Rocky Valley is magical. A lot of people do."

Andrew recalled all the little offerings tucked into niches by the carvings, and the bits of fabric tied to tree branches nearby.

"Just because maybe the labyrinths aren't so old doesn't mean there isn't magic there anyway," she concluded.

This was a reasonable position, Andrew mused, so long as you believed in magic in the first place.

Certainly, Rocky Valley was an enchanting place, and he had to admit it was more than just that the place was visually dramatic. Was there a sort of continuum from "enchanting" to "enchanted"? From "magical" to "magic"? Maybe this was somehow similar to the inexplicable way he had gone from being attracted to Nicola to understanding—very much to his own surprise—that he loved her. How had that transition occurred? What was the point along that particular continuum where certainty emerged? If that was a question that eluded rational analysis, that could not be ascertained through deductive reasoning, then why not other aspects of being? Why not magic?

It was an odd morning, the air close, almost sticky on the skin. There was almost no birdsong, as if there were insufficient oxygen from which to create trills and chirps. Andrew was moving slower than usual. After the unpleasantness at Rocky Valley, he'd moped around his cottage a bit and finally gone down to the Cobweb late Sunday afternoon. He wanted to talk to Flora, but it turned out that she'd gone off duty after the lunch crowd cleared out. So he sat at the bar and had a bag of salted crisps and couple of pints, then a couple more, then ordered a dinner of shepherd's pie and another pint, and finally wandered unsteadily home, collapsing into bed before eight.

"Gonna rain this afternoon," Lee announced, apropos of nothing. "A lot."

Andrew looked up at the milky-blue sky. "What makes you so sure?"

"I just know. Dad was gonna cut hay today, but I told him not to. He always listens to me about stuff like that."

This sort of thing no longer surprised him. Lee seemed to live closer to nature than anyone, much less any child, he'd ever known. It was as if she occupied some sort of nether zone between the world of humans and that of animals and plants. More magic, perhaps. Or just the magic of childhood.

They stopped by the weir that had once fed water to the mill downstream.

"This is as far as I go," Lee said.

"Got plans, do you?"

"Uh-huh."

"What kind?"

"Just out and about. You know, exploring."

"Okay, kiddo. Thanks for the company this morning. And the advice."

Lee smiled, turned, and skipped back the way they'd come. He watched her until she rounded a bend and disappeared. The girl was enough to make you believe magic was an everyday occurrence. Then he turned downstream to meet Jamie and Becky.

THE NEW HEDGING crew had been at it for nearly four hours when the rain started. As had been the case the week before, it had taken only a couple of hours for the group to sort out their respective roles and settle into a steady rhythm as the new recruits gained skill and confidence. Stone by stone, section by section, the new hedge lengthened beside the car park along the bank of the River Valency. Jamie had been levering a particularly large grounder into place when one of the volunteers pointed out the cloud, like a massive black-and-blue bruise, that had appeared in the otherwise blue sky to seaward. The valley was so narrow, they hadn't seen it coming.

Jamie squinted at it for only a moment, laid down the iron pry bar he'd been working with, looked at his watch, and shouted, "Right, lads, time for lunch. Indoors, I should think. The Cobweb!"

The rain began as a mist. As they put tools in Jamie's van, it settled on the crew's dusty clothes so lightly that it was like dew on leaves. But by the time they'd hurried across the road to the inn and ordered drinks, the clattering hiss of raindrops on the steaming pavement outside could be heard even within the pub.

HIGH UP IN the Valency valley, near the village of Lesnewth, which Andrew had walked through two days earlier, the rain gauge recorded that it was raining at the rate of nearly two inches per hour.

• • •

JAMIE WAS SITTING on a stool at the bar, chatting up Flora, who was wearing a deeply plunging, décolletage-revealing, knit blouse—in keeping, she would have said if asked, with the sultry weather.

"You mark my words," Flora said as she leaned on her elbows opposite Jamie, "in fifteen minutes, this place'll be cheek-by-jowl. Here we are a seaside village, and everyone comes to walk the cliffs and see the harbor, but when the rain comes, everyone wants to be in the pub. You watch."

"I don't know, Flo," Jamie said. "Might be the scenery in here that draws 'em."

"Go on, you dirty old man," Flora protested, with a grin. She slipped off to attend to another customer, but not without giving the stone craftsman a lascivious wink.

And sure enough, in they came, tourists who'd been nosing about the harbor and the gift shops and had dashed up the street to shelter, ramblers in dripping anoraks who'd been out hiking the coast path, and passers-through who decided a shower was a good excuse to stop for a pint. In no time at all, the pub was jammed, and Flora and the manager, Alan, were working at full tilt taking people's orders.

Andrew had been standing to one side, talking with the new volunteers but also enjoying the spectacle of his mentor, Jamie, courting Flora in his sweet if awkward way.

He envied Jamie. He would have liked nothing better than to have the kind of warmly affectionate relationship with Nicola that Jamie and Flora seemed to have, one in which intimacy had grown, like a hedge, stone by stone, upon a foundation of history and mutual acceptance. Andrew had no such history with Nicola. And as for mutual acceptance, well, that seemed to come and go like the tide in the harbor. What Andrew knew with certainty was that whenever he was with Nicola, his heart felt like it was about to become airborne, to lift, as if winged, from his chest. And yet whenever he tried to really reach her, whenever he tried to offer her some part of himself, share some part of his mind or heart, it backfired. She could be so warm and playful and, on occasion—like that moment by the waterfall the day before when she'd pressed against him to cover his eyes—downright sexy. And then, as if someone had thrown a switch, she could turn distant, withdrawn, even icy. He felt perpetually off balance, and none of the crutches he'd relied upon in the past—rational thinking, walling himself off from feeling too much, being an observer rather than a participant—worked. He wasn't rational when he was with her; he was flooded with emotions he hardly comprehended—awe, excitement, affection, need, protectiveness, tenderness. The sturdy stockade he'd always been able to depend upon to shield him from uncertainty, cupidity, dissatisfaction, and anger from Katerina was gone. When Nicola flared, it was as if his heart were made of dry tinder and she was intent on immolating it. Try as he might, he could not maintain a safe distance; there did not seem to be a distance that was safe. She flashed so quickly between warm affection and blowtorch anger—or fear, or something else he didn't yet fully understand but thought was connected to her dead brother—that it was dizzying.

And yet despite all this, despite the damnable and persistent prickliness of the woman, he was more sure every day that he'd finally found the woman he was meant to be with, the woman who was both his match and his counterbalance, the woman with whom anything was possible.

If only he could stop screwing up.

The rain stopped entirely at about 12:45, and the sun came out a few minutes later. Jamie's gang returned to their labors. Jamie had given Andrew the task of overseeing the hedge builders, while he and two assistants found and laid big grounders ahead of the crew. It was so humid that everyone was soaked with sweat. Quick, sometimes fierce, sun showers swept over the valley from time to time over the course of the next hour and a half, but the hedgers were grateful for the cool rain, and afterward their shirts steamed in the sun as they worked. The hedge progressed at a pace that seemed glacial, and yet when Andrew stopped to check their progress, he was amazed to see that they'd advanced several feet.

LEE WAS GETTING cranky. All morning, acting on advice from Elizabeth at the Visitor Centre, she'd been hunting newts in the boggy spots higher up in the Valency valley, without success. Among the lush, violet-strewn water meadows far upriver, she'd seen legions of pearl-bordered fritillary butterflies and, every once in a while, a dive-bombing dipper flying right into the water to seize aquatic insects. In the oak copses there were flashes of color from electric-purple hairstreak butterflies, too. And hovering just above the surface of the river, she'd seen two linked golden-ringed dragonflies, whose wings fluttered so fast they seemed invisible. It wasn't until she began returning downstream again, to the shadier parts of the valley, that she began to find the newts, along with creepy slow worms—a bronze-colored kind of legless lizard. Apart from the on-again, off-again bursts of rain, she'd had a lovely time. The showers were more an annoyance than anything else; they came and went so quickly it was hardly worth one's while to look for shelter. But she felt sticky and dirty as she poked around under rocks beside the river.

She'd been having a streamside lunch just below the little cluster of cottages called Newmills when she heard the dull rumble of thunder. She looked at her watch and was surprised that it was already coming up on three o'clock, and she still had a long way to go to get back down the valley toward home. She'd just tucked her Harry Potter into her backpack when a bolt of lightning flashed directly above her. There was a moment of absolute silence, and then the air sizzled and erupted into the loudest, closest, scariest crack of thunder she'd ever heard. This was no low growl; this was like Zeus cracking a spectacularly big whip directly over her head, just like in the Greek myths she'd learned about in school. Almost immediately, the rain hit. She grabbed the backpack and raced downstream to a spot where, in another time, the curving river had cut overhanging ledges out of a cliff of night-black slate. She ducked beneath one of them and was amazed that she could barely see the other bank of the stream; the rain was falling so hard it was like being behind a waterfall.

THOUGH IT WAS at that moment sunny in Boscastle, Andrew heard the thunder and looked up at Jamie. Jamie, in turn, was looking up at the sliver of sky above the narrow valley. Downstream, over the harbor, the sun threw diamonds across the ruffled surface of the water. Upstream, though, the sky was black as a crow's wing. Andrew noticed that the river—only some twenty feet wide and clasped in its ancient stone channel—was rising. Though the afternoon showers in Boscastle had been tolerable, clearly, somewhere else it was raining much harder. There was another flash of lightning, and, as if there was an intuitive channel of communication between them, Jamie and Andrew nodded to each other.

"Lads and lasses, you're in luck," Jamie announced. "It's an early day we'll be having today. But I'll expect you all bright and early tomorrow, raring to go!"

The novice crew cheered and groaned, in rough proportion to their respective ages, and began the process of cleaning up the work site and putting away tools. A few headed for their cars, but several returned to the Cobweb. Jamie locked the van, looked at Andrew, and they, too, repaired to the pub. Becky had already left for an appointment with a local landowner.

A LITTLE AFTER three o'clock, beneath the darkest of the clouds, the Lesnewth rain gauge far up the valley registered rainfall at the rate of nearly six inches per hour.

THE COBWEB WAS even more crowded than at lunchtime. The two men eased their way through the throng, and when Flora saw them coming, she had two pints of Doom Bar ready for them. Jamie executed an awkward bow in her direction.

Andrew took a quick slug from his glass but found himself feeling oddly restless.

"Back in a bit," he shouted into Jamie's ear above the din, but the older man just nodded, his attention otherwise engaged by the fluid movements of the voluptuous woman behind the bar.

Out in the street, Andrew was struck by how loud the rain was. What had sounded like the noisy hiss of static earlier was now a low roar. He pulled the drawstring on the hood of his anorak tight and wandered down the street past the row of attached buildings called Bridge Walk, ducking under awnings where he could. When he rounded the corner of the Riverside Hotel and followed the sidewalk onto the two-lane bridge, the sun came out, and he realized the roar was not the rain, but the river. He peered over the parapet and was stunned by what he saw. A stream that was normally clear as tap water was now black as graphite and flowing at a terrific speed, its normally comforting burble an angry, fraught rumble, as stones carried by the flood tumbled along the bedrock in the streambed like dice in a cup, punctuated now and then by the dull thud of rolling boulders. And in the few moments it took to take all this in, he realized it was only a matter of time before the muddy flood reached the cottages downstream, including Nicola's. He ran off the bridge and down the lane along the south bank of the river to her house and pounded on the door. No answer.

He opened the door and called again. Again, no response. He stood there for a moment, then looked across the tumbling river and saw the Museum of Witchcraft. Of course. She was at work. He dashed across the footbridge and saw the river, so thick with sediment it was viscous, slip over its banks just upstream and spread, slowly but without interruption or hesitation, like an ugly tide.

LEE KNEW IT was time to do something. The thing was, she wasn't sure what. She had been huddling beneath the ledge for nearly half an hour and there had been no letup in the rain. For most of that time, she'd been excited by the scene before her. She loved lightning and thunder; it thrilled her to feel the air shudder, the vibrations penetrating into her bones. But that part of the storm seemed to have passed now and there was only the relentless rain. She'd been staring at it for a while now, enjoying the way it made all the familiar features of the landscape soften into a blur, as if they were melting.

She didn't notice until it was too late that while she was safe in her niche in the cliff, the footpath had been flooding both above and below her. Where earlier had been a well-beaten path, there was now only swirling, frothy water, dark as licorice. And the slightly elevated platform beneath the slate overhang where she'd been sheltering was getting smaller by the moment as the water rose.

A high-pitched screech, like hard chalk scraped across the blackboard at school, but much, much louder, pulled Lee's attention to the river upstream. This was followed by a strange whooshing sound, and then a thud. And suddenly, she knew it was a tree that had crashed into the river. Almost as suddenly, she realized the footpath was reemerging; the river was dropping. She picked up her backpack, slung it over one shoulder and ran pell-mell downstream toward home.

IT TOOK A while, given the amorous distractions, but eventually Jamie realized Andrew hadn't yet returned to finish his pint. Now, a pint of real ale was, in Jamie's expert opinion, a delicate thing, and something one did not want to let sit for very long. That slight effervescence, so much more subtle than the assertive fizz of an imported lager—he could not for the life of him understand the attraction among young Britons to gassy American swill like Budweiser—that gentle tang, did not survive long out of the cask. So, naturally, he drained Andrew's pint and set off through the bar, thick with dampish humans, toward the front door to see what had become of his friend.

He knew almost the moment he stepped into the street that something was wrong. Unlike Andrew, he understood instantly what the deep, thundering noise was, and he took off at a dead run to the car park. It was almost completely filled with cars, and dozens of people stood beside the stone hedge his crews had been building, watching the roiling river, which even here upstream was close to bursting its banks.

"People," he said calmly as he reached them, "I think it might be wise for you to stand back from the river and, if you have autos in the car park, to remove them to higher ground. You are in some danger here."

One or two men nodded and moved away toward their cars, pulling their gawking spouses after them, but the rest seemed hypnotized by the scene before them: the churning black water, the chunks of debris flowing downstream, the steady rise in the river level. It had now topped the channel edge and was inching toward the base of the new hedge.

He turned from them and climbed into his van, reversed out of the lot, and drove up the steep road to the north, pulling onto the verge just above the newsagent's shop. He locked the doors and jogged back downhill to the pub.

Inside, no one seemed to have the slightest idea what was happening outside, or to much care. He wrestled his way to the bar, catching nasty looks from more than one bloke waiting to order, and got Flora's attention.

"Listen, luv, this is important: The river's topped its banks, and I reckon there's more to come. So we need to get these folks out to their cars and heading up the hill. I want you to promise me you'll stay upstairs, in the dining room, out of harm's way. You'll be safe here. Tell Alan he needs to assume there'll be water in the bar. I don't know whether it will get this high, but he needs to deal with it. He needs to deal with it right now."

There wasn't the slightest indication of a problem in the cozy confines of the Cobweb, and Flora lifted an eyebrow and gave him a look.

Jamie caught it. "Flora, I'm going to tell you right here and now: I love you, lass. But you're in danger. We all are."

Flora stood stock-still for a moment, then grabbed Jamie's shirtfront, pulled him across the bar, and gave him the wettest kiss of his life. Then she released him, and while he tried to catch his breath, she bellowed, "All right you lot, here's the latest news: The river's risin' fast and the car park's about to be flooded! If you value them fancy BMWs and Land Rovers out there, you'd all better look to your vehicles. No rushin' about, mind you; nice and easy out the door, please."

No one moved.

She slammed her beefy hands on the bar. Glasses danced. "Oi!" she shouted. "Is there somethin' about *out* we don't understand? Bar's closed, got it? Drinks are the least of your worries, people. Out you go, then, everyone." Like a plump-breasted mother hen, Flora came out from behind the bar and, arms spread wide as if to corral vagrant chicks, edged the crowd toward the door. It was only when they got outside that they truly understood. The river, which normally slipped quietly through its channel beyond the car park and behind the connected stone buildings of Bridge Walk, had formed a second route, a shallow but fast-flowing delta that spread across the lot and consolidated again to speed down the main street, oblivious to the constructions of man on its headlong rush to the harbor.

Some of the Cobweb's customers gathered up their family members and dashed through the intensifying rain to their cars. Despite the fact that it was midafternoon, the light was sepulchral, as if a shroud had been thrown across the roof of the village. Cars started and headlights snapped on. Taillights reflected on the surface of the water streaming across the macadam. The cars bunched up at the entrance as drivers tried to decide which direction to take. Those who had been to Boscastle before knew to turn right and head uphill to the north, in the direction of Bude. Those who did not, or were simply too stubborn to recognize the obvious, turned left toward the bridge over the raging river, only to be stopped there by the flood. Many of the Cobweb's patrons stood as if paralyzed along the pavement, too fearful to move uphill or toward their cars. Flora shooed them back into the inn and up the stairs to the formal dining room, a space typically reserved for weddings and funerals.

Jamie strode across the street, itself a fast-flowing rapids, to help people in the car park. He'd only got twenty feet when the water swept him off his feet.

Lee reached the footbridge for the path up to Minster Wood and the farm just in time to see the river lift the delicate wooden structure off its footing on the north bank. Slowly, even gracefully, it pirouetted some ninety degrees until it angled downstream, dangling from the footing on the south side. Then it toppled sideways into the flood and was gone.

Lee watched this event transfixed. She'd had no idea water could do such a thing, and the born observer in her was fascinated. In fact, she found the entire experience of being in the storm—of watching the placid river she knew so intimately turning into something altogether different and powerful—thrilling, exhilarating.

But as she continued running along the sodden path downstream, for there was nowhere else to go, from upstream she heard a groan like that of an agonized beast, a crash, and then a low rumble, lower in pitch than any thunder she had experienced before, followed by more crashes. She was at the edge of the meadow above the weir when she turned to look backward, even though she'd already intuited what had happened: The fallen tree that had dammed the river and lowered its level downstream had given way. Squeezed between the slate outcroppings on the north bank and the steep, forested slopes on the south, a ten-foot wall of water, black as night, was twisting its way down the valley with the speed of a train, tearing at everything in its path and carrying a tangled mass of roots, limbs, trunks, and shrubbery at its crest. And in a moment, her excitement turned to panic.

Lee did the only thing she knew to do, the only thing she had time to do: She sloshed through the rising, fast-moving water by what had once been the riverbank and threw her arms around "her" tree, the one steadfast, familiar thing left in a landscape that was changing from pastoral to diabolical before her eyes. The wall of water and debris hit when she'd climbed halfway up to her accustomed perch. The gnarled sessile oak lurched, but its deep roots held. Lee clung to her tree with the passion of a child clutching a parent; the oak was her protector. After the first surge passed, she climbed higher. She expected the flood would lessen after the wall of water passed, but it did not. It kept rising, inching up the twisted trunk of the ancient oak.

A FEW YARDS downstream from the witchcraft museum, Trudy Walters was watching the river from one of the arched windows of her shop, the

Harbour Light. The store, which specialized in nautical clothing and gifts and also served rich Cornish ice cream in the rose-bedecked garden terrace out front, had been busy all morning. The sporadic rain had driven most of her customers to cafés or either the Cobweb or the Wellington Hotel after lunchtime, but now the sun was out and the garden was once again filled with ice cream customers. Though she could see the river rising, she wasn't much concerned. The building that housed the shop, a whitewashed former pigsty with a picturesque swaybacked stone roof, had been there for more than three hundred years. It had seen everything.

But by 3:30, Trudy decided it was time to take precautions. The river had risen before. Indeed, there had been serious flooding back in 1959. The exterior frame of the shop's front door was equipped with slats to hold storm boards. Trudy and an assistant thanked their remaining customers, locked the garden gate, and slid the storm boards down the slats to protect the door. Then each of them headed home.

AT 3:35, THOUGH the sun was shining in Boscastle, the rain gauge at Lesnewth recorded rain at the astonishing rate of nearly a foot an hour.

COLIN GRANT WAS descending the exterior stone stairs from his library and office at the Museum of

Witchcraft just as Andrew arrived. Colin had been working with his usual bookish concentration upstairs and had only just noticed the river out his window. He'd come down more out of curiosity than worry. Andrew changed that instantly.

"River's over its bank just upstream, Colin," he yelled above the din of the rapids behind him. "Where's Nicola?"

"Ticket window." Colin peered around the corner of the building and immediately returned. He yanked open a door beneath the stairs and pulled out a uniform jacket for the coast guard. "Tell Nicola and the others to shift what exhibits they can to the upper floor. I'm the town's coast guard; I've got to get to the bridge and warn people away."

Andrew went into the museum. The light was dim and there was soft, New Age music playing. The river's roar barely penetrated the museum's ancient, thick stone walls. Nicola looked up and smiled. Then she saw the tension in Andrew's face and the smile vanished.

"The river's flooding. Colin says you're to get your visitors out and take what you can upstairs. He's gone to warn people on the bridge. The water's already risen to within a few feet of your cottage." Nicola came out to the door and looked across the river to her house. Randi stood beside her, his body vibrating with anxiety.

"Shit; I should have paid attention."

"What are you talking about?"

"Randi's been barking all morning. He knew."

Andrew looked at them both, shook his head in disbelief, and said, "I'm going to go help Colin."

"You got your white horse tied up outside?"

"Horse?"

"You know, knight in shining armor on his white horse; protecting the citizenry . . ."

"Not funny. Look, the sun is shining, right? But the river is full to overflowing. That means it's raining hard somewhere up in the hills. And the way this valley's shaped, there's no place for that water to go but straight through this village. The tourists are strolling around the flooding banks and standing on the bridges gawking like this is some kind of a spectacle staged for their benefit. That's how people get killed: by not thinking. Don't be one of them, okay?"

This was something new for Nicola. Until now, Andrew had seemed a shy but brainy chap, sort of an intellectual, though also easygoing. But here was another Andrew: assertive, direct, responsible, taking charge. But caring, too. His worry was palpable.

"You're right," she said. "I'm sorry. Go; I'll tend to things here."

A moment after he left, she ran out of the building and called after him, "Take care of yourself, okay?"

But the noise of the furious river drowned her out.

• • •

JAMIE HAD ROLLED and slid across the car park in the swift floodwater until he slammed up against a parked car. He got to his feet and leaned on the vehicle to catch his breath and discovered there were two middle-aged women inside, rigid with panic. In the same instant, he felt the car lift slightly and begin to drift. He yelled for help to the crowd gathering on slightly higher ground near the pub. People looked at one another helplessly, but finally a couple of heavyset men waded out into the flood, holding each other's hand for stability, and inched toward the car. Jamie yanked open the door and coaxed the first of the women out of the passenger seat, passing her to the nearest man in what was becoming a human chain. The other woman seemed incapable of moving, paralyzed by fear.

"I can't swim!" she cried, and tears etched tracks through her heavy pancake makeup.

"I'll tell you a secret, luv," Jamie said in the kindest voice he could muster given the circumstances. "Neither can I. Which is why we both need to get away from this car before it goes bob, bob, bobbing along right out of here and into the harbor. Ready, then?"

The woman managed a single nod.

"You'll have to climb over here to the passenger door, then, dear; I don't want to risk us being on the downstream side. Understand?"

She nodded again. Finally, she hitched up her skirt, clambered over the gearshift, and fell into his arms. She even found the presence of mind to kick off her heels. Then he passed her to the outstretched hands of the other men. He looked around and could see other people trying to get to their cars, becoming frightened, and giving up. A couple with a small child in the middle of the lot had climbed up to the roof of their Mercedes, and now Jamie headed for them, placing each foot carefully, moving crabwise across the current. Some of the other men who had been helping saw where he was going and followed. It took some persuading, but Jamie finally got the mother to release her hold on the little boy, and the men passed the child from hand to hand like a water bucket at a fire until the boy reached safety. The mother followed, but the husband hesitated.

"It's brand-new!"

Jamie was momentarily confused, then understood the man was talking about his car.

"That's why God invented auto insurance, mate; now get off of that roof before your wife has to check into your life insurance as well!"

By 4:15 P.M., the rain gauge at Lesnewth had recorded rain averaging between 100 and 150 millimeters (4 to 6 inches) per hour for more than an hour and a quarter.

• • •

BY THE TIME Andrew reached Colin on the south side of the upper bridge, it was raining torrents again. Colin had the coast guard vehicle parked there with its emergency lights flashing. They were joined by a team from the fire brigade from the nearby village of Delabole, who were wading about shepherding people toward higher ground.

"It's still rising!" Colin shouted. "I just phoned an incident report to headquarters in Falmouth. You can hardly credit it, but people keep trying to get on the bridge to watch. Bloody idiots! Help me string emergency tape across the road."

Andrew nodded. They stretched the blue and white tape between two poles on the north side and were just crossing to the south side again when, upriver, they saw a small red Ford shooting down the river's channel like a kayak. Colin looked at it in disbelief as it swept beneath the bridge toward the sea.

"Definitely speeding," he deadpanned.

"Nobody in it, thank God," Andrew noted. Seconds later, it slammed into the smaller, lower bridge downstream. The water there was already too high. The car twirled like a top for a moment and finally got wedged, nose down, beneath the bridge arch, the ebony flood churning like surf around and above it.

As they were cordoning off the south side of the road bridge, Andrew looked up Dunn Street, the steep one-way road that ran from the upper village to the harbor, meeting the main road just past the Wellington Hotel.

"Jesus," he said. The narrow street had become a river itself, channeling water nearly a foot deep downhill at frightening speed. People parked there were trying desperately, and largely unsuccessfully, to reverse their cars uphill away from the flood. Pedestrians trudged up the same hill in muddy shin-deep water, clinging to walls and fences as they went, slipping often.

"Oh, bloody hell!" he heard Colin cry. Andrew thought Colin was looking up Dunn Street, too, but when he turned he realized the man was facing upriver, his mouth open. Andrew followed his gaze and froze. Far up the Valency, at the curve just above the car park, a wall of water at least a building-story high was bearing down on the village. And not just water. Tons of debris and entire uprooted trees, their root masses upturned like hideous bouquets, were borne along, bouncing and twisting, on the foaming crest of the wall like so many weightless straws. And as it advanced, it mowed down everything in its path.

Andrew had been worried about people's safety ever since the river broke its banks. Now he knew people would die.

With rainfall readings now confirmed in the vicinity, it seems likely that nearly 200 mm fell in the space of four hours.

Boscastle Flood Special Issue,
Journal of Meteorology 29, No. 293

fifteen

Lee's special friend Elizabeth Davis, manager of the Visitor Centre at the south end of the main car park, was at a distinct disadvantage as the flood-waters rose. The center was designed to face the lot, not the river behind it, so it was a surprise to her when she realized there was water flowing through the entry hall. The storm had been an annoyance all afternoon, and the power in the building had failed several times, but she'd been too busy rebooting the center's computer to pay much attention to what was happening outside. When she understood that a safe exit was no longer possible, she closed the double doors and called both the fire brigade and the Environment Agency, to whom she reported. She also turned off the power. There were two families of five in the Visitor Centre at the time, along with Elizabeth's assistant.

Despite the closed doors, water rose in the center. First, the group moved to a raised children's play area. Then, when Elizabeth realized that this area, too, would soon be underwater, she shepherded parents and children up a ladder into the storage loft. They had just reached safety when the wall of water smashed into the building. The whole structure shuddered. There was nothing upstream of the Visitor Centre; it was the first point of resistance. Though it was a relatively new stone building, the front doors could not withstand the attack and failed. The ground floor was immediately inundated. Upstairs, what had seemed to the children an exciting adventure now became frightening. While trying to keep them occupied and their parents calm, Elizabeth called her husband, who worked for the county council, so he could let the police know where they were hiding. It was one of the last cell phone calls from Boscastle; immediately afterward, the phone service failed. Soon thereafter, so did the power. Each time Elizabeth peered down to the ground floor from the loft, the water had risen another rung on the ladder.

JAMIE HAD SEEN it coming, or rather had heard it—a thunderous rumble as the cresting river churned through the upper valley, tumbling boulders beneath its surface and lofting anything that floated to its surface. Thankfully, when it hit, there was no one left in the dozens of cars and camper vans still stranded in the lot. The instant he saw the wall of water, he understood that its effect would be catastrophic. Though it hadn't come from schoolbooks, Jamie knew his physics. He knew a cubic foot of stone weighed between 100 and 150 pounds. He knew that a cubic foot of water weighed only a little over 60 pounds. But he also knew that water moving at ten miles an hour exerted a force of more than 250 pounds on a given cubic foot of stone, and guessed that this mass of water and debris was moving at more than forty miles per hour.

And he knew the new hedge would fail.

It did so with grace, however, and this gave Jamie some semblance of comfort. The wall of water ignored the curve in the riverbend and aimed directly at the car park. It hit the hedge of stone and, to his amazement, passed right over it. It was only a few moments later, as the stronger force far beneath the surface of the flood worked on the base of his creation, that the entire structure seemed to soften before his eyes and slowly, elegantly melt away. It put him in mind of something without real substance, like a bowl of ice cream dissolving on a sunny café table. It made no sound as it vanished—at least no sound he could hear above the thunder of the flood itself—and Jamie thought this a form of passing he would like to emulate when his own time came. It was dignified, a sort of yielding to the inevitable.

THE CONNECTED SHOPS along Bridge Walk—the continuous block of stone-built structures that included the Cornish Stores general store, the Spinning Wheel Restaurant, the Rock Shop, the Boscastle Bakery, and the sixteenth-century building that housed the Riverside Hotel—had become an island in the stream. The Valency normally ran peacefully behind the buildings, and the apartments above the shops had balconies to take advantage of the river view.

There was a small footbridge over the river leading to tables in a popular tea garden on the bank opposite the hotel. Both had vanished. The front side of this block of buildings normally faced the main road through town. The road, too, had disappeared, to become an entirely new branch of the Valency—a vicious, snarling water beast that ripped at anything in its path and carried with it a swirling, pitching stew of half-drowned automobiles, trees, recycling bins, fences, and traffic signs, all of it just so much detritus purged by what seemed an insanely vengeful God of Street Sweeping, intent on flushing the entire village into the ocean.

Jeffrey and Sheila Miles, owners of the Riverside Hotel, had evacuated guests from their rooms and diners from the restaurant sometime after 4:00 p.m., when water began seeping under the back wall, behind which the river flowed. The guests fled quickly; no one paid his bill, but it hardly mattered. Jeffrey had decided that the newer concrete building that housed the Cornish Stores at the other end of the block would be better able to withstand the flood and had hauled Sheila uphill through the now knee-deep water to shelter with the owners, their friends André and Trisha LeSeur.

Jeffrey and Sheila were so intent on reaching the

Cornish Stores, and on doing so without being swept away, they barely noticed the fire brigade volunteers frantically working to secure the front door of the Boscastle Bakery against the rapidly rising floodwater. Inside, Ethan and Debbie Churchill and their two young assistants had been baking batches of saffron buns in the bakery's massive gas ovens when, as at the Riverside, water began seeping through their back wall. The fire brigade volunteers, who'd ducked into the bakery to phone for more emergency assistance, knew what those outside did not: that it was suicidal to be wading through the flood at the rate it was rising. They ordered the bakery staff upstairs and, once the outside door was secured, they plodded—in firemen's boots that having been overtopped by the floodwater now felt like lead weights on their feet—to the next shop, the Spinning Wheel Restaurant. Once inside, they struggled to force the doors closed against a thigh-deep torrent. Neither they nor the restaurant owners, Rory and Jennifer Dunn, would ever use those doors again, because at that moment, the wall of water that had crashed through the car park now swept past the shops and instantly raised the water level to halfway up the restaurant's windows. The fire brigade members and the owners retreated to the apartment upstairs.

At the Rock Shop, Sandy White had sensed trouble the moment she noticed water gushing through the street. She did a quick assessment of the shop, locked the front door, and calmly began boxing up what was most valuable: the wine. When she'd carried the last of the cartons upstairs, she phoned her husband, Ron, who was off on a buying trip in London, and told him to double his orders. "I think we may lose some inventory," she said. In fact, they would lose almost everything.

Next door at the bakery, the river smashed through the back wall and flushed everything in the shop, including the massive oven, out into the street, where it was gripped by the current and ripped downstream to the harbor.

The sheer force of the cresting river shook the Cornish Stores to its foundation, and André and Trisha led Jeffrey and Sheila and a crowd of other people who were sheltering in their shop to what they thought would be the safety of the apartment above. Soon afterward, however, they all fled across the rear balconies, directly above the churning main course of the river, to the apartment where the Dunns and the firemen were. And still the water rose—ugly, brown as porter, and furiously fast—until it had reached half a foot above the floor of the Dunns' apartment. It was time for the crowd, now numbering forty souls, to climb to the roof.

ANDREW AND COLIN, still on the south side of the main bridge, had been astonished when the wall of water Colin had spied failed to follow the course of the river and disappeared behind the Visitor Centre and the Bridge Walk block. Moments later, they watched helplessly as, one after another, waterborne vehicles careened down the road, past the turning to the bridge, and carried on downhill, following the lower ground along the lane that paralleled the north bank of the river. As each sped past, they strained to look for passengers, but at times the rain was so dense it was like a curtain between them and the opposite shore.

Something had been nagging Andrew's subconscious ever since he'd watched people struggling uphill against the current on Dunn Street, and now it came to him: Last Wednesday, on his way to the weekly sing in the bar of the Wellington Hotel, he'd learned that the River Jordan, the main tributary of the Valency, passed directly under the venerable building through an ancient stone culvert. Now, as he and Colin had been left no task other than to watch as what felt like the whole village was being washed into the sea, he yelled to Colin, "Back in a few minutes; need to check something!"

Colin nodded but did not turn his gaze from the flood before him.

Andrew plodded uphill—"upstream" would have been more accurate—along Dunn Street until he reached the back of the Welly. He wasn't surprised to find its owner, Peter Williams, there as well.

Williams looked up, recognized Andrew, and

said, "It'll never hold. It's just not meant to carry so much water."

"We need to get everyone out," Andrew said.

"My wife's already going from room to room," Peter said, "but half the village is in the bar."

"Then you'll just have to evict them, won't you?" Andrew said, grinning, the rain streaming off the tip of his nose.

"And the sooner the better, though I don't imagine they'll much appreciate being driven out into this; it's pissing down."

Peter was right, they didn't. At first, he was genial: "Ladies and gentlemen, neighbors and friends, I know it's far from closing time, but we're closing just the same. I think we may be in danger here."

There was a rumble of voices, a murmur of dissent. And there was very little movement.

"Right, then!" Andrew said as loudly as he could while still sounding friendly, his arms spread wide. "The landlord says out, and out it is! May I just invite each and every one of you to exit the front door with as much speed and grace as you can manage. I have it on good authority that while it is indeed tipping down out there, you are unlikely to dissolve."

With remarkable good humor, the crowd dissipated. Andrew followed them and headed down the street to rejoin Colin. Peter and his wife exited the hotel from a door upstairs. Moments later, the

River Jordan, carrying a careening burden of boulders, trees, and mud, smashed through the upstairs wall of the hotel, broke through to the floor below, and cascaded through the Welly's famous Long Bar, shattering its beams, flooding it with thirteen feet of debris-choked floodwater, and filling it with 120 tons of mud.

TRUDY WALTERS LIVED in a cottage on the south side of the river, across the footbridge from her shop, the Harbour Light. She had just brewed a pot of tea. She took a cup to her front window and saw, for the first time, that the main force of the river was no longer in its neatly bordered channel, but racing full throttle down the lanes paralleling the channel, and, on the far bank, sweeping debris and cars through the garden in front of her shop.

At the same moment, floodwater burst through her own front door, quickly filling the ground floor of her cottage. She hurried out the rear, up to the garden terrace cut into the hillside above, and then up a ladder she'd had built to enable her to ascend to the main road, which did a switchback above her house. She had no opportunity to look back. Thus it was that she was spared the moment when the venerable, three-centuries-old Harbour Light building, with a sigh like a last breath, collapsed into the flood and was sucked downstream like so much driftwood. It made hardly a sound, as if its seniority rendered complaint undignified.

ONCE THE CAR park was clear of people, Jamie retreated to the flood's edge, where crowds, unaccountably, still milled about in the downpour, gazing at the disaster before them as if hypnotized. He tried one more time to urge them up the main road north out of town, and then turned toward the Cobweb, which, because it was on slightly higher ground, had thus far avoided the kind of massive inundation its neighbors had suffered.

Flora met him at the door.

"I thought I told you to stay upstairs," he snapped.

Flora ignored this and pulled him toward her in a full-body embrace.

"Be quiet, you," she whispered.

Jamie relented. He was exhausted.

"I've been watching you from upstairs, you maniac. Did you think you could rescue the entire car park?"

"It was worth a try," he said weakly. "Any chance of a pint?"

ELIZABETH, HER ASSISTANT, and the two-family brood in the loft of the Visitor Centre had been able to keep their spirits up in the dim light by means of the stories, games, and songs she improvised to distract the children. This strategy had been largely successful . . . until, at about 5:00 p.m., another massive wall of water and debris smashed into the building. The upstream two-thirds of the structure imploded and was torn away in moments, engulfed in the torrent. By some miracle, the loft was in the portion of the building that survived. But when Elizabeth saw that the water now was up to the top rung of the ladder they'd used, she pushed the Velux skylight open as far as it would go and she and her assistant helped the parents and the children up to the apex of what was left of the roof.

Exposed to the downpour, straddling the roof peak and the lower apex of the building housing the Visitor Centre's public restrooms, Elizabeth and her stranded families felt that if they didn't drown from the flood, they would surely drown from the rain itself. Visibility was nil. So when a new sound found its way through the thunder of the river and the scream and thud of collapsing buildings, Elizabeth struggled to place it: a rhythmic *whomp-whomp-whomp* that throbbed in her bones, not just in her ears.

"And then I realized what it was," she would later tell a reporter. "I felt like Radar O'Reilly on that American television show *M*A*S*H*. Incoming helicopters!"

Earlier, in far northern Scotland, the rescue coordination center at the Royal Air Force base at Kinloss, on the Moray Firth near Inverness, had responded to initial police and coast guard reports of a flood at Boscastle by scrambling rescue helicopters based at RAF Chivenor, fifty miles north of Boscastle, in Devon, and the Royal Navy Air Squadron base at Culdrose, forty-five miles to the southwest, in Cornwall. Rescue 169, a big yellow RAF Sea King, was first on the scene. It made its initial pass through nearly impenetrable rain and hail, with lightning strikes happening almost continuously at higher ground. Moments later, another Sea King, the red and gray RNAS 193, approached from the south along the coast. Marine captain Pete McLelland, peering down from his copilot's seat through the teeming rain, watched as a swollen fan of coffee-colored water surged out of the harbor into the bright green sea, followed almost immediately by a churning mass of debris, trees, and automobiles. They dove close to the sea to look for trapped drivers, but could find none, and, in any event, most of the cars were tipped nose down, like feeding ducks, by the weight of their engine blocks.

Responding to a police report, the yellow RAF helicopter went off to deal with a reported heart attack. RNAS 193 then dipped into the mouth of the valley.

Several of the crew members were veterans of the first Gulf War, but what they saw below horrified them nonetheless: the valley, from hillside to hillside and in both directions—indeed, the entire lower village—was one vast, raging river. "My God," McLelland heard someone say through his earphones. He looked at his wristwatch; it was 5:10 p.m. Then he radioed the rescue center at Kinloss: *Pass to all emergency services. This is a major incident. Repeat, major incident. We require all standby aircraft and all available land-based emergency crews, as we are in danger of losing Boscastle and all the people in it.* Within minutes, three more rescue helicopters had been scrambled and were en route to the disaster site.

Hovering only fifty feet above the rooftops, Rescue 193 first winched to safety a family of four from a rental property near the bridge. They had barely cleared the helicopter doors when McLelland saw something that clenched his heart: two little girls in pink blouses sitting atop the spindly remains of a structure he would later learn had been the Visitor Centre. The closer they flew, the more survivors he saw stranded there, atop a ruined building that was the first line of defense against the tons of water that tore through the valley.

ANNE TRELISSICK WAS in her flagstone-floored farmhouse kitchen, warming herself by the Aga stove, drinking tea, and trying to shake off the last vestiges of the cold or flu or whatever it was she'd been fighting for several days. She was listening to the afternoon program on BBC Radio Cornwall, when the host, Rosie Dunkley, was interrupted by Matt Small, the newscaster, with breaking news that roads around Boscastle were being closed due to flooding. Though the rain had been unusually heavy, up on the hills above town there hadn't been the slightest indication that something terrible was happening down in the valley. Anne's first reaction was skepticism. Her second sent her flying out into the rain to the barn, where Roger was mucking out manure.

"Roger! Where's Lilly?"

Her husband looked up, smiling. "In a world of her own, I expect." Then he saw the fear in his wife's eyes.

"Annie. What is it?"

"The radio says Boscastle's flooding. Lilly told me she was going hunting for newts in the valley today. She's not back."

"Lilly's a smart, resourceful girl, Anne."

"Roger! The valley's flooding; she could be anywhere!"

Roger put down his pitchfork, walked up to his wife and gave her a hug, and said, "I'll attend to it. I'll pop down to the bridge below Minster Wood and give a shout."

Roger Trelissick was by nature unflappable, and while his wife worried about their daughter all the time, he did not. His family had lived in this part of Cornwall for centuries, and the fact that there were "most people" and the "special people" was just second nature to him, passed down through the generations. He didn't discuss it with his wife, but

342

he knew, as certainly as he knew the temperament of his animals on any given day, that his daughter was one of the rare ones. He viewed her with a combination of pride and awe. Lilly knew things. Sensed things. Appreciated things "normal" kids did not. And he felt as if she was a timeless treasure left in their safekeeping. He climbed up onto his four-wheel all-terrain vehicle and raced up the farm track, the little motorcycle engine screaming. For the first time in his life, he was afraid for his girl.

Just beyond Minster church, where the footpath down to the river began, he skidded to a stop and, careful to keep from breaking an ankle or a leg on the steep, muddy footpath, ran as fast as he could down through the woods, calling out his daughter's name. But before he'd descended even two-thirds of the way into the valley, his ears told him what his heart had been trying not to admit: that the valley was inundated. The river's roar was deafening. The charming, pastoral, stair-step shelves of riverbed slate, their shallow, musical waterfalls and limpid pools, were buried far beneath a pandemonium of churning chocolate fury. So high was the river that Roger was forced to stop well above what he knew to be the valley floor. If the footbridge still existed, which he doubted, it was at least ten feet below the current level of the flood. And even as he stood there, stunned, the river was ripping trees whole from the saturated ground and spinning them down-stream as if they were made of nothing more sub-stantial than milkweed. The sleepy Valency, he would later tell others, had become evil, a destroyer.

Running, hunched, ducking under sagging branches and stumbling over ivy vines, Roger ran along the hillside as far upstream as Newmills, calling Lilly's name, only to be halted by the fierce rapids of a tributary stream-turned-river that barred further passage. He reversed and clambered back along the same east bank, ducking beneath ancient oaks, weaving around thickets of wild rho-dodendron and laurel, still calling. But the river was so incredibly loud, like a cacophony of tim-pani, it was as if his words were snatched from his mouth and drowned before they could become sound.

He did not know what to do but return to his wife, banking, insanely, on the strange but com-pelling wisdom of his odd little daughter.

WHEN ANDREW RETURNED from the Welly, he was elated by the sight of the two helicopters sweeping in from the harbor. But Colin was nowhere to be seen. He glanced around in the murky light and caught a glimpse of the coast guard jacket to the south of him, in the direction of Nicola's cottage on the south side of the river. Colin was clawing his way back upstream;

Andrew waded down to help the man, who looked at the end of his tether.

"Had to check the cottages," Colin gasped as they reached higher ground. "All empty, I think."

"You think?" Andrew said.

"I hope," he said between breaths. "Nicola."

Andrew's head turned as if jerked by a wire. "What about her?"

"I tried to get her out, but she was adamant about having to save someone called Ella," Colin shouted over the noise of one of the now-hovering copters. "Don't know who she was talking about. A friend staying with her? I couldn't get her to come with me. She said she'd be fine. Nothing more I could do. Now look," he said, jerking his head downstream.

Andrew looked and was stunned.

Far downstream, he could just make out Nicola's cottage—or what was left of it. The river had gnawed its way through the front wall on the ground floor. The door, the two small, multipaned windows, all were gone, leaving only a gaping hole with the upper story suspended above it.

"I have to find her," Andrew said. He set off into the water, but Colin grabbed him.

"Don't be an idiot!" he shouted. "She's either safe or gone, and you can't do anything to change that. God only knows how many we've lost already!"

Much as he struggled, Andrew knew Colin was

right. The river, if that was even the right word for the roaring beast before them, was destroying everything it encountered in its headlong rush to the sea. He wouldn't have stood a chance. He felt something now that he hadn't throughout the entire afternoon: a crushing personal terror. It swept aside his habitual rationalism the way the flood flushed cars effortlessly to the sea. It was simple and basic. It was beyond analysis. It was pure fear: Nicola might be gone.

"Andrew!"

He spun on his heel and looked uphill toward the voice. Just above the cordon, Roger Trelissick was climbing down from his ATV.

"Have you seen Lilly?" her father yelled.

Andrew glanced downstream again to the ruins of Nicola's cottage and then trudged up to meet Roger.

"Not since this morning. We walked together for a bit. Said she was going up-valley."

"Lord help her; she's missing!"

"Jesus, Roger; did you check below Minster Wood?"

"Tried, but the bridge is gone. Hell, the whole bottom of the valley up there is underwater! I was hoping she was with you. Or Nicola."

"Nicola was alone when Colin saw her a while ago."

Roger stood in the rain, drenched. And Andrew watched as the man's face went from hopeful to desperate. Andrew was suddenly overcome by the sheer extent of the devastation around him: physical, financial, human. Only this morning, he and Lee had been strolling happily through the meadows along the quiet riverbank in the sun . . .

And suddenly, Andrew knew.

. . . much of Cornwall had a dry and fine sunny day, with a maximum temperature of 22.6 degrees C. Beaches were well-populated.

Boscastle Flood Special Issue,
Journal of Meteorology 29, No. 293

"Roger!" Andrew shouted.

The farmer had just climbed back onto the ATV.

"I might know where she is!"

Andrew raced up the hill.

"Can we get to the river below your farm?" Andrew asked as he climbed up and straddled the seat behind his friend.

"The Jordan's overtopped the road. Police have everything closed off. We'd have to go overland. Where is she?"

"I want you to understand it's only a hunch, Roger, okay?"

"I'll take whatever I can get!"

"Right, then: she has a favorite tree—"

"What?"

"Yeah. A big twisted oak by the river near the weir. She likes to climb into it and read. It's like she thinks she and the tree are friends."

Roger shook his head. It didn't surprise him in the least. He gunned the ATV. "Hang on!"

Andrew gripped the handles at his hips, and they raced up the switchback main road south out of the lower village. Instead of taking the main road to Camelford, Roger jerked the four-wheel farm motorcycle up a narrow lane, around the ancient Napoleon Inn, uphill past medieval cottages, and east.

"We'll cut through Paradise!" Roger shouted, and Andrew wondered if Roger was hallucinating. The landscape looked anything but: The lane was more like a stream than a thoroughfare; the gardens and fields were ripped bare by sheets of floodwater. He later learned that the lane paralleled a stream called the Paradise. They seemed to be going a long way away from the valley, but Andrew just hung on. When they reached the high fields at the crest of the valley, Roger jerked the handlebars left and they plowed through the flooded bed of the upper reaches of the Paradise. The rear end of the ATV slewed sideways in the current, but Roger gunned the engine and powered out of danger.

Then they were plummeting downhill through fields Andrew knew were Roger's.

"Do you have any rope at the farm?" Andrew bellowed into Roger's ear.

Roger simply nodded, and they barreled across fields and farm lanes. They lurched to a stop by one of the barns. It was still raining, but not with the intensity that it had been. In moments, Roger was back with a thick loop of rope tossed over his shoulder, cowboy-style.

"Where's this tree?" he yelled as they rocketed off downhill again.

"Below the footbridge and just above the weir!"

"We'll have to go down through the woods on foot!"

Andrew just patted the man's back. He could only imagine the fear the father felt. He prayed—something he was unaccustomed to doing—that his hunch about Lee was right.

Roger finally stopped at the edge of a thicket of brush and trees and tore off into the woods. Andrew followed. The two men crashed through the undergrowth and clambered down the steep slope of the valley toward the river roaring below. The ground was as slick as grease, and they fell, slid, stood, and fell again, repeatedly, as they struggled downhill.

When they reached the racing river, Andrew could recognize nothing.

"Where's the weir?" he called.

"Under there!" Roger called back, pointing to the swirling maelstrom of water and debris below them.

Andrew headed upstream, most of the time on his hands and knees, gripping branches to give him stability in the slimy morass of mud and leaves on the hillside. Roger was right behind him. A few minutes later, Andrew stopped. Below him, leaning more than he remembered, but still stubbornly clutching the ground with its roots, was Lee's tree. Around it swirled a torrent of brown, whitecapped water. The noise was incredible. There was no way Lee could have heard him if he called, so he peered through the rain looking for a sign of her in the tree's canopy. He searched to no avail until the wind picked up and shuddered the leaves, and there, in the crotch of two branches, was a little girl in khaki shorts and a T-shirt. She was clutching a battered red and white umbrella.

NICOLA HAD BEEN standing on a dining chair in front of the fireplace, lifting Laura Knight's exquisite *Ella: Nude in a Chair* from the wall above the mantel, when the river tore her front door off its hinges and flung it across the room as if it was made of balsa instead of thick pine.

Instinctively, she leaped from the flimsy wooden chair to the floor as a three-foot wall of inky water surged through the room, the flood rising as fast as water filling a bucket beneath an open faucet. Moments later, when she reached the stairs to the studio, the portrait under one arm, both front windows imploded, sending glass shards and wood fragments skimming across the oily, roiling cesspool that had once been her sitting room.

With the water rising quickly, she clawed her way up the rest of the flight to her studio. Upstairs, she pulled a drop cloth from the floor and wrapped the painting in it, clutching it to her breast not so much because of its monetary value, but because it was her one tangible connection to Sir Michael.

She stood at the long window as if nailed to the floorboards. Outside, the scene before her would have been unimaginable, a nightmare, were it not so obviously and hideously real. The humpbacked stone footbridge, across which she'd fled after locking up the museum, was buried beneath the flood. Cars, vans, recycling bins, even the venerable red public phone booth that had stood across the street from the Welly, sped by below her on the waves. Suddenly, she felt very alone and wished she hadn't left Randi with the museum staff when she ushered them out to the terrace above the building—not that he'd be anything but sympathetic company. A power failure had thrown the windowless museum into pitch darkness and halted their work rescuing artifacts. Now, beneath her, furniture thudded against the walls as water whirlpooled through the sitting room. She had the bizarre, if momentary, sensation that she was watching an old black-and-white newsreel with modern Dolby sound effects. Despite the maelstrom downstairs, she felt safe in her sturdy seventeenth-century fisherman's loft.

This illusion lasted for perhaps two minutes. Speeding out of the gloom on the surface of the rushing river, an entire tree, big as a bus and stripped of its August leaves and most of its branches, hurtled directly toward her house. It was just like what she'd read about in stories: a disaster approaching as if in slow motion, the kind that gives you plenty of time to think, which is to say the worst kind. She grabbed *Ella* and fled to the back of the loft, praying the tree would slide by.

But her prayers went unanswered.

• • •

ANDREW GRABBED ROGER'S shoulder and pointed toward the swaying oak in the middle of the flood. Roger's face flashed from desperation to almost heartbreaking relief when he, too, saw the umbrella. While Roger tried vainly to call out to his daughter, Andrew sat on the muddy slope and studied the current. It was an architectural problem, he realized: a matter of angles and forces. After a few minutes of silent calculation, he started crawling upstream, pulling the rope behind him. Roger understood immediately and followed. The idea was to fix the rope to a tree on land and have one of them go downstream with it to Lee's tree. If they could get to it, and get Lee down, they might be able to get her back to the hillside to safety.

There was a brief shouting match about who would stay ashore and who would go with the rope. But Roger was a much bigger and stronger man than Andrew, and they agreed he needed to be at the pulling end. They clove-hitched one end of the rope to a well-positioned young alder that so far had survived the flood, and Andrew wrapped the other end around his waist, cinching it with a quick-release knot—glad now he'd helped Katerina learn her climbing knots. And then he entered the river.

His plan was to ease himself into the flood, slip downstream, and use his feet to stop him whenever he got swept away. This strategy worked well for perhaps twenty seconds, at which point subsurface debris knocked his legs out from under him and he spun on the end of the rope, alternately above and below the water, until his feet found purchase again and he sputtered to the surface. The principal advantage of this unintentional maneuver was that Lee saw him.

"Drew!" she screamed. It was the scream of a very frightened, very little girl.

"It's okay! Come down!"

"No way!" A stronger, more Lee-like voice this time.

Andrew ignored her and concentrated on his footing, inching closer to the tree. The boulders in the streambed were constantly on the move. He'd steady his feet on one and, almost immediately, it would be swept out from under him. His ankles and shins were constantly under attack from shifting rock and branches. Twice more he went under, but each time Roger held him tight and he was able to right himself in the rushing, mud-choked water. After perhaps ten minutes of this battering, Andrew was closing in on the tree, though still swinging wildly in the current. He began wondering how Roger would ever get them back to shore. Lee's father let out one last length of rope and timed it perfectly; Andrew slammed into the trunk of the tree, caught his breath, and began climbing toward Lee, the climb made easier by the fact that thanks to the flood, he was already in the lower branches.

• • •

LIKE A HUGE, out-of-control lorry, the massive tree trunk tore through the front of Nicola's cottage, as if the whitewashed wall were made of paper instead of stone. The entire building shuddered and the massive beams and pegged joists supporting the upper story groaned.

Nicola clung to the banister at the top of the stairs as the house lurched. The glass in her beloved studio window shattered, but the frame held. There was no way to know how long the structure would last, and she knew she needed to flee. But like many old cottages, there was only one way out: down the stairs. And the lower floor was flooded to the ceiling. Unlike her neighbor Trudy, she had no back garden; her house was backed by a sheer slate cliff face.

When she heard the rescue helicopters thumping up the valley, her head instinctively jerked upward and she saw, at last, her escape. She placed the wrapped portrait on her paint stand and, with her eyes clenched tight, smashed a wooden chair through the glass of the old skylight in the loft's sloping rear roof. On the second try, it splintered like an antique Christmas ornament, raining razor-sharp shards on her head. She shook them out of her hair as best she could, then pulled a folding step stool beneath the hole. With a pillow from her bed, she snapped off the remaining bits of glass in the window frame. Then she tied the drop cloth holding *Ella* around her neck and, grateful at long last for her height, pulled herself out onto the wet slate roof.

But that was as far as she could get. The distance to the roof peak was too great and the slate too slick for her to climb higher. And so she sat there in the downpour, her feet braced against the frame of the skylight, and prayed the cottage would hold.

BY 5:15, THE rain gauge at Lesnewth had recorded no significant rain for nearly forty-five minutes; in Boscastle, however, the rain was so diabolically heavy and the visibility was so poor that Captain McLelland called to the crew in Rescue 193, "Check your orientation points in case we ditch!"

ANDREW HAD JUST managed to coax Lee down through the tree limbs toward the rushing water and the rope when he heard a shout.

"Andrew!"

He peered through the branches and saw Roger scrambling furiously upslope, and, a moment later, he saw why: yet another wall of water was funneling down the narrow valley, one so choked with debris that the water was barely visible, as if the surging mass were a torrent of trash. Effortlessly, the tidal wave ripped the young tree that held their rope from the ground like so much brush. Andrew tore open the quick-release knot at his waist and watched the rope whip away through the branches like a line on a harpooned whale.

"See?" Lee yelled, and just for a fraction of a second, he wanted to throttle the wise little kid. Instead, they climbed higher into the venerable old oak.

And there they sat. Roger had disappeared.

"Where's Daddy?" Lee cried, clinging to Andrew's soaked shirt. And Andrew prayed that he hadn't been sucked into the flood.

What Andrew didn't know was that Roger had heard the helicopters farther down the valley. Now, with their own rescue plan destroyed, he'd scrambled back up the hillside to his ATV. At the edge of the woods, he threw downed limbs, leaves, and a bale of just-mown hay into a pile until he heard the hammering rotors of one of the helicopters again. Then he poured half the contents of his spare fuel can on the pile and lit it. There was a towering explosion of flame, and then a thick, white cloud of smoke as the wet leaves and hay burned.

Then he waited. He looked at his watch. It was nearly 6:00 p.m. The rain had stopped. He willed a helicopter up-valley.

Nicola was desperately cold. It might have been August, but the rain felt arctic, and as if it were trying to suck the life out of her. Her calves, flexed to hold her against the skylight frame, kept cramping. The hard roof slates felt like ice cubes through her wet slacks. She was at the limit of her courage, and her consciousness. She drifted off to that night, not even a week ago, when Andrew was caressing her on her chaise—how flushed with warmth she had felt, how full of life and joy and tenderness, how loved. And it was to this memory, as much as to the roof, that she clung, waiting, praying to be seen. But the helicopters seemed fully occupied upstream, above the heart of the village itself, and not down here near the harbor.

IT WAS THE copilot of one of the second wave of rescue helicopters, a bird from RAF St. Mawgan, who noticed the pillar of smoke in the valley. The chopper was on its way to respond to a report of stranded motorists in a shallow valley near Otterham, where the deluge at times had been even heavier than at Lesnewth, when Tim Llewellyn, a Welshman who, like the crewmen in Rescue 193, had also seen service in the Gulf War, tapped his pilot's shoulder and pointed down. A hundred feet below, beside the smoky fire, a man was pointing frantically west, toward the center of the flooded Valency valley. They circled once but, seeing nothing obvious, continued to Otterham. It was fifteen minutes later, as the helicopter returned to Boscastle after having lifted and dropped the motorists to safety, that the copilot saw the smoke again and, almost immediately thereafter, a flash of orange flame. Roger had thrown the rest of his gasoline onto the smoldering pile.

This time, the helicopter dropped and pivoted around the signal fire. Again, the fellow below was waving them toward the center of the valley.

Llewellyn peered into the canopy of trees as the pilot banked sharply and brought the aircraft low into the valley and hovered. And then, amid the mass of green and brown that was the valley floor, a flash of red appeared. Bizarrely, a man in a tree was waving an opened red and white umbrella. Llewellyn radioed his winchman in the back to prepare to descend again.

As they held position above the raging river, the downdraft from the blades tore the leaves from the old oak and its neighbors and whipped them into a green storm. In moments, the winchman was down, and, to Llewellyn's surprise, a child appeared from the foliage beside the man with the umbrella.

Robbie Campbell, the winchman, balanced on a limb and cinched the girl—who, to his amazement, was grinning broadly, as if this was the best adventure yet—to his chest, then signaled to be lifted. And up they went, spinning slowly in the back-wash, until another crewman pulled them both in through the side door. Then Campbell descended again for the man, and Andrew, too, was carried up to the hovering craft.

In the field beside the smoky bonfire, Roger Trelissick waved with both arms like a madman. Then he sat down in the wet grass and wept.

21:00 hours: First fire brigade relief crews mobilized from St. Ives, St. Austell, Newquay, Camborne, and Penzance. Helicopters return to bases. Over 150 people have been airlifted to safety by the emergency services. Cliff rescue and lifeboat teams continue to search for casualties.

Boscastle: The Flood (North Cornwall District Council, 2006)

seventeen

Lee clung to Andrew's soggy shirt like a limpet to a rock once the helicopter dropped them at the football pitch above town, like everyone else who'd been airlifted. Volunteers guided them down to the rectory, where Janet Stevenson, the vicar, enveloped them in care, served hot tea, and found them dry clothes. Andrew realized, with a suddenness that seemed like someone had thrown a switch, that he was utterly spent. He slouched in an easy chair, and Lee, dry now, curled into his chest. He held her there for all he was worth, as if she were life itself.

But his love for Lee—who'd turned out to be a little girl after all—and his joy at having found her, could not ease the dread he felt about Nicola. No one had seen her. No one knew where she was. And the people gathered at the rectory were so overcome by their own traumas they had little emotional energy left to give to someone still missing. Elizabeth, from the Visitor Centre, was the exception. Having herded her flock to safety, she moved through the little clutches of refugees asking after everyone's health, offering encouragement, reminding them how lucky they were.

"Nicola's missing" was all Andrew could say to her, and he whispered this, so Lee, who was dozing, wouldn't hear. Elizabeth looked stricken at first, and then smiled.

"If anyone is tough enough to get through this, it's Nicola."

But Nicola, the woman he knew now with absolute clarity to be the love of his life, the matching half of his splintered heart, had not been seen or heard from for hours. And he knew she was nowhere near as tough as she pretended to be.

Colin appeared out of nowhere with a van, and began shuttling survivors from the rectory to the village hall at the top of Fore Street, where arrangements were being made to take those who needed medical attention to the clinic in Camelford and those who needed shelter to the big leisure center there. The police were letting no one near the lower village, where the river still raged and the destruction continued.

At the village hall, Roger and Anne arrived, having had to drive miles out of their way to avoid the roads the police had blocked. Lee was asleep in Andrew's arms. Instead of waking and startling her, both parents knelt on the floor on either side of the mat on which Andrew sat holding her, and, very gently, stroked her hair and bony legs until she awakened.

"Mum! Daddy! It was so cool! You should have been there, up in my tree! It was like the whole of Cornwall was swimming by—trees, bridges, bits of buildings; I expected to see cows and sheep."

Roger looked at Andrew, lifted his eyebrows,

and just shook his head, as if to say, *She's a complete mystery to me . . . but thank you.*

Andrew smiled. Anne stood, kissed him, tears in her eyes, and gathered her gangly daughter in her arms. "Come home, Drew; we're dry up there."

"I need to find Nicola," he replied, and Anne nodded.

"Do it for all of us," Roger said. "Lilly needs her."

And then they left, and Andrew ached at the completeness of them: mother, father, daughter . . . family.

ANDREW HAD JUST left the hall and turned down Fore Street, toward the ruins of the lower village, when she arrived in the van from the rectory. She stepped down to the road hugging a rag-covered package and looked around, blinking, as if she'd been left on another planet. Andrew would remember this moment for the rest of his life: She was shattered, lost, a waif in borrowed clothes. He didn't call out, for fear he'd frighten her. He reached her just as she entered the village hall.

"Nicola . . ."

She turned toward the sound of her name, in a stiff, twitchy motion, as if the turning were a reflex, not entirely of her own volition. She stared hollow-eyed for a moment, and then the light came on. A smile rose from somewhere deep and she held it for a moment. Then she began to sag, like a leaking balloon. Andrew slipped his arms under her armpits and lifted her toward him.

"Nicola," he said again.

"I saved her," she said into his shoulder.

"Of course you did," he said quietly. He had no idea what she was talking about.

After they'd been fed by volunteers and had their dried clothes returned, they spent the night, side by side, wrapped in blankets on gym mats at the leisure center in Camelford, along with dozens of others—residents and tourists alike. Though she was dry and warm, Nicola trembled uncontrollably. Andrew wrapped his arms around her and held her close until the trembling passed and he could tell by her breathing she was asleep. Then he unwrapped the package and understood whom she'd saved.

TUESDAY, AUGUST 17, was cruel. The heavy weather having passed, the morning dawned sunny, warm, and preternaturally clear—the kind of storm-rinsed clarity that made you think you could see right over the horizon into the next time zone if you were only tall enough. A perfect day for tourists, but the only people moving in the lower village were emergency workers.

Nicola and Andrew were standing on the edge of the main road at the top of the switchback, halfway up the hill above the harbor. Though they were told the police had cordoned off the area, they'd hitch-hiked back to Boscastle from Camelford anyway.

Nicola had been adamant about returning. Now the two of them, along with a small crowd of others, tried to take in the scene before them. No one said a word. The only sound was the muted roar of the river, still flowing filthy and fast through the ravaged town, but no longer at full flood stage. The main road through the lower village had survived, but the bridge that carried it over the normally sparkling river had been stripped of most of its stone railing walls. The Clovelly Clothing Company, the shop on the other side of the bridge, had vanished, leaving only a section of thick stone wall. At the Riverside Hotel—and, for that matter, at all of the buildings as far as they could see—the ground-floor doors and windows had been ripped out, and tree branches hung out of them like claws. The river had gouged out ravines at least eight feet deep, exposing and destroying water lines, sewer pipes, and underground cables of all sorts. And everywhere were towering piles of destruction—uprooted trees, poles, bits of twisted metal, signs, rock, and crushed cars.

Downstream, it was worse. The verdant lawns that had graced the riverbanks were knee-deep in charcoal silt and strewn with rocks that had once been parts of buildings but now lay embedded in mud as if trying to return to their native habitat. The lower bridge was invisible, buried beneath a tangle of trees and cars. The historic Harbour Light building was gone. Down at the harbor, the tide was out, and the entrance was choked with sand-bars of mud from which dead trees and the corpses of cars and vans protruded.

"It's still there," Andrew heard Nicola say.

"What is?"

"My house."

A weary-looking man beside Andrew said, "Fifty people missing."

"Fifteen?" Andrew asked.

"Fifty. Five-oh."

"Jesus."

At the bottom of the hill, they could see that the police were refusing to let anyone across the bridge. Nicola grabbed his left arm and pulled him away.

"Come on," she ordered, leading him to a foot-path along the hillside that led west to the coast. "We'll go in the back way."

"What in the name of God for? There's nothing left down there."

"I need to get Lee."

"Lee's at home, Nicola," he said gently, wondering if Nicola was still in shock.

She stopped amid the yellow gorse and magenta heather and turned to face him, a hand on one cocked hip, one eyebrow raised.

"The *painting* of her!"

"Oh. Right."

"How did you ever get to be a professor? Affirmative action for the hopelessly dim?"

"Nicola?"

"What?"

Andrew grinned. "Nice to have you back again, love."

To his utter surprise, she stepped forward, held his face in her hands, and kissed him.

"Thank you," she said. "Now get a move on!"

When they reached the cliffs, they picked up another footpath that dropped down to the harbor entrance along a series of slate ledges as regular as stair steps. With Nicola leading, they ran along the edge of the ancient stone wharf and ducked behind the backs of buildings so the police and firemen at the center of town wouldn't see them. It was slow going, either plodding through stinking mud or picking their way across expanses of debris. They were both wearing what they'd worn the day before—Andrew his hedging work clothes and boots, Nicola black slacks, sandals, and a museum T-shirt printed with a pentagram. They were filthy in minutes.

When they finally came out of the shadows and turned the corner, Nicola gasped. Where only yesterday there had been a postcard-worthy cottage—whitewashed wall, two small, multipaned windows with sagegreen window boxes flanking the granite-linteled doorway—there now was nothing but a raw, gaping hole, much of it filled with a huge, mud-caked tree trunk.

"My God, what's keeping it from collapsing?" Nicola said.

"Post-and-beam construction," Andrew replied, missing completely that the question was rhetorical. "The stone walls really just function as filler; it's the posts and beams that hold it up. If they're intact, the structure will survive. Problem is, there's no way of knowing the condition of the upright posts without going inside."

He was peering into the dim interior when he heard shouts from upstream. Men in yellow hard hats were waving at them. Nicola bolted inside, clambering over the tree toward the back.

"Nicola! I don't know whether—"

"Neither do I, but I'm getting Lee! Hold off the goons!"

Daylight cascaded down the worn stone steps from the hole in the roof as she crawled upstairs. Her heart leaped when she reached the top and saw Lee's portrait, clean and dry, leaning against the wall. She grabbed the spread from her bed, wrapped it around the canvas, then glanced at the wild, dark painting she had just finished—so different from anything she had painted before. And suddenly she knew it had been a premonition of the flood. She left it on the easel, turned, and started back down the stairs. But the treads were greased with mud, and she hadn't even descended halfway when her feet shot out from under her. Desperate to protect the painting, she twisted and fell heavily on her side, landing on the sharp edge of the stone treads and slithering to the bottom, into the mud. Pain like a knife blade shot through her rib cage and took her breath away. She lay still for a moment, breathing shallowly.

Andrew was beside her in seconds.

"Are you okay?"

She shook her head. "No, but Lee is; I think I cracked a rib."

"Take a deep breath," Andrew ordered.

"I'd rather not, doctor," she said.

"Do it!"

There's that intensity again, she thought. *It always takes me by surprise.*

She took a deep breath and let it out again.

"No change?" Andrew said.

"No."

"Good. Sharp pain would mean you'd actually broken a rib, which could puncture a lung if you moved. Now, let's get out of here."

They'd just stumbled out through the ragged arch of the front wall when one of the policemen arrived in his reflective yellow emergency jacket.

"Oi! What you think you're doing, then?"

"Visiting my house, dammit; what does it look like?" Nicola barked.

"She lives here," Andrew said, as if that explained everything.

The policeman, who had probably been up all night, maintained his composure. He looked at the ruin behind them and then said, almost tenderly, "Not anymore, she doesn't. Look, we can't have people trying to enter buildings that may be on the verge of collapse. I'm afraid everyone's got to be evacuated. I'm sure you understand."

Nicola softened, and the three of them made their way up the debris-cluttered lane to the main road. Andrew carried the draped canvas.

"Which way are you heading?" the officer asked when they reached the bridge.

In pain, emotionally spent, stunned by the destruction all around her, Nicola looked first one way and then the other, and said, "I don't know; I have nowhere to go." Tears zigzagged down her cheeks through the dirt.

"Yes, you do," Andrew said, taking her hand.

"I don't know, Andrew . . ."

"I know you don't, Nicola. But you will." And he led her toward the road to the upper village.

They'd just reached the switchback above the harbor when Roger found them.

"You two are even more trouble to find than that vagabond daughter of mine. Been to Camelford and back trying to locate you. Somebody back at the farm wants to see you; truck's at the top of the hill."

It was nearly four o'clock before they finally jounced into the yard at Bottreaux Farm. They'd had to detour south to Tintagel, east to the main Atlantic Highway, then north past Camelford, and finally through the few narrow lanes that didn't cross rivers or streams to get back to the farm. All the other routes had washed-out or badly damaged bridges and were closed.

There were animated voices in the kitchen, and they could smell the heavenly aroma of a beef rib roast as they came through the side door of the house.

"Drew! Nicki!" Lee threw herself at Andrew and scaled him as if she was climbing her oak tree. Andrew was laughing from someplace deep in his belly and realized he couldn't remember the last time he'd done so. Nicki was ruffling Lee's hair and showering her with kisses.

"And aren't you two an attractive pair," a voice cracked. "Look like a couple of mud wrestlers." It was Flora; she and Jamie were sitting at the end of the big scrubbed pine table in the middle of the kitchen, drinking red wine from thick tumblers. Anne was bent over the big solid-fuel AGA stove, checking the roast. When she straightened up again, she screeched, "Out! Out of my kitchen, you two; look at you!"

It was the first time Andrew and Nicola realized just how filthy they were. Their trousers were encased with dirt to the knees, and the rest of their clothes were plastered with caked silt. They looked at each other as if coming out of a trance and began giggling.

The ever-gentle Roger said, "Perhaps you'd like a bath . . ."

"Not till I get a drink!" Nicola protested.

Jamie took charge, and poured three more glasses. Then he held his up and suddenly his aging, weather-browned face lost its levity.

"You gave us a hell of a fright, lass," he said to Nicola. "Thank God you're with us again. Thank God we're all here and safe."

"Amen, brother," Flora intoned. "Now pour us some more of that plonk, will ya? Sermon's over." And she pinched his rear for good measure, making him jump.

Andrew nudged Nicola. He still had the covered painting under his arm. She looked at him and understood, then took the package, unwrapped it, and laid the painting of Lee on the table before Anne and Roger.

"This was meant to be for your anniversary, but maybe now's the right time," she whispered.

Anne's hand flew to her mouth. Roger slipped his arms around his wife and tears inched down his weathered face.

"Way cool!" Lee cried.

"ANNIE! I DON'T have any clothes!" Nicola was standing at the top of the stairs wrapped in a big white Turkish towel.

"Music to a man's ears!" she heard Jamie shout from the kitchen. And then, "Ow!"

Anne called from her bedroom, "In here, Nicki!" She'd laid out several pieces of clothing and was shaking her head. Anne was petite; Nicola was not.

"These are the biggest things I have, luv," she said as Nicola entered. "The only thing we share is a shoe size. Good luck!"

There was an ankle-length black challis skirt with an elastic waistband and a hand-knit, V-necked yellow jumper in a fluffy angora-blend yarn, clearly the work of some loving but inaccurately knitting maiden aunt. Still, with Nicola's lush figure, it left little to the imagination. She slipped into a pair of flats Anne had left and descended to the kitchen again. Andrew was there in his own clean clothes; Roger had fetched them from his cottage.

"Woo-hoo," Jamie crowed when she entered. This got him another cuffing from Flora.

"Go on, ya randy old man," Flora said, smiling.

Nicola was stricken. "Oh my God; Randi!"

"Not to worry, luv," Anne said. "Colin's got him and he's safe, if a little lonely."

Andrew slipped his hand around Nicola's waist and she leaned into him, feeling safe, too, for the first time in what seemed forever.

Dinner was the sort of event that often follows a disaster, a mix of giddy exultation at having survived and recognition of just how close some of them had been to perishing. They ate in the kitchen, around the big table, a battery-powered radio tuned into BBC Radio Cornwall the whole time. Gradually, the news reports from Boscastle turned brighter. The number of people thought to be missing had dropped sharply. No bodies had been found in either the ruined cars or in the buildings that had been searched. With their usual penchant for hyperbole, the reporters already had begun calling it the "Boscastle Miracle."

Jamie and Flora had spent the night on the floor of the dining room above the pub, along with others. "Gettin' too old for that sort of nonsense," Flora complained. Jamie allowed as how it was the most romantic night he could remember.

Flora snorted. "Either your memory is rubbish or you need a better life!"

"I'm hoping for the latter," Jamie said with a grin. Under the table, Flora squeezed his hand.

The police had cleared them out of the Cobweb in the morning, as part of the general evacuation; with no fresh water, the sewage lines broken, and many structures unsafe in the lower village, officials were taking no chances. Jamie had bundled Flora into his van, and they were bouncing along single-track lanes around the fields above town when they ran into Roger on his ATV, moving cattle. Roger told Jamie his chances of making it home were slim, given the closed roads, and invited the two of them to stay at the farm.

They lit candles as the August light waned, but, between the rich food, the wine, and the nearly continuous stress of the last two days, the celebrants were flagging by nine o'clock. It was Flora who called a halt to the proceedings.

"Right, then; I don't know about the rest of you lot, but I'm knackered. Where're we kippin'?"

Anne looked from Flora to Jamie, and then back to Flora.

"Yeah, yeah; we're regular sleepin' buddies now, we are. Just point us to a room, luv; we'll take care of the rest."

Andrew was almost certain he saw Jamie blush. He felt a tug at his sleeve.

"Let's go home," Nicola whispered.

"Are you sure?" he asked.

"Oh, yes," she said, smiling.

"Me, too!" Lee cried, jumping from her chair.

"No, you don't, you little ragamuffin!" Roger said, sweeping his daughter into his arms. "It's early to bed for you, too. For all of us, I should think."

"THE SHEETS AREN'T clean," Andrew apologized as he pulled back the coverlet on the antique double bed in his cottage.

"Good," Nicola said, pulling the fuzzy yellow jumper over her head. Her full breasts swayed and came to rest against her surprisingly spare rib cage as she stepped out of Anne's skirt. She had nothing else on underneath. It flashed through Andrew's mind that he wished he'd known that all through dinner.

She slipped into bed, pulled up the sheets, and patted the mattress beside her. He sat.

"Andrew?"

"Yes?"

"Do you love me?"

"Yes. I do."

"That's what you were trying to tell me on Dunn Street that night I ran away, isn't it?"

"Yes. Although, honestly, I'm not sure I really knew it then."

"I didn't know it then, either—well, maybe I did but couldn't deal with it."

Andrew leaned down and kissed her.

"I know I love you, too, Andrew . . . but sweetie, it scares me to death," she said.

"I know it does. We can take this slowly. I don't want you ever to be afraid again."

Nicola sat up, the coverlet sliding to her waist. Andrew did not think there could be a more beautiful woman in the world.

"Andrew?"

"Nicki?"

"When are you going back to the States?"

"Never."

"What?"

"Never. I'm staying here. I'm resigning my position at the university."

Nicola stared at him for a moment.

"Andrew?" she asked again.

"You certainly have a lot of questions."

"I only have one more: Will you please get undressed and come to bed?"

They did not go to sleep immediately. As the light outside failed, they traced each other's contours with their fingertips and their lips and their tongues, as if they were archaeologists deciphering an ancient, sacred text etched on their skin.

And later, when it was finally dark, Nicola put her lips to Andrew's ear and whispered, "Would it be okay if I just curled up with you? Could you do that? Just hold me? I'm afraid."

And he did, drawing her into his arms, her back curled against his chest, her rear cupped in his lap.

She pressed herself into him and he felt her tension ease. They were both asleep in moments.

During the afternoon of the 16th, an incredible amount of rainfall fell, conservatively estimated to have been over 1,422 million litres (310 million gallons) in just two hours. That's over 197,500 litres (43,000 gallons) falling per second, the equivalent of 21 petrol tanker loads of water flowing through Boscastle every second.

Boscastle: The Flood (North Cornwall District Council, 2006)

eighteen

Andrew was frying eggs and bacon when Lee burst through the cottage door Wednesday morning.

"Mum says to tell you that the radio says folks will be allowed into the lower village to collect valuables later this morning! Where's Nicki?"

"Here, sweetie," Nicola said, emerging from the bedroom wearing one of Andrew's shirts and the skirt from the night before. Lee threw herself at her, and they hugged as if each of them was a source of nourishment for the other.

"Mum also says your clothes will be out of the dryer in a few minutes."

"Have you ever considered a career as a newscaster?" Andrew grumped. He hadn't had his tea yet.

Lee shot him a look. "Is that supposed to be funny?"

"I'm never funny before lunch."

"You got that right," she said.

God help the man who marries her, Andrew thought, but he was chuckling. He was deeply happy. Awakening earlier with Nicola beside him had felt like a miracle; he'd lain motionless for a long time, watching the slow rise and fall of her chest, the tumble of dark hair across her face, the relaxed curve of her full lips in slumber. When the morning sun had reached her face, she'd opened her eyes, seen him watching her, and smiled. Without saying a word, she'd pulled him atop her and guided him inside her. Then, very slowly, they made love.

"Good morning, darling," she'd said afterward, grinning.

" 'Darling'?"

"Yes. Because you are. I'm just a slow learner is all."

"I'll say."

She'd punched him playfully. "For that, you get to make me breakfast!"

"You call that punishment? I'd gladly do that for the rest of my life!"

She'd grinned. "You may have to."

He'd wanted more than anything to make love with her all morning, but he also hadn't wanted to break this spell, to send her back to the dark place that he knew still lay within her.

"Tea, then?" he'd asked.

"That's a start . . ."

"Yes, madam; coming right up, madam."

He'd hopped out of bed. She'd sat up, then leaned toward him. "Do you suppose you could leave part of you here?"

"What part."

"You know damn well what part!"

"I don't think that will be possible, madam; I shall need my wits about me."

"Is that where you keep them?"

"Yes, madam."

She'd pouted. "I should have known."

"I'll just be getting that tea now."

IT WAS PAST noon when the two of them reached the bridge. A crowd of shell-shocked residents milled about behind an emergency cordon waiting for the police to let them through, but there was a holdup of some sort. Nicola elbowed to the front and found the elderly but formidable Joyce Manley, who lived in a little cottage on Valency Row, yelling and waving her walking stick at the police officer manning the tape.

"'Ow come all them media jackals can wander about the village willy-nilly and us what lives here can't, eh? Where's the justice in that?"

"I'm sorry, dearie, I am; I'm just following my orders," the officer said calmly.

"That's what the Germans said in the war!"

Nicola looked around. There were television satellite trucks positioned in the road and cameramen and reporters everywhere, many interviewing local and county officials. Off to one side, a Salvation Army emergency services van had been set up, and there were a lot of fire and rescue staff milling about in full emergency outfits. The Royal Society for the Prevention of Cruelty to Animals had teams of veterinarians and volunteers combing the wreckage for lost pets.

Then the walkie-talkie on the policeman's lapel squawked. He mumbled "Roger" into the device and then unhooked the tape, gently herding everyone away from the bridge, which only infuriated Mrs. Manley more.

"Please, madam," he said, his arms spread wide to move people back, "it's only for a few minutes. The prince is arriving, you see."

"Bloody hell," Joyce bellowed. "I just knew someday my prince would come, and me hair wouldn't be done!"

This got everyone, including the cop, laughing just as a cavalcade of funereally black vehicles rounded the switchback, descended the hill, and swept past the cordon and across the bridge. A few moments later, Prince Charles emerged from a large black Range Rover. He was deeply tanned and wearing a dove-gray double-breasted suit in a faint glen plaid. Andrew noticed that he also had on brightly polished brown shoes and wondered whether no one had told him about the mud everywhere. The prince waved to the clutch of residents on the other side of the bridge and was immediately escorted by officials around the corner of the ruined Riverside Hotel and uphill toward the Cobweb. As if on cue, it began sprinkling again. He felt sorry for the fellow; you could tell he'd wanted to visit with the residents, but he'd been commandeered elsewhere. Some meeting, no doubt.

"He's very short," Andrew commented.

"And very rich," Nicola said. "Let's hope he's come to offer assistance; in addition to being Prince of Wales, he's also the Duke of Cornwall. They say he cares a lot about rural England; here's his chance."

They stood there for a moment, taking in the spectacle, and then Nicola nudged him. The officer was letting people in.

"Come on; we've got work to do."

They headed downstream toward Nicola's cottage. On the opposite bank, they saw Colin beside his coast guard vehicle and called to him.

"Hang on a bit," the museum director yelled back.

He pulled open the rear door of the car and Randi leaped out. The dog looked around, then danced like an acrobat across the debris pile that once had been the lower bridge, and tried to launch himself into Nicola's arms.

"Bloody ungrateful, I call it!" Colin called, smiling broadly.

"Thank you, dear man!" Nicola called back as she struggled to calm her dog, who now was leaping at Andrew with equal enthusiasm.

Then they entered the wreck that had once been Nicola's home.

NICOLA HAD FINISHED packing her paint box and was stuffing clothing into a valise when Randi barked, just once.

She looked up wearily at Andrew. "Would you see what that's about?"

"I'm on it."

He picked his way down the muddy steps. A few moments later, he called back: "Nicola? A gentleman to see you."

She cursed and descended. Then she saw him. "Dad!"

Sir Michael stood in the shelter of the hole that had been her front wall. Andrew was at his side. Randi panted happily.

Muddy from climbing over the tree lodged in what remained of her sitting room, she hesitated. The elegantly dressed old man stepped forward and she threw herself into his arms.

"Nicola, thank God. Oh, thank God." That was all he could say. There were tears in his eyes. The two of them, the old man and the woman, clung to each other as if they'd drown if they let go.

Andrew had no idea what was happening.

Nicola lifted her face, saw his bewilderment, and laughed.

"Andrew Stratton, allow me to introduce Sir Michael Rhys-Jones, my father-in-law. Well, former, actually. Dad, this is Andrew, an American architect, a formidable Cornish hedge builder, and the man I love."

Now it was Sir Michael's turn to be flummoxed, but he recovered quickly, scrutinized the man beside him for a moment, and then said, "Nicola, I am very pleased indeed."

Andrew bowed slightly, took the old man's extended hand, and said simply, "Sir Michael; my pleasure."

"What the hell are you doing here?" Nicola erupted.

Sir Michael laughed. "That's my girl; right to the point! All right, I'm here with Charles."

"You know the prince?"

"My dear, there are many things you do not know about me, but you will; you will in time. Yes, I know the prince. I've been one of his financial advisers for most of his adult life, and I'm on the board of the Prince's Trust. There are certain other connections I have that made it possible for me to prevail upon him to let me come along on this visit. I was desperate to know how you were, and the local authorities hadn't a clue."

The penny dropped for Andrew. "You're MI5, Sir Michael, aren't you?"

Sir Michael lifted his bushy eyebrows and then smiled. "Goodness, you are a clever devil, aren't you? Only in an advisory capacity, my boy, I assure you. But it brings me certain perquisites. Like finding my dear Nicola."

He turned to his former daughter-in-law. "I will have to leave in a few minutes, dear. You will need a place to live . . ."

"I have one, Dad," she said quietly, nodding toward Andrew.

"Yes," he said, scrutinizing Andrew once again. "Yes. Good. That's for the best. But I shall be in touch. And please, Nicola, stay out of this place in future; it is dangerous."

Nicola nodded. The old man turned and began walking back upstream toward the bridge and the prince's entourage.

"Daddy?"

He stopped and turned.

"Wait." She took his arm and walked with him.

Andrew held Randi and let her go. Except for earlier that morning, he had never seen her so happy.

THAT NIGHT, THE word went out through Boscastle that the Wednesday night sing would go on as usual, as close to the Wellington Hotel as possible. Andrew and Nicola were there, along with Roger and Anne and Lee and many of the regulars. A bonfire had been built outside from the ruins of the Welly's Long Bar, and a full keg of ale had been delivered, gratis, by Skinner's Brewery. They sang the old songs for more than an hour, with a fierceness that attested to their stubborn refusal to let this disaster kill the traditions that made living here unique.

Then, sensing the winding down of the evening, Jack Vaughan began the first lines of a ballad they all knew, a song about the shipwreck of a vessel called the *Mary Ellen Carter*. It was a lengthy ballad, as most sea shanties are, but it was the last stanza that gripped the singers:

> *Rise again, rise again,*
> *Though your heart, it be broken;*
> *and your life about to end,*
> *No matter what you've lost,*
> *a home, a love, a friend,*
> *Like the Mary Ellen Carter,*
> *Rise again.*

"DREW!"

It was Nicola. It was September now, and she had adopted Lee's nickname for him. She dashed across the lower bridge to where he and Jamie were working to repair the witchcraft museum. She waved a letter she had clutched in her hand.

Andrew put down his mason's hammer and stretched his back muscles.

"It's from Dad!"

It had taken Andrew a while to get used to Nicola's calling her former father-in-law "Dad," but now he smiled and sat down on a rock pile.

"Listen!" she demanded.

> *My Dear Nicola,*
> *For various boring tax reasons, I have arranged to donate Trevega House and its*

lands to the National Trust. But I have done so with the proviso that it remain in a lifetime tenancy so long as my family is in residence. I have named you as the family tenant. I have also named you and Nina as my beneficiaries. Jeremy is no longer employed in my firm and I no longer acknowledge him as my son. I have settled an amount upon him with his promise that he will relinquish any claim on Trevega or on my estate. Having little choice in the matter, given the information I have about his recent behavior, he has accepted these terms. No one since my dear wife has loved Trevega House as you have, Nicola, and it should be yours. Nina agrees.

I have also—I hope you will forgive me— examined the background of Andrew Stratton. You have chosen well. I should like to request that Andrew begin at once a survey of the properties appurtenant to Trevega House—the cottages, the mill— and advise me as to their restoration, renovation, and potential as rental properties, all income therefrom to go to you.

Please advise if this is acceptable . . . and please say yes, Nicola.

With love abiding,
Michael

Nicola was dancing around with excitement, in exactly the way Lee so often did.

Andrew smiled. "Tell me about Trevega House, Nicola."

And she did, sitting on a pile of rocks beside him, the joy pouring out of her like sunshine.

When she was finished, Andrew said, "Do you think I could finish what I'm doing here first? It seems like Sir Michael's work will be long term, and I'd like to invite Jamie to be my partner."

"And Flora and Jamie could have one of the cottages!" she enthused.

"Let me just see, okay, babe?"

"Yes. Yes of course."

"Nicola?"

"Yes, love?"

"What will we tell Lee?"

Nicola winked. "She and I already have something planned," she said. "She'll spend summers with us; she wants to learn how to paint."

"I see. So you just assumed I'd agree to all this?"

"No, I didn't. That's why I threw Lee in as the clincher," she said with a mischievous smile. "I know you're a sucker for her, and I didn't want to take any chances."

Andrew grabbed Nicola and pulled her onto his lap.

"C'mere, you; I'll show you the clincher!"

Epilogue

The two women sat on the ground beside a primitive well, framed in rough stone, from which a spring seeped. They were just a few hundred yards downhill from Minster church, in the woods above the River Valency. It was the last night of the waning moon, and thus pitch dark but for the thick black candle flickering between them. Above them, the papery autumn leaves of the sessile oaks rustled like static.

They had been here for some nights now, quietly going through the same ancient rite.

The older woman reached her hand into the water bleeding from the hillside and then flicked it over the head of the younger woman.

"Amen, hetem," intoned the older woman.

"Amen, hetem," the younger one repeated.

"What's mine is thine," the older one continued. "What's thine is mine.

"Mighty ones and old ones:

"Witness Flora and Nicola anointing themselves, that we might be great like you.

"Thout! A thout! Throughout and about!"

The women sat quietly, taking in the sounds and spirits of the place—listening for owls, badgers, deer, and foxes. As it had during the nights before, time both stretched and compressed. Some nights they sat for what seemed like hours when in fact only minutes had passed. Some nights it was the other way around. After a while, Flora held up the remains of a photograph—the one from Nicola's bedroom that depicted her and her two brothers at the beach—and began a chant: *"Johnny DeLucca, be dead and past; Nicola DeLucca, be whole at last."*

The younger woman joined in the chant, and gradually it built in volume and power. After perhaps ten minutes, Flora held up her hands and they stopped. Then she took what remained of the photo—just the head of Nicola's dead brother—tore it, and set it afire in the flame of the candle.

Both women let out a *whoop!* And then Flora shouted into the night: *"The work is done; so mote it be!"*

Nicola shuddered involuntarily and suddenly fell to one side.

Not far away in the darkness, Andrew Stratton struggled to get to his feet, but the girl beside him dragged him down again.

"Drew!" Lee hissed. "It's all right; it's what has to be."

Jamie put his arm around his friend. "Let it happen, lad; let the magic work. Flora knows what she's about."

FARTHER UP THE hill and just beyond the parish boundary, Colin Grant, unbeknownst to any of them, tied together two small sticks—one from

Andrew's yard, the other from Nicola's former cottage—with red string, and left them as an offering beside the secret grave of a witch who had been known to have success with love spells.

Then he slipped into the darkness.

Author's Note

Boscastle is a real village on the north coast of Cornwall in southwest England. On August 16, 2004—a warm, largely sunny day at the height of the tourist season—a bizarre coincidence of meteorological events combined to create a highly localized series of torrential downpours in the hills immediately above and east of the village. The valley in which the lower part of Boscastle sits acted like a vast funnel, and the result was one of the worst floods ever recorded in Britain.

The meteorological data in this novel, and the sequence of events during the flood, are all factually accurate. Some of the characters, though renamed, are real people, and their actions during the flood, as well as those of their rescuers, were nothing short of heroic. Miraculously, despite the fury of the flood and the massive destruction, not a soul was lost.

Everything else is fiction.

Acknowledgments

One of the joys of writing and publishing books is that you get to thank the people who helped make them possible. This is important, because even a work of fiction like this one depends upon the wisdom and assistance of many, many people. A novel is not so much the work of solitary imagination as it is a collaboration of generous folks.

Because this story is set in a real village on the Atlantic coast of Cornwall—a village that was severely damaged by a catastrophic flood a few years ago and which has resurrected itself since—there are many residents to whom I owe a deep debt of gratitude for sharing with me not just their time and hospitality, but also their harrowing personal experiences. I want to especially thank Graham King at the Boscastle Museum of Witchcraft; Rebecca David at the Boscastle Visitor Centre; and the Reverend Christine Musser, for their support, their fact-checking, and their patience as I turned them into fictional characters. I am also in debt to David Rowe, Cornish journalist and author of a moment-by-moment account of the flood who gave me permission to use his time line of events. A nod of special respect is due John Maughan, the "Boscastle Busker," who has been singing at the Welly (and elsewhere) for years and who has, thanks to his splendid voice and huge repertoire, raised thousands of dollars to support a local hospice. I also want to thank Nicola Collings (no relation to the Nicola in the story) at Hillsborough Farm for her hospitality and for the pleasure of living at Hayloft Cottage, and Jackie and Robin Haddy, at Home Farm, for the inspiration for Bottreaux Farm.

I am also grateful to Richard Boden-Cummins of the Stone Academy, and Robin Menneer of the Guild of Cornish Hedgers, for instruction and advice on the construction of traditional Cornish hedges. In the same spirit, thanks are due to Steve Jebson at the United Kingdom's National Meteorological Library and Archive for the scientific accuracy of my description of the meteorological events leading up to the flood.

For sharing with me both the technical and emotional wellsprings of their art, I extend my appreciation and affection to two formidable Cornish painters, Kathy Todd and Edwinna Broadbent. Their work, while utterly different, has captivated me.

There is a deeply serious subject at the heart of this story, which is the lifelong psychological effects of childhood sexual abuse—a horror that is far more widespread than I ever could have imagined. For insight into this subject, I thank Lorie Dwinell, teacher and friend, and Dr. Lucy Berliner at Seattle's Harborview Center for Sexual Assault and Traumatic Stress. To Dr. Berliner I am deeply grateful for the simple but powerful observation that, "Just because there isn't a clinical psychological condition doesn't mean there has been no long-term effect from abuse."

I am thankful, as well, to a few trusted and sharp-eyed readers of earlier versions of this story: Ann Vaughan, Cindy Buck, Kate Pflaumer, Lawrence Rosenfeld, Yvonne Price, and my delightful Portuguese translator and favorite witch, Marta Mendoncas. I am also deeply grateful for the friendship and hospitality of my many British friends, including Claire Booth, Valerie and Hugh Edwards, Ann and Malcolm Vaughan, Phil Budden and Melissa Hardie, and Malcolm and Anne Sutton. Thank you all.

And then there is the splendid team of professionals who turn these words into books, beginning with my publisher within Crown/Random House, Shaye Areheart Books: a more enthusiastic and supportive publisher, editor, and friend than Shaye one could not even begin to imagine. Working with her, and on my behalf, I extend my appreciation to Kira Walton, Sarah Breivogel, Christine Aronson, Karin Shulze, Anne Berry, and Christine Kopprasch. At Three Rivers Press, my paperback publisher, thank you to Philip Patrick, Julie Kraut, and Annsley Rosner. And for his wonderfully inviting cover designs, thanks to the talented Whitney Cookman. Thank you all.

As always, a toast of gratitude to my agent,

friend, and candid adviser, Richard Abate at the Endeavor Agency. It was Richard who nudged me into fiction from nonfiction, and Richard who believed in me for years. There is nothing I can do, no sentiment of thanks I can express, that can possibly equal the meaning of his support. Richard, you are a prince.

Finally, and closer to home, I must honor the patience, love, and encouragement of my family—Hazel, Nancy, Tom, Eric, Ardith, and Baker. But more than anyone, I thank Susan for the joy she brings to my life and the love she extends without reserve.

About the Author

Water, Stone, Heart is WILL NORTH's second novel. His debut novel, *The Long Walk Home,* was a selection of the Doubleday and Rhapsody book clubs and was chosen by *Reader's Digest* as a 2008 Select Edition. In addition, it has been translated and published in several foreign countries, including Germany, Japan, Spain, Portugal, and Israel. A condensed translation has appeared in many other countries. Formerly the ghostwriter of more than a half-dozen nonfiction books, Will has just completed his third novel. He lives in Washington, on an island in Puget Sound, with his partner, Susan, and their two dogs.

Visit the author's website at www.willnorth-online.com.

Center Point Publishing

600 Brooks Road ● PO Box 1
Thorndike ME 04986-0001 USA

(207) 568-3717

**US & Canada:
1 800 929-9108**
www.centerpointlargeprint.com